THE TASK OF
THIS TRANSLATOR

THE TASK OF
THIS TRANSLATOR

STORIES

Todd Hasak-Lowy

A Harvest Original · Harcourt, Inc.

Orlando   Austin   New York   San Diego   Toronto   London

Requests for permission to make copies of any part of the work should be mailed to the following address: Permissions Department, Harcourt, Inc., 6277 Sea Harbor Drive, Orlando, Florida 32887-6777.

www.HarcourtBooks.com

A version of "On the Grounds of the Complex Commemorating the Nazis' Treatment of the Jews" first appeared in *The Iowa Review*.

Library of Congress Cataloging-in-Publication Data
Hasak-Lowy, Todd, 1969–
The task of this translator/Todd Hasak-Lowy.
p.   cm.
"A Harvest Original."
I. Title.
PS3608.A7895T37   2005
813'.6—dc22   2004017846
ISBN 0-15-603112-4

Text set in Garamond MT
Designed by Cathy Riggs

Printed in the United States of America

First edition
C E G I K J H F D B

To Taal

In this room Goldman wrestled with his problems and the problems of the world, and out of wonder and despair created for himself in his imagination a life of liberation, intensity, and vitality for the future to come, happily preoccupied by it all, but in this room he also learned to renounce this life with great sorrow and an oppressive sense of failure, only to return desperately after a short time to create for himself, out of jealousy and longing and immense hope, a life even more beautiful and brazen, a life transcending all laws and possibilities, and between one and the other he trained himself to live his slow and certain death with complete acceptance, even readiness, although he yearned to live a thousand years.

—Yaakov Shabtai, *Past Continuous*

CONTENTS

1

On the Grounds of the Complex Commemorating
the Nazis' Treatment of the Jews

21

Will Power, Inc.

61

The End of Larry's Wallet

117

The Interview

149

The Task of This Translator

179

Raider Nation

211

How Keith's Dad Died

The Task of
This Translator

ON THE GROUNDS OF THE COMPLEX
COMMEMORATING THE NAZIS' TREATMENT
OF THE JEWS

The smarter-than-average, smaller-than-average Israeli man in his middle thirties had been for a time a freelance journalist in Jerusalem, the city in which the state of Israel constructed its massive complex commemorating the Nazis' treatment of the Jews. His work of late had been subpar, and was never exceptional to begin with, but he had, for a few years, enough persistence to carve out a living. He was single again after a three-year marriage to a woman taller than him, who doomed the marriage by formally announcing her reluctance to reproduce at any time with her husband despite the implications of their marriage contract, though they both agree now, not that they talk much, that it was for the best they never made another person. But his work had slipped, along with his enthusiasm for his trade, and he stopped writing, stopped looking for projects, and was eventually replaced on a list of regular contributors to a

Jerusalem weekly by another shortish Israeli journalist, of which there are many.

One of his friends managed the coffee shop at the Jerusalem complex commemorating the Nazis' treatment of the Jews, and this friend offered the failing journalist a job working the cash register. The offer was a joke, made in response to a three-minute monologue by the failing journalist about his professional woes and financial constraints, but the failing journalist professed interest in the offer. He hoped, in vain it would turn out, that such work would serve as a welcome respite from the doldrums he had arrived at as an idle journalist. He hoped, in vain, that the mindless labor of working a cash register in the complex commemorating the Nazis' treatment of the Jews would afford him the opportunity to gain perspective on his situation and summon the energy necessary to get his life back on track. When accepting the job and its low pay, he did not consider at length the effect working within the complex would have on his larger attitude and condition. The friend who offered him the job did ask, bewildered, "You want to work at *Yad Vashem?*" stressing the name of the place in order to draw his friend's attention—that is, the failing journalist's attention—to the fact that he would be working in the complex commemorating the Nazis' treatment of the Jews, and that in other words this was no typical workplace, that this was exactly *not* just another coffee-shop cash register he would be sitting behind for hours each day. The friend who offered the job could have, and under different circumstances perhaps would have, detailed what precisely working in the coffee shop of the complex commemorating the Nazis' treatment of the Jews involved, in terms of the general mood and atmosphere of the site, the impossibility of either ignoring the purpose of the complex or engaging it fully, the frustration one encounters time and again alternating between disdain and pity for the endless stream of customers, customers from all over the globe, who somehow have an appetite after touring the complex commemorating the Nazis' treatment of the Jews, even those customers who do or don't go to great lengths to conceal those numbers poorly written under the surface of their skin by the Nazis *while* they were being treated by the Nazis, but who luckily, one imagines with important reservations, were not given the full treatment, as it were. The failing journalist soon to be cashier at the coffee shop in the complex commemorating the Nazis' treatment of the Jews both did and did not hear his friend's words, in the sense that he heard the sounds, the words themselves, but did not make the intended connections, this failure itself loosely akin to the impossibility of ignoring or understanding what it means to work in the complex to begin with, which the manager friend could and would have detailed, again, under different circumstances.

Six weeks into the job, the onetime failing journalist had come to view himself as the on-edge, almost maniacal cashier in the coffee shop in the complex commemorating the Nazis' treatment of the Jews. He had come to realize that he was in no condition mentally, both in general and most certainly recently, to be in such regular contact with the complex commemorating the Nazis' treatment of the Jews. He did not benefit from the brief walk through the main doors of the complex each day affording him a glimpse of a few distant photographs detailing some unhappy chapter of this most unhappy story. He could not tolerate or cope with the unique strain of mostly silence that filled and made heavy the very air of the complex. He did not enjoy constantly thinking, hearing in his head the word "Nazi" once he began tending the cash register, propped up on his small black stool which made his back sore, nor did he enjoy think-ing and in his head hearing "Treblinka," "the final solution," "Dachau," "gas chambers," "crematorium," "Zyklon B," "SS," "Hitler," "six million," etc., or their Hebrew equivalents. He took no pleasure in watching the occasional beautiful woman who en-tered the coffee shop, for he felt bad coveting in such a place, felt bad if he smiled due to his coveting, felt bad if he denied him-self and her such a harmless smile if he censored the smile and resisted his coveting. He did not like working in the coffee shop in the complex commemorating the Nazis' treatment of the Jews. Not at all. Lucidly he concluded his life was falling apart, collapsing inward as he manned the cash register in the coffee shop of the complex commemorating the Nazis' treatment of the Jews. He sensed a loose but meaningful affiliation obtaining between the endless stream of random numbers appearing on the cash register each day and those overwhelming numbers as-sociated with the events commemorated in the building at which he worked. Somehow all these numbers meant something simi-lar, he thought. He felt a pathetic, lonely urge to address his cus-tomers, to let them in on some of his misery, to ask directly for their assistance or at least their sympathy and prayers in his effort to return his life to what it had once been. The absolute restric-tion on such behavior was painfully clear to him, and this only increased his suffering. He tried somehow to bond with his cus-tomers as they filed past him unceremoniously each day, to com-municate with his eyes and those muscles around his mouth his hope they enjoy their meal, snack, or drink. He strove to brighten their day with his Israeli equivalents of "thank you," "you're welcome," and "have a nice day," yet knew even the most heartfelt deliverance would not penetrate most patrons' oblivi-ousness to his very existence. He yearned to offer jokingly

"B'ta'avon," that is, "Bon appétit," but he restrained himself, knowing how vastly inappropriate such levity was in this heaviest of coffee shops. So he sat, hunched in his melancholy, hoping for incidental finger-to-palm contact between cashier and consumer, hoping for some misunderstanding requiring an extended dialogue to clarify things. He wanted to no longer work in the coffee shop of the complex commemorating the Nazis' treatment of the Jews. But he was quite poor and quite unmotivated, and during the five weeks and three days following the first two days of his employment as the afternoon cashier, these two days more than enough time to conclude that this was no place for him to work, he had yet to muster up the energy sufficient to find another job. He was, he concluded, depressed. His shame at suffering from such a condition during a time and in a place worlds better than the world in which the Nazis so mistreated the Jews did nothing to improve his state. Nor did it motivate him to find another job.

The American, three-plus inches taller than the cashier, was in mid-level management in a technology firm located in the American state of California. He entered the coffee shop in the complex commemorating the Nazis' treatment of the Jews to purchase and consume a baked good and some juice. The American had been sent to Israel along with a coworker to meet with an Israeli firm to discuss the possibility of undertaking a joint project developing technologies related to computer automation in the Middle East. The American was Jewish, albeit assimilated. He spoke no Hebrew, and despite three years of bar mitzvah training during his pre- and early adolescence, he recognized only a handful of that language's letters, and could do nothing concrete with this limited knowledge. He had for a time

in his early twenties considered investigating his Jewishness further, this inspired by the enthusiasm for the same faith shown by
his then-girlfriend, whom he admired very much and loved
dearly, but who eventually terminated their relationship when
she concluded that though this American boyfriend was physically attractive and above average in intelligence, he was not extremely intelligent or intensely attractive or really interesting for
that matter. She concluded that out in this great, big world was
a man who was simply more of a man than this American
boyfriend, so she slowly, methodically, and intentionally undid
the ties connecting them until that was that. During his brief,
five-month tour of his Jewishness, he read a handful of books,
attended four lectures, and waded through the newspaper with a
slightly altered sense of purpose. As best he could tell, when one
got past the American Jew's interest in who else in America—
from celebrities to closeted coworkers—was Jewish, American
Jews' two main interests seemed to be the Holocaust, as he often
heard it called, and the state of Israel. He, of course, was familiar with both entities on some superficial level. Right below the
threshold of consciousness he sensed he should, as he explored
his Jewishness, choose either the state of Israel or the Holocaust,
as he often heard it called, as his main Jewish interest. Both ap-
pealed to him in different ways, though the Arab component of
the state of Israel—Palestinians, Israeli Arabs, wars, refugees,
occupations, terrorist incidents, etc.—confused him terribly,
so he drifted toward an interest in the Holocaust. Reading
Leon Uris's *Mila 18* and attending the first six hours of Claude
Lanzmann's film *Shoah,* as the Nazis' treatment of the Jews is referred to in Hebrew, confronted him with an intense set of emo-
tions he could not express to his then-girlfriend. He felt that his
effort to become a newly aware Jewish adult, or more precisely

his effort to communicate to his girlfriend his program of becoming a newly aware Jewish adult, hinged on his ability to speak with some degree of adroitness about these feelings and the confusion they bred within him. But he could not, really. He had a few ideas, but nothing unique and certainly nothing compelling enough to raise him above the host of clichés that so dominate the world's understanding of the Nazis' treatment of the Jews. For a time during idle moments he would contemplate the numbers tied to the events, dividing the figure 6,000,000 by days in the week or months in the year, or estimating the average height of the victims, something along the lines of "if all the victims of the Holocaust were lined up end to end they would stretch from here to…" When this macro approach bore few fruits in terms of girlfriend-impressing eloquence and profundity, he swung to the other extreme, concentrating on individual stories, searching for that single anecdote from among the rat-filled cellars and benevolent gentile attics of survivors' memories able to express all by itself the meaning and significance of all those events. To no one's surprise he failed, and in time his girlfriend left him, though it would be unfair to blame the Nazis' treatment of the Jews for the demise of their once promising union.

Some years later, informed he was to be sent to the Jewish state on a business trip, he decided he would visit the complex commemorating the Nazis' treatment of the Jews. Near the end of the trip, when most of the significant meetings concerning Israeli automation and efficiency had concluded, he excused himself from his coworker and commandeered a taxi and instructed its driver to take him to the complex. He was impressed by its gardens and outdoor sculptures, but entered the main building with a foggy trepidation, the cause of which he had difficulty locating. As he navigated his way through the main time line of the events, past placards bearing photographs of the ghettoed Jews of Europe, past reproductions of anti-Semitic brochures boasting caricatures of sex-starved Jewish men with absurd hook noses, past diagrams explaining the Nazis' racial theories, past a German tour group stumbling slowly along as well, he discovered himself wistfully recalling, not once or twice, but upon nearly every footfall, that bright, comely, strikingly beautiful Jewish woman whom he so admired as to undertake an intensive-for-him five-month independent study of the Nazis' treatment of the Jews. That this complex commemorating the Nazis' treatment of the Jews activated his memory of her did not surprise him, but the stubborn regularity of this recollection, the refusal of the image of her face in his mind to retreat to accommodate a paltry ninety-minute reflection on the Nazis and their treatment of Europe's Jews disturbed and upset him greatly. The farther he walked into the narrative of the Nazis and the Jews, many rooms past the well-lit entrance, past 1935, 1938, 1940, into the years of the gas chambers, to the photographs of countless anonymous skin-and-bones corpses piled one on top of another in vast pits, the more he was overcome with the bitter disappointment of his inability to win over his beloved's heart in the early years of the previous decade. He continued, intermittently passing the same German tour group the way you encounter again and again a fellow supermarket patron who has chosen a slightly different route through the aisles, but a route managing to still overlap at times with your own. He was nearly certain they were indeed Germans and this only confused him more, as if they were sent there en masse to remind him of his reason for coming in the first place. This is not to say that he was as coarse as to be unaffected by the complex's effort to communicate the full horror of the Nazis' treatment of the Jews. He was alternately saddened and outraged, and this did not make things any better. But after years of working through the injuries of her rejection, after convincing himself of the worth of his present lover and soon-to-be wife, he could now almost smell the devastation to be realized as his pure love for his past girlfriend rekindled before a glass case exhibiting the blue-striped uniform of a concentration-camp prisoner.

Near the end of the tour he stood inside a final room (with the strikingly downtrodden German tourists) summarizing the numbers generated by the Nazis' treatment of the Jews. Mostly numb, nervously fumbling Israeli change in the right pocket of his well-pressed American slacks, he reviewed the country and camp totals presented on plaques throughout the room, different ways of breaking apart the number six million. He stopped at the number one million five hundred thousand, the number of children murdered by the Nazis. He decided this was a truly novel way to think of the events, but soon dissociated into a consideration of the cutoff age for children as determined by whoever computed this figure—thirteen, sixteen, eighteen? These damned children caused him to miss the unborn children of his stillborn union with that paragon of Jewish beauty and wisdom. All this made him hungry and thirsty. Tired and hungry and thirsty.

In the coffee shop, the American bought an Israeli baked good, an odd hybrid between the cinnamon roll and marble cake, a large, dense, doughy thing promising mass if nothing else. To wash it down the far-from-home businessman selected a grape-juice drink, bottled in a comically small container, the capacity somewhere in the area of 280 ml. The American had discovered the beverage earlier in the week, its unashamed brownish purple spoke to him. Back home the size would have served as a deterrent. But abroad, meticulously collecting receipts without further care, his need to purchase two such grape drinks at a single sitting bothered him not at all. As he made his way toward the aforementioned down-and-out cashier, he made a mental note of the likely ratio of grape drinks to baked goods this snack was likely to require (2:1), but elected not to buy two when there was still an outside chance that one would be enough.

The problem, it would turn out, would have nothing to do with the grape drink and everything to do with the baked good. It was not fresh, and while certain baked goods age well, while in fact certain baked goods are manufactured, indeed mass-produced, with the phrase "long shelf life" in mind, this particular baked good was made with the express purpose of being consumed within seventy-two hours. The company rep, who coordinated this particular account here in the coffee shop in the complex commemorating the Nazis' treatment of the Jews, communicated this to the manager of this same coffee shop (the aforementioned friend of the cashier) when the two met for the first time. He told the manager that his company would deliver twice a week, and that he should order only for the three-day period between deliveries (the week rendered essentially six days due to cessation of all activity on Saturday). The manager eventually ignored this advice, choosing instead to place his orders with less precision, erring on the overorder side, thereby forcing the standard baked good to inhabit the halfway house of the coffee-shop display case for, on average, over a hundred hours. The manager made this policy decision because he did not believe typical patrons of this particular coffee shop—that is, the coffee shop in the complex commemorating the Nazis' treatment of the Jews—would bother to voice complaints concerning the freshness of their baked good, what after spending the afternoon contemplating all varieties of starvation, emaciation, etc.

Our American, on this day, was different. He entered the café in a state his mother used to refer to as "ungy," a term describing that childhood mood of crabby self-pity specializing in the generation of yet more crabby self-pity. As a boy in a restaurant not of his choosing, or in the car on the way to visit family friends not of his liking, our American would cross arms pouting, defiantly intransigent in his self-absorbed protest. His mother—who today back in the suburban Midwest drank her diet-formula milk shake with pride, beaming because her son was bringing economic prosperity to the Holy Land, preparing it for the next century, this generation's Ben-Gurion—would, after a short round of negotiations and pleas, announce with sarcasm the arrival of this ungy attitude, often using the third person even if the two were the only ones in the car. Among his elaborate arsenal of manipulative childish behaviors, unginess was among the less effective, yet he employed it often. There is no reverse out of this mode, he could only ever trudge forward, until exhausted and bitter his tears or screaming would ignite. Then Mom would respond impatient and bitter, another painful family episode concluding only because it must.

It took only two bites of the once-fresh baked good for the American to realize the substandard quality of his purchase. He tugged and tore at it for a minute more, verifying with his eyes and fingers what his mouth had already discovered. Falling swiftly down his ladder of global historical consciousness, past the Nazis' systematic murder of the majority of Europe's Jews, down beyond even his self-centered remembrance of his own past, past his former girlfriend's dismissal of him as unworthy, this American fixed his sights firmly on the poor baked good, and put his proverbial foot down as he rose to voice his displeasure with who else but our equally troubled Israeli cashier.

PATRON: This is stale.

VENDOR: Stale?

CONSUMER: Yes, stale, it is not fresh, it is no good.

CASHIER: I know what this is, "stale."

AMERICAN: Well, then, it is stale.

ISRAELI: Why are you thinking that I will know what this is, "stale"?

BUSINESSMAN ABROAD: Well I wasn't certain, I tried to explain—

EX-JOURNALIST: This is the American arrogance at its finest. You are in Israel, in the middle of the Mideast, and you are saying "stale." Why am I needing to know what this says?

PRESSED SLACKS: But you knew.

JEANS SHORTS: This is not the matter. What if I am not knowing? If I am entering an American café and complain *"Zeh lo Tari,"* no one is helping me, until I say this thing in English.

SCORNED BOYFRIEND: Please, I just want my money back.

SCORNED HUSBAND: A refund? Say it, I know this word. I lived in your decadent, yes I know also this word, decadent United States for two years, less or more, reading your idiot newspapers, watching your stupid television, speaking this ugly language.

UPWARDLY MOBILE: Sir, please, I just want—

BOTTOMING OUT: Don't fucking call me "sir"! I'm a cashier worker, you motherfucker son of a whore!

EXASPERATED: Fuck you. Take your fucking shitty roll, fucking Israeli asshole!

And in a gesture wildly out of character, the American, before storming angrily out of the coffee shop in the complex
commemorating the Nazis' treatment of the Jews, seized the
surviving remains of the roll and threw them with some force at
the Israeli, who sat no more than four feet from him, hitting him
squarely on the left cheek, causing physical pain for a moment or
two, leaving a line of sticky sugar goop just below his glasses.
A much older Israeli man, originally from Galicia, who lost
much of his extended family during the Jewish genocide at the
hand of the Nazis, who spent at least two days a month here
in the complex commemorating these events, muttered loudly,
"Enough, stop," in heavily accented Hebrew. Others in the café
turned their heads to look, vaguely sensing the need to intervene
after internalizing the lessons of this complex, the need not to
remain passive and silent in the face of injustice, etc., but they,
too, were tired, and the brief quarrel ended before anyone could
summon the resolve to act. The tension subsided as the furious
cashier removed the ex–baked good from his face and shirt collar, cursing to himself in Arabic, because Hebrew has no good
curses.

Just outside the central building in the complex commemorating
the Nazis' treatment of the Jews, the confused and upset businessman sat upon a bench and caught his breath. The late-
afternoon sunlight dazzled him, and he felt as if he had just left
an engaging matinee, the bright day smashing to bits in his recent, receding memory the world projected upon the screen
just inside the dark movie house. He laughed to himself,

embarrassed, amazed, still hungry. The regular foot traffic of the complex passed him unaware, though he felt a palpable need to respond to these people, to show his amused disbelief at the events that had recently transpired. If he still cried, like the ungy boy he had once been, he would have cried. It had been an exhausting day, not what he expected, and he wished he smoked cigarettes. He thought this would be a good time to concentrate on the smoking of a cigarette.

After a time the American rose to wander about for a few more minutes on the grounds of the complex commemorating the Nazis' treatment of the Jews. His business was done here, but he wasn't ready to leave. He wanted to add a layer of pleasantness to cover over the coffee-shop incident. He welcomed eagerly the mood of the sprawling complex, centered by the sense of purpose this site of perpetual mourning enjoys, however somberly. He walked lazily. He grinned slightly. He fumbled the new combination of Israeli coins in his left pants pocket. He would need to get these pants pressed before his final meeting tomorrow. He should call his fiancée when he returned to the hotel, but he couldn't decide if he would tell her about today.

Meanwhile the Israeli cashier, nearly spinning out at the edge of self-control, sat stewing in his fury a few moments more. Embarrassed, confused, humiliated, and further embarrassed, confused, and humiliated by his embarrassment, confusion, and humiliation, he noticed how difficult breathing had become. His vision seemed blurred. He motioned to a coworker, muttered something unintelligible in any of the thousand tongues of this planet, and stumbled toward the exit of the main building in the complex commemorating the Nazis' treatment of the Jews. The cool air immediately soothed him, lowering his anxiety to something merely disturbing. He lowered himself on a large rock and began to smoke a cigarette.

"Sliha." It was the American trying out the one word he had learned on his trip, Israel's version of "excuse me." If he had known the condition of his addressee, he would not have addressed him at all, but he did not know, and, as stated earlier, he did want a cigarette.

The Israeli on self-imposed break raised his head in a jerk and mustered up just enough control not to respond initially. He lowered his head, sucked on his cigarette. "It's 'slicha,' there's a 'cha' sound, you must feel it in your throat."

The American tried again and almost succeeded. "Slichka, you wouldn't happen to have an extra cigarette?" He thought they might laugh about what had transpired inside. His embarrassment, confusion, and humiliation manifested itself as giddiness. The Israeli reached into his front pocket and removed the box of cigarettes, the word "Time" written on the white container. He continued smoking with his head down as he extended the cigarettes to the American. The American removed a cigarette from the box, placed it in his mouth, and removed the book of matches that had been tucked smartly in the cellophane wrapping that still covered two-thirds of the box. His hand shook a bit because he felt naughty. He didn't smoke. He had smoked, all told, eleven cigarettes in his life, seven of them during the same drunk evening/night in college thirteen years ago. But seeing so many Israelis smoking everywhere in apparent apathy to its effects roused in him a desire to join in, to go native in this very way. He lit the cigarette, and inhaled, pleased to have embarked on this adventure. For a moment the enduring silence bothered him, then he concluded it enhanced the absolute coolness of the moment. He wished his pants and shoes were not in such good condition.

The Israeli dared not raise his head. He had entered the unpleasant territories of irrationality and paranoia far enough to suspect that this American was not the cheery tourist he pretended to be. The on-break cashier worried that a security guard had already been summoned and was on his way to confront him. He considered rising and walking straight to his Vespa scooter, driving home, or even better to a bar he visited on rare occasions. He smirked, catching himself in such senseless worry. But, still, he preferred staring at the ground straight ahead. Anything else was too much just now.

The American experimented with different holds, with inhalations of varied length, with exhalations both vigorous and casual. Then came a lull of foolishness, of anticipated regret for how his mouth would feel in ten minutes. Heavy, puffy, somehow dying ever so slightly. Smoking is stupid after all. He broke the silence by apologizing to the cashier for throwing the roll at him. The Israeli remained silent, and the American felt uncomfortable. "Forget it," the Israeli said, his voice calm in the way one's voice is calm when trying extremely hard to sound calm: a bit too loud, slow, finally cracking to betray the speaker.

If either the Israeli or the American had eyes on the back of his head, he would have been able to see an Israeli guide lead around the grounds of the complex commemorating the Nazis' treatment of the Jews, of all things, the same German tour group. The tour guide, fluent in German of course, but not a survivor in any literal sense, specialized in the German tourists visiting his country. Initially he took sadistic pleasure in the day each tour visited the complex, something few Germans had the guts to sidestep, though most of them were there, that is in Israel and its occupied territories, to see where Jesus had been during his brief but vital to them life. Later on he began to sympathize ever so slightly with the Germans, most of them just young enough to be mathematically eliminated from direct responsibility for their nation's treatment of the Jews. Each tour at least one or two would have a really tough time of it, breaking under the cruel burden of something too big for even the broadest Bavarian shoulders, and the whole tour group would project a nearly sour smelling dark disappointment, their pilgrimage in honor of the Son of God rained upon. And of course this rain and the Son of God in the final account were not totally inseparable, the Jews and the Jewish Jesus did dovetail for a while there with unfortunate results; one of the longer misunderstandings to date. But now he had come to dread this day. Often on this day he would sigh slowly and remove his spectacles to clean them with his shirt. He spoke with little drama and allowed long silences to prevail. Not for effect, but because he didn't want to be involved in the day any more than necessary. After the trip he would round up his sheepish, nearly lifeless tourists and return them to their hotel, each one of them silently grateful to have a Jew tell them what to do. He would then retire to a nearby bar and drink a few bad Israeli beers. The Germans would remain in their hotel rooms, ashamed and stone-faced, watching television.

"Please get away from me," the Israeli pleaded after another silence.

The American sat quietly, and almost rose, but weathering the first instant of defiance realized he could, if he wanted, remain right where he was.

"Get away from me, please," the Israeli's speech crescendo-ing, his abnormally round head filling with blood.

The American, his courage and giddiness inflated by his

initial refusal, offered, "It's 'go away.' Not 'get away,' and you don't need the 'from me.'" He smiled, quite pleased with himself.

There was a pause during which the American concluded that this section of their dialogue had ended, that the Israeli had been won over by his cheerful cleverness. The American could only understand this moment by identifying himself as yet one more incarnation of one-half of any of a few hundred odd couples from television and the movies. Men, who despite all varieties of difference, ranging from dress to political convictions, come to like and even rely on one another. The American took an extra-long drag on his cigarette, they really were different and would make a great team.

"Go away, fucking bastard." The Israeli pushed the American in the torso, causing the American to lose his balance on the rock. He prevented a complete fall by quickly placing his open palm on the rocky walkway, skinning his hand just a bit. His clenched lips alone had to maintain their purchase on the cigarette, but they failed, and the much-shortened cigarette fell lazily to the ground. It rolled swiftly, drawing out a half circle, bits of ash here and there.

"You son of a bitch," the American responded. He picked up the cigarette, suffering from ice-cream-cone-on-the-pavement thoughts. He threw the still-lit butt at the Israeli. "What the fuck?!" he added, like a good American.

The Israeli did not mean to stand fully erect and so challenge the American, but he was drawn by a blunt urge to close the distance between himself and the American, and there was no way to do this but to stand. Scooching over was all wrong in this situation. He had no plan, no concrete intention, just a base need to encroach on the other man's space. As he neared, the American, 0-1-1 all time in fights, lifted his right hand toward the Israeli's face. The hand was neither fist nor palm, had not been instructed to function as either punch or push. But this mattered little. The Israeli was, after all, a onetime soldier (who still served in reserves six to eight weeks a year) trained in a very basic but effective Israeli military form of martial arts, a combination of judo and simple street fighting. Without much thought, his left hand intercepted the American's right hand. After redirecting the American's hand past his own left shoulder, the Israeli redirected his own hand, landing the ball of his palm squarely on the American's lower lip with adequate force. The lip split and blood rushed unabated out of his face and into the air where it fell to the ground of the complex commemorating the Nazis' treatment of the Jews, the dozen or so wide drops drawing out aesthetically pleasing shapes and images, in some abstract sense, as they hit the ground. The American stumbled backwards and fell. The Israeli stood, heaving, his hand partially bloodied. The cigarette smoldered. The sky was blue with the right amount of clouds.

The tour guide continued in his impeccable German, standing between twenty-six mute Germans—each trying in his or her own private way to figure out how to apologize to an entire religion, each wishing collective memory and state policy showed no interest in genealogy, now or then—and a massive bas-relief sculpture. The sculpture was a weighty snapshot of eventual, allegorical genocide etched deep into a sixty-by-twenty-foot wall of stone. The elongated figures, the Jews and their persecutors, bent up and away from each other, stuck in a moment but stretched over time in silence and horror. The guide, in his worn-out shoes, clutching his day pack lazily, addressed his Germans, pausing often to allow the others to consider the frozen scene. "And this boy, this innocent child, seemingly not of this scene.

He is both in the center, and yet somehow he steps out of the rock toward us. How? Why? Because he alone looks out at us, at each one of us. With his eyes he transcends this stone and enters our world right now. The pure eyes of simple youth ask us, demand from us an answer, 'Why do you just stand and look? Why do you do nothing?' Finally he asks, 'If it is too late now,' and surely it is, 'will you act next time, will you prevent this next time?' This is the question and this is the lesson." And the guide lowered his eyes, dominated from all sides by fury and shame. This boy, the one from the famous photo. His arms raised in the Warsaw Ghetto, too young to possibly understand. The same photo produced by that maniacal bastard Begin when asked to justify Beirut. That boy.

The American eventually stood back up, dabbing his lip with some of his receipts. He found a bathroom located on the grounds. He washed up and considered the small rip near the knee of his slacks. Inside the coffee shop of the complex commemorating the Nazis' treatment of the Jews, the Israeli, whose hands were recently washed but who continued sweating slightly, returned to his stool indifferent to his possible futures. In a few moments the Germans would enter, passively led by their Jew. They would buy all matters of food stuff, including stale baked goods, and they would eat every last bite, tasting nothing. The guide with his coffee would come through last, his heavy, full red beard just on this side of prophecy. Looking at our Israeli, he would enjoy the pleasure of his discomfort abating slightly. He would smile and say to the cashier, in a soft, intimate Hebrew, "How's business?"

"Not bad," the Israeli would respond with a tired grin, clutching his scalp pensively below his close-cropped hair, "not bad."

WILL POWER, INC.

I. DINNER

It doesn't matter how wealthy or hungry you are: If at 7:30 P.M. on a Saturday night you don't already have a reservation at Chez Panisse, you're pretty much going to have to kill someone to get a table. The birthplace of California Cuisine, Alice Waters's influential Berkeley landmark could well be the best restaurant in the country. And it knows it. The upstairs dining room—with its wood-burning oven, custom mahogany fixtures, and brass trim—is at once doggedly immaculate and refreshingly relaxed. The waitstaff buzzes about, not so much handsome as interesting and competent. I'm stunned that all the other patrons have overcome the urge to whoop and holler in celebration.

Our party numbers five, and we're seated in this order: Don

Trammell,[1] Peter Stone, Diane Chadwich, Craig Dannon, and myself. Prior to the introductions outside, I only knew Peter, who works for Don. Everyone else seems to be Don's friend or a business associate. These are the kind of people (i.e., really rich people) for whom such distinctions are meaningless. Our menus, printed out today, arrive with bread. Peter casually moves the plate toward Diane and Craig's edge of the circle, tearing off a piece of the hearty brown loaf first.

I order from the unintelligibly sophisticated menu using a random-selection method not worth getting into here. Thankfully, Diane chooses the wine. Peter and Craig order without ceremony, Don doesn't even consult the menu. Also, he skips the opening course. The bread stays at the opposite end of the table from him, but he doesn't seem to mind.

Though I still have no idea what it is, my appetizer is yummy, as in really yummy. I can't believe we aren't hugging each other. Instead, we (okay, they) discuss the commodity markets. Peter asks a single question and is otherwise silent. Don whispers something to Peter, motioning to his lonely bread plate. Peter shakes his head and rises to consult with our waitress.

Don's entrée materializes on our table a few minutes later while the rest of us are still working on our first course. Peter softly clutches Don's forearm and whispers something in his ear. Don nods almost imperceptibly.

By the time our entrées arrive, Don is only a third into his, apparently pacing himself. Craig orders a second bottle of wine, while Don asks the waitress to remove his wineglass. Peter smiles a bit. The conversation turns to politics, and I try to join in, though soon I realize that we're actually talking about fiscal

[1] Name changed.

policy. Everyone chews and nods. Don, who I should mention is fairly heavyset, suddenly picks up his pace, and, in something of a masticatory sprint, clears his plate in seconds. Peter notes this as well.

Our second round of menus appears, and once again I'm lost. The language is more familiar, but are these the kind of people that order desserts at all? They're so different from me— a poor graduate student who definitely wants to order his own dessert—maybe they forgo dessert entirely in the spirit of their brand of turbo capitalism ("Just a double espresso for me, thanks."). Suddenly Diane suggests sharing three desserts. Peter politely objects or declines. Don says nothing, just chews on his lip. I agree with everyone, however impossible that may be at a table in disagreement. But three desserts it is. Peter tells the waitress: No fork or spoon for me.

Four spoons arrive with our three desserts, and Peter, to my surprise, does take a spoon. Don lowers his head to the side toward Peter and with an odd smirk says something I can't make out. With the desserts half dismantled, each immeasurably delicious, Don says, "Peter, let me see that spoon." Peter doesn't say anything, nor does he offer the spoon. Don grabs it. "C'mon," he chuckles. Don furiously starts making up for lost time, his recently acquired spoon a silvery blur. I'm simultaneously relieved and appalled by Don's assault on our collection of endangered desserts. Relieved, because it won't be me who blows it in the manners department, appalled, because, well, reread this sentence. Diane turns away from Don and asks Craig a question about his upcoming trip to Rome.[2] Craig responds, trying to fix his gaze squarely on Diane, but he can't, as Don is a sight to

[2] Not Italy, just Rome.

behold. "Don," Peter admonishes him softly. "That's enough," Peter blurts out, but Don is not to be stopped. Finally, as yet another heaping spoonful of the unfairly rich chocolate event heads toward his mouth, Peter grabs Don's wrist, squeezing quite hard. The tendons on the back of Peter's powerful hand rise tensed, Don's thick fingers redden instantly. Don drops the spoon, its creamy chocolaty bliss spilling onto the white table-cloth. "Thanks," Don admits with some shame.

Peter works for Don. His job is to prevent Don from overeating, to prevent Don—through encouragement, cunning, and, if need be, physical restraint—from eating too much.

Don retreats to the bathroom, returns a few minutes later as if nothing has happened, and says, "Let's go," having picked up the tab somewhere along the way.

II. TRYING TO DIGEST THE RIDE HOME

"Last year fifty million Americans spent $30 billion trying to lose weight." Driving me in his beefy Ford Expedition to my apartment in nearby El Cerrito, Peter informs me of these numbers with little passion, he's presented this information before. "Within five years, and in most cases within the first year, any weight lost will be put on again. Five years after going on a diet, more than 95 percent of adults fail to keep off the weight they lose." This is my first ride in an SUV. I despise them, the useless bulk, the asinine status they promise, the gluttonous consumption of natural resources. "Ninety-five percent. Let's say that the average initial weight loss from any diet is twenty pounds— that's an extremely generous figure, but never mind." Yet I can't imagine Peter in any other type of vehicle. At six feet four and, I'm estimating, 220 pounds, a Honda Civic just wouldn't do the trick. "Americans pay $30 billion to lose one billion pounds. That's $30 a pound." Being such a pure instance of masculinity—he could effortlessly beat me to a pulp—the obvious alternatives for Peter are the pickup truck or the sports car. "But only, at most, 5 percent of that weight stays off. So, in fact, Americans pay $30 billion to lose fifty million pounds." He needs a car that resonates with, indeed accommodates, his physical might. "That comes out to $600 a pound—$600 *per pound*." Also, he's intelligent, sophisticated, urbane. A pickup truck, therefore, is too brutish, too overtly physical. The sports car betrays a need to prove one's virility, and too small besides. "So, in fact, paying $12,000 to keep twenty pounds off for five years is the going rate." Thus, Peter deserves, in a way that is true of very few people, an SUV. I make a mental note to use public transportation and carpool as much as possible to compensate for Peter's rightful place in the transportation hierarchy. "But Jenny Craig doesn't offer a money-back-guaranteed $12,000 program. Our service is guaranteed. To be sure, it costs more, but it works."[3]

Were Hollywood to produce the film adaptation of this story, John C. Reilly, the fleshy-faced actor in *Magnolia* and *The Perfect Storm*, would play Peter, as long as the actor agreed to six months of intensive workouts. Peter's heavy brow and bulbous nose aren't up to the standards set by his Apollonian physique, but they do make it easy for me to accept that he's nearly as

[3] Peter's numbers, if not necessarily his math, more or less check out. I say "more or less" not because they're only sort of accurate, but because when dealing with the notoriously unregulated diet industry there's just no way to know. It should be noted that nearly half of the $30 billion spent annually on dieting goes toward diet drinks, like Diet Coke. So perhaps the bottom line is a little inflated, since it's hard to equate drinking a Diet Coke with dieting. But then again, "Just for the taste of it!"? Hardly.

bright as he is strong. Otherwise it would be unfair. Peter grew
up in a middle-class suburb of Cincinnati, where he was a three-
time varsity letterman in wrestling and football. His senior year,
1992, Peter made the All-State football team as an honorable
mention and graduated in the top 10 percent of his class. At
Ohio State University, Peter walked on his sophomore year, but
played only four plays all season. Leaving organized athletics
behind, Peter focused on academics, graduating with a 3.95
GPA and an economics degree in only seven semesters. He
scored in the ninety-sixth percentile on the GMAT, was accepted to Stanford's MBA program, and at the age of twenty-
one moved to Silicon Valley with plans to make millions in the
new economy.

Alarmed at the outrageous cost of living in Palo Alto, Peter,
despite taking out tens of thousands of dollars in student loans,
was forced to find part-time work to make ends meet. "I became
a bouncer at a club in San Jose. It was usually an easy gig. Wear a
black leather jacket, look imposing, act swiftly on rare occasions.
But it only took one rough night to teach me why the pay was so
good." We're waiting at a red light, and Peter pulls up his right
sleeve, revealing a five-inch white scar along his forearm. Hoping
to continue earning the high paycheck available only to men of
his rare size and strength, Peter found work in "personal security" for a high-tech tycoon who had just gone through a nasty
breakup with two former business associates. Peter became a
bodyguard.

We're stopped in front of my humble complex. Peter's
Expedition idles in silence. "Mr. Trammell is the smartest man
I've ever met. How can I put this? It's similar to the experience I
have with physical activities. Tasks that require extreme effort
for a normal person mean nothing to me: running five miles,

climbing a mountain, lifting heavy objects. Mr. Trammell can learn an obscure, complex computer code in half an hour. I've watched *Jeopardy* with him when he's known every answer without hesitating: opera, chemistry, ancient history, you name it. When his weight finally got down to where he could travel again, he went to Spain. He studied intensively with a private language tutor for eight weeks. He was fluent, I mean absolutely fluent. He made millions in the early and mid-nineties. I'm not at liberty to say what he's worth, but if you want to do the research, check out the *Forbes* 400."

Don Trammell, I'd wager, traveled the start-up, IPO, buy-out path more than any other man. In six years, Don worked for or started seven different companies, all of which were bought by Sun Microsystems, Lucent, or Cisco. Don's short tenure with each start-up—indeed, the abbreviated life span of each company—is not coincidence. According to Peter, early on, years before the bottom fell out of the new economy, Don sensed that the boom was not going to last. "By about 1994 Mr. Trammell's goal was to make as much as he could, retire early, ride out the bust, and then return to the industry when things steadied out. He had gotten interested in some radical projects, artificial intelligence, universal translators, but with the amounts of money moving around, things were too unpredictable for the long-term stability that type of research requires. Mr. Trammell was adept at starting a company, quickly raising its value, and selling it. The only problem was that some of his partners weren't as eager as he was to be bought out. There were some misunderstandings that got quite ugly, as I'm sure you can imagine with the amounts of money we're talking about. Mr. Trammell made some enemies, there were numerous threats to his personal safety. That's where I came in."

Don retired in 1998, worth over $400 million, bought a mas-
sive home in Tiburon, watched his assets nearly double as the
NASDAQ continued through the roof, and waited for the bust.
And ate. "Mr. Trammell, when I met him in 1999, was already
obese. Bigger than what you saw this evening. I don't know, 250,
260. He has significant difficulty controlling his diet. He never
had so much time for himself, and quite honestly he didn't know
what to do with it. He developed a chronic eating disorder,
which manifested itself primarily in binge eating. He tried a few
diets. He would lose five or ten pounds, only to yo-yo back up
and over his initial weight. He tried personal trainers. He hired a
live-in chef. But he was unable to stop eating. He would start a
day off determined to limit his intake, 'Today no junk. No snack-
ing, no ice cream,' he would say. Everything would be going fine
until mid-afternoon, then he'd have a handful of potato chips.
And that would be the beginning of the end. Nonstop eating
until he fell asleep in front of the home-theater system. Ice
cream, pizza, sushi, steaks, anything and everything."

By early 2000, Don weighed 372 pounds. Clothes became
difficult to find. Travel impossible. He rarely left his house,
where he couldn't ascend the stairs, or even sleep lying down for
fear of asphyxiation. Effectively restricted to a single recliner,
Don's millions were nearly irrelevant. "He considered gastro-
plasty, stomach stapling, but he was concerned about complications. Finally one day he turns to me, nearly in tears—this is a
very strong, proud, wealthy, brilliant man—and he says, 'Peter,
what can I do? I'm my own worst enemy.' I don't know what I
was thinking, I just responded, 'Mr. Trammell, would you like me
to protect you from yourself?'"

Thus, Don Trammell became, before Will Power, Inc., officially existed, the company's first client. In the beginning, opera-

tions were a bit crude. "I just wouldn't let him eat very much. Cold turkey. Like a movie about a recovering alcoholic. Flush it down the toilet, throw it in the garbage. That's what I did with the food in the house. Soon I realized that when I wasn't around he would binge, ordering junk through Webvan. So we had to hire more diet escorts, to share twelve-hour shifts and weekends." Their dynamic changed considerably, since Peter now told Don what he could and could not eat and when. Since Don was largely immobile, Peter rarely had to restrain him physically, though it happened. "The first month was very difficult. He went through withdrawal, like any addict would. Mr. Trammell tried to fire me repeatedly, but I knew that's not what he wanted. Finally we signed a contract, a basic single-page document that stated, 'I, Don Trammell, rescind the right to terminate Peter Stone as my diet escort until the year 2002.' Of course, legally, it was meaningless, but I fell back on it often. We use a similar contract with our other clients."

After two months Peter thought he could see a slight change in Don, but he was concerned about the lack of a long-term program. "The two of us had started reading dieting books, medical journals, Don even invited doctors from UCSF and Stanford to his home for advice. Everyone warned us against low-calorie 'starvation' diets. We worked with dieticians and nutritionists, placing him in a range of 1,500 to 1,700 calories a day, mostly lean meats and vegetables. When Don got below 325, we started him on light exercise. He got back under 300 around this time last year. That convinced me to start the business. This morning he was at 234." Peter smiles, not smugly, just proud of the role he played in effectively saving another man's life.

When I ask Peter if his pay has increased with his new responsibilities, he responds, "Not officially, but Mr. Trammell has repeatedly demonstrated his gratitude to me through bonuses and gifts," and then pats the dashboard. "Also, he provided the funds to start the company. But he expects no money in return. He thinks of it as a philanthropic act. As you can imagine, he believes in this quite deeply."

I thank Peter for arranging my invitation to dinner. "My pleasure," he says, extending his hand toward mine. Wishing we knew each other well enough to hug, I brace myself, attempting to wrap my meager hand around his massive, powerful palm. "I'll call you tomorrow," I tell him casually, as if he wasn't crushing my poor fingers.

III. HOME ALONE WITH MY GIRTH

Just inside my apartment, I immediately ditch my tight khakis for more forgiving sweatpants. Like most Americans, I have an infinitely complex relationship with my body, a running interior dialogue detailing the fluctuations of its mass, which swings back and forth around a point probably twelve pounds over my (the, an, its?) ideal weight. Five years ago this point was closer to eight pounds of excess. But as my metabolism slows, as the constraints of my career require a more sedentary lifestyle, as minor recurring injuries limit certain physical activities, I, like the bulk of my fellow Americans, steadily grow fatter. I'm not obese, but at this rate I will be, I estimate, by my fiftieth birthday. And even if I'm only marginally overweight this evening, I feel fat after eating so much. The last thing I want to be conscious of, the last thing I want to feel, is my waistline, so praise the Lord for sweatpants. But even after a wardrobe change, I still can't get myself to sit at the computer to enter the notes buzzing around my head from tonight's events. Sitting would involve too much belly and waist sensation. Instead I pace my apartment and try jotting some notes down on a dry erase board mounted on the fridge. It's no use. My sudden self-disgust overwhelms any desire to describe the group dynamic at dinner. All I can manage—as I scribble on my frozen-food chest, some six inches from my always-ready reserves of ice cream—is: "More than envying Don Trammell for his wealth, I empathize with him for his size."

Such self-induced suffering and discomfort—as much as the steady dissemination of personal technologies, the ever-widening gap in income levels, the unstoppable growth of the war on terror—is a main story line of our country here in the early days of the twenty-first century. We are, in short, a nation of heft. If we represent only 5 percent of the world's population, we are probably responsible for 6 to 8 percent of global human biomass. We don't merely consume a disproportionate amount of the world's resources. We stubbornly, and against our collective will, internalize, integrate, literally incorporate much of these resources into our very bodies. The concentration, per capita, of matter in the American national body is without precedent in our planet's past, and tomorrow we'll break our own record. Every day is the fattest day in the history of the United States.[4]

---

[4] Some numbers from the Centers for Disease Control and Prevention (CDC): Since the early 1960s, the percentage of men in a "healthy" weight range (Body Mass Index (BMI) between 19 and 25 kilograms/meters squared) has dropped by over 10 percent in every age category except one. Nearly two-thirds of all men are overweight (BMI 25 or more); 27.2 percent of men age 55–64 are obese (BMI 30 or more), tripling the 9.2 percent figure from thirty-five years ago. While a marginally larger percentage of women still fall in the healthy range, the female descent

Peter Stone's company, Will Power, Inc., offers an extreme service in our ever-increasing, ever-more-futile efforts to lose weight. For a sum that Peter himself admits is exorbitant, his company will design an extensive and personalized long-term weight-loss program combining the expertise of dieticians, nutritionists, personal trainers, psychotherapists, personal chefs, and ex-bodyguards. The latter group doesn't actually participate in devising the program, they merely ensure that you stick to it. As Peter astutely notes, even the most comprehensive weight-loss strategies—those employing the latest research on diet and nutrition as no more than a foundation upon which is constructed a far-reaching, individualized lifestyle program addressing the physical, emotional, and spiritual needs of each client—cannot solve the inconsistency of said individual's resolve, motivation, and self-control. The bold addition of an outside will to the weight-loss equation neutralizes this volatility and is Peter's addition to the weight-loss industry. It is also the secret to his company's striking success.

---

into weight gain is more precipitous. In other words, once a woman hits the 25 BMI mark, she is much more likely than her male counterpart to break the 30 BMI barrier as well. In fact, over one-third (33.7 percent) of women in the 55–64 age range are obese. Oh, and these figures are actually taken from research conducted during the first half of the 1990s. Things are even worse now. According to a 1999 CDC report on the "obesity epidemic," obesity in the general population rose from 12 percent in 1991 to 17.9 percent in 1998 and continues to rise. No one is being spared, to wit: "The obesity epidemic spread rapidly during the 1990s across all states, regions, and demographic groups in the United States." While this means misery for millions of Americans nationwide, one can only imagine the satisfaction it would have brought to Foucault to see a situation (a bodily situation nonetheless) in which "abnormality" has become the norm.

IV. WILL POWER, INC. OFFICES,
SAN RAFAEL, CALIFORNIA

Only forty-two years old, George Bissell has a CV that looks like the professional itinerary of an overachieving workaholic who at the age of seventy is still chugging along. At twenty-five, with an MBA and master's in Public Health, George, every bit ambitious as he was precocious, set off to make quality public health care viable. Yet by his thirtieth birthday, perhaps unable to resist the exponential pay increase, George was lured into the private sector. Alternating between upper-level hospital administration and restructuring insolvent insurance companies, George became the wunderkind of the health-care industry. Always eager for the next challenge and more than willing to consider the latest eye-popping financial package from another high-caliber head-hunter, George occupied seven powerful positions in nine years. Then, three days before turning forty and on the verge of his first and only "professional identity crisis," George came across a small piece on a radical new dieting company. Two weeks later George was CEO of Will Power, Inc.

We've been talking for a few minutes, cordial and friendly, but everything from his body language to the way he says my first name every time he addresses me (I'm the only other person in his office) gives me the creeps. I figure as the journalist it's time for me to ask the difficult questions: "Your company, its service, it raises some ethical or moral questions."

A smile rises on Bissell's tight face. He was expecting this, it has made things a bit unpleasant, but he's more than ready. I don't frighten him. He's not about to get exposed, he's about to get exposure. Because as I'm learning, people will do anything to lose weight. Ends kick means' ass in the world of dieting. Just to have fun, Bissell stalls, tossing the question back at me. "Such as, Michael?"

My turn to manufacture the "you're fucking with me, aren't you, well, no big deal" smile. I shift to the inflection of an intellectual graduate student at the top research university in the world. I want to problematize the hegemonic discourse constructing modernity's representations of the body, or at least try. "Well, it seems to me that your service promises each subject an opportunity to achieve the body he or she has always wanted by, ironically, surrendering control over this body."

"Ironically, yes, Michael, you're right there. But I'm not convinced that otherwise there are any serious ethical or moral questions. Our clients elect to use the service we provide at their own volition, and they may terminate this service, unilaterally, at any time."

"At *any* time?"

"Yes."

"So last night, when Don Trammell nearly had his wrist broken by your partner, what could he have done?"

"He could have said, 'Peter, I would like to terminate our professional relationship, effective immediately.'"

"Don't your clients do that all the time?"

"At first, many do, yes."

"And if they regret that?"

"As they almost always do."

"Then what?"

"Then, Michael, we, for a fee, restart service, at times including the 'cool-down' clause in their contract."

"Cool-down clause?"

"It stipulates that they relinquish the right to terminate service while in the middle of any given redirection incident." He pauses to see if I've understood Will Power's technical jargon. "That if, for instance, a client surreptitiously orders a large pizza with mushrooms[5] while our employee leaves to use the bathroom, and upon arrival of the large mushroom pizza our employee disposes of the pizza, mushrooms and all, as he is required to do under the agreed-upon contract, the client cannot terminate the employee during the act of disposal, cannot terminate the employee, in fact, for one full hour after this incident."

"So then"—I'm a bit pleased for observing this, though I know he's ready for it—"the client *can't* actually terminate service immediately, at any time."

"No, Michael, not if they've agreed to forgo that right."

"Is that legal?"

George wets his lips, preparing to remind me about what really matters here. "None of our seventy-nine clients has resorted to litigation. They're too busy sending us $1,000 flower arrangements"—he motions to a miniature Rose Bowl Parade float nestled in a corner—"and signing up for three-year extensions."

In sharp contrast to Peter's awe-inspiring physique, George looks what I imagine I might look like—minus the generous

---

[5] Surreptitiously?! In deference to Mr. George's request I did not tape our conversation, but I did take detailed notes throughout and tried to re-create our discussion in its entirety moments after leaving his office, and I know for a fact that he said "surreptitiously orders a large pizza with mushrooms." In the history of pizza ordering, not a one has ever been ordered *surreptitiously*. Secretly, for certain, on the sly, no doubt, I'll go so far as to entertain the possibility that a pizza or two, possibly even a large pizza with mushrooms, has been ordered furtively, but surreptitiously, absolutely not. It was at this moment that I—against my better judgment and at the expense of even the most lowly journalistic standards—assumed an overtly contrary stance to George and the company he represents.

application of hair products—in fifteen years: well-dressed, be-spectacled, and a little heavy. And whereas I found Peter to be as sensitive and even compassionate as he is strong—a guy who unexpectedly wound up in health care simply because he cares about other people—George immediately strikes me as the hard-nosed, calculating, even ruthless type. The kind of guy who found success in the health-care industry because he was willing to choose, time and again, the bottom line over quality medical care.

"And all this costs?"

A minor grin. "Our fees vary, depending on the package chosen. The basic package requires an extensive consultation with one of our nutritionists, including weekly follow-up meet-ings for the first three months, and monthly follow-ups there-after, and, of course, some consistent use of a diet escort, for a minimum of two hours per day, five days a week."

"How can ten hours a week be effective?"

"Oh, you'd be surprised. Some people develop temporally bounded behaviors that have devastating consequences. We have a client in New York, the wife of an influential investment banker, who every day at 5:45 P.M. returned to her Park Avenue residence, and ate, without fail, two pints of premium ice cream, chocolate based, and one five-ounce bag of salt and vinegar po-tato chips. By pairing this woman up with one of our diet escorts from 5:15 to 7:15 each workday, and by having our escort engage the client in an alternative, healthier, but equally compulsive be-havior—racquetball, a movie, yoga, and walks in the park were all tried until we hit upon the combination of Rollerblading to a gourmet grocery store—our client lost fifty pounds."

I'm impressed. "But your fees."

"Yes. The flat fee, Michael, for participation in the program

for six months, which is the minimum we agree to, which includes initial consultation, follow-up visits, and the services of a
diet escort for up to eight hours a day, seven days a week is
$120,000."

I have absolutely no idea how to respond to this. All the obvious options—(1) no fucking way; (2) wow; (3) holy shit—however sincere, are too dissonant with the conventions of my
present role. Yet to do anything but laugh out loud would bestow
upon our conversation a certain legitimacy I'm reluctant to be
party to. I do, however, want more details. I gather myself. "How
did you come to that figure?"

"We pay our diet escorts at least $50 per hour, not including
benefits and other expenses. Nutritionists' fees come out to
about $10,000 for the six-month period. There are additional ad-
ministrative costs, etc."

"And how much is profit?"

"That I won't divulge. We're doing well, though most of it
we reinvest in the company."

I want more numbers. "You said that's the basic package,
what does something more elaborate run?"

"Let me give you the average scenario, to the extent that
there is one, because, Michael, as you can imagine, each of our
clients comes to us with a truly unique condition. Most clients
elect a much more extensive diagnostic evaluation: doctor, dietician, analyst for certain. Some add personal trainer, hypnothera-
pist, acupuncturist, live-in chef, applied kinesiologist, you name
it. Many of our clients visit with one or another specialist numerous times a week, at least in the beginning. Then, of course, for
some eight hours a day is not enough. Some require twenty-four-
hour support, the average is fourteen. So for one year, because
most of our clients elect to go that route, as we encourage them

to do, about $500,000 for the year. And most of our clients look
like they'll be lifers."

I rub my eyes and giggle nervously, unable to maintain my
composure. "That's nuts," I announce. "George," I say it slowly,
the "or" sound steadily rising in pitch, like we're old friends and
we're going over the same misunderstanding for the fortieth
time, "who the hell is going to pay half a million dollars a year
for life in order to lose weight?"

"Mr. Diamond"—he addresses me condescendingly—"all
of our clients, without exception, come to us with two central
qualities: one, they are exceptionally wealthy. The average net
worth of a client of Will Power, Inc., is just under $100 million.[6]
Two, they are exceptionally obese. The average Body Mass Index

---

[6] While considerably smaller than that of, say, Blockbuster Video, Will Power's potential client base—in northern California alone—is nothing to scoff at. Before
the utopian bubble of unprecedented prosperity over Silicon Valley burst during
the second half of 2000, 20–60 new millionaires were created there *per day*. Of the
somewhere between 5–10 million millionaires in the United States, at least 10 percent live in Silicon Valley. And though the bear market bloodbath of 2001 cut
more than a few one-time millionaires down to semiaffluent size, the ultra-rich,
Will Power's true client base, is hardly going hungry. The NASDAQ-centered free
fall cost investors some $4 trillion in paper money by May 2001, but having only
$550 million still kept you off this year's *Forbes* 400. Moreover, the filthy rich know
a thing or two about diversifying their holdings. And don't even get me started with
hedge funds and futures, the kind of stuff that (a) you need a bundle just to get
your foot in the door, (b) you can actually make money when the economy is
in the toilet. All told, and these numbers change daily, there are at least 10,000
Americans—as in 10,000 heads of household, some, you've got to figure, have
rather chunky dependents (juvenile diabetes, anyone?) and cousins—with the
money to sign up. And even if the super-rich and their loved ones reach obesity at
only half the rate of the general population, you're still looking at a few thousand
who are soon to wind up on Will Power's mailing list. In conclusion: It's a viable
market.

for our clients is in the upper forties. A healthy range is between 20 and 25. Your net worth is, I'm guessing, under $50,000. Well, $500,000 for our clients is equivalent to $250 for you. Tell me, Michael, do you have cable TV?"

"Yes," I concede reluctantly.

"This is a similar expense for them. In fact, I believe that if we could go back three years to start all over, we could double our rates and lose virtually none of our clients. We have seventy-nine clients. We elected to accept eighty-one to the program. Two have chosen not to participate, and only one cited cost as the reason."

George has silenced me by clarifying with two broad strokes the alternate universe that is Will Power, Inc. I don't belong here, I couldn't, can't, for a host of fundamental reasons, ever find myself in the shoes of a client.

But then:

"Perhaps, Michael"—George's voice trained in the art of never allowing the nastiness of commerce to come across as anything other than perfectly civil—"perhaps you'd like to undergo our screening process followed by a couple days with a diet escort?"

To my surprise I'm scared, so I hide behind my role. "I don't know, George, this isn't supposed to be about me. I'm just a journalist. An observer."

"Think of it as a mutual favor. We have a new diet escort getting ready for his first assignment. Typically, one-on-one training runs are too risky for an actual client, so you'd be helping us out. All the explanation in the world from me won't ever give you a true picture of what Will Power is all about. Take a couple days to think about it. My secretary will contact you by the end of the week."

When I call the local free weekly that has tentatively agreed to accept my piece in order to discuss this latest development, my editor, a gregarious type to begin with, moans with pleasure. She can't believe I failed to accept on the spot, let alone called the paper for her approval. I mumble an excuse while she rants about all the possibilities and how she'll talk to the head editor about moving up the date of my piece and how I better call them right back to accept before they change their mind. Our conversation ends, I hang up, still holding the phone, planning to call George at once. Then I sit there for fifteen minutes, paralyzed. A week ago the story was a great idea: an opportunity for me to research and offer my intellectual two bits about a strange company that has emerged at the unsupervised intersection of American wealth and weight, not to mention a little pocket change to supplement my meager stipend from the university. But like one more self-absorbed postmodern anthropologist who just can't get enough of armchair cultural criticism, I'm sensing an unnerving conflation between the writer and his subject. Not because my research is so extensive, but because the subject hits a little too close to home.

I call George and accept, since I have no other option. An hour later I meet a friend at nearby Albany Bowl. We drink a few beers and play pinball. I tell him all about my upcoming research project. My friend imagines the grounds for my future interventions: taking too much dressing at the salad bar, abusing free-refill privileges, buying M&M's from a seventh grader to support his junior high soccer team. Drunk, we go on like this for hours, laughing moronically. By the time I get home the carefree affect I projected all night long nearly feels authentic.

V. THE PAPERWORK

Though it will forever be unclear to me if the people at Will Power actually have any idea what they've got all of us, if only by historical association, into, one can't fault them for a lack of thoroughness. The introductory packet consists of seventy-two pages of forms and questionnaires. They range from run-of-the-mill medical history to a forty-eight-hour "eating journal."[7] There are even mini-essay questions, like this one on page fifty-two:

"What is your first memory of being overweight?"

The answer I gave, which took up but a line of the blank half page provided:

"I was ten. I put on a T-shirt before school, and I saw that I had breasts."

Filling out, or barely filling out, such queries for nearly six hours over the course of a weekend is a potent form of self-inflicted torture. My answer to question #6 of the twelve-page mini-essay section was accurate, if suspiciously brief.[8] I have,

---

[7] Not too many surprises here. Up to about 3:00 P.M. I was a model of healthy self-restraint. Things, however, got progressively worse as the day continued, with the post-dinner section of the chart (Will Power, of course, provides a date book–style time-line chart) an unruly arabesque of uninterrupted snacks, both sweet and savory.

[8] Other questions/prompts: #4, describe your body; #11, describe the healthiest day of eating you've had in the last three months; the bold #22, why, in your opinion, are so many Americans overweight?

from the earliest days of self-consciousness, been, well, self-conscious about my weight. Ever since I developed the ability to look at myself from the outside, to think about *me* as a concept, when I lost that original childhood Zen of just *being* me, I've been thinking about me as a fat guy. In fact, that was precisely how I became self-conscious. Forget that I never was technically obese, not even during the rough days of my stubbornly prepubescent bar mitzvah year, when I measured five feet one and 140 pounds.[9] I was heavy, chubby, plump, even fat, but never obese. I was never what one of the dieticians at Will Power calls an "O.A." for "one adjective(r)," that is, a person whose identity is subsumed by a single descriptive term: "tall," "thin," "short," and, of course, "fat."[10] Nevertheless, I worry, however irrationally, about my weight each and every day. And all that I can think about after the first half hour of my sobering six hours of Will Power paperwork is that I've got it good. It's not just that there are people much heavier than me, that's obvious, it's that there are people many times more obsessed about their weight,

---

[9] Not that I've ever checked or anything, but that comes out to a BMI of 26.5, placing the thirteen-year-old me in the overweight range, but still almost 20 pounds shy of obesity. The whole scale seems a bit fishy to me. Today, at five feet nine, and, to my mind, a much fitter 175 pounds, I'm still officially overweight at 25.9. And this is using different scales for each age, since bone density changes over time. Of course, BMI doesn't actually measure body fat, so maybe I'm just "big boned."

[10] As a rule, the staff at Will Power is a serious bunch, earnestly policing the edge of the slippery slope separating the unusual from the preposterous that informs the service they provide. The "O.A." dietician, Peggy, was the single exception to this norm, a giddy, spirited woman with a horrible sense of comic timing who most certainly, when behind closed doors, admitted to finding the whole thing more than a bit funny. If I had to guess I'd say that by now she's found new work. Either that or she's enlisting the support of one of her psychoanalyst colleagues to keep the wheels from spinning off entirely.

people two, three, even four steps deeper into this agonizing obsession than myself, people whose preoccupation with their own
bodies would make a yoga master appear only mildly aware of
his corporeal self.[11]

And that's why my answer is so brief. Not because I don't
have more to say about what it was like, at the precious age of
ten, to realize you don't want to be in your body, to try on all sixteen of your T-shirts before school one day, hoping that a certain poly-cotton blend or a particular iron-on decal will magically
cloak your sudden tits, to settle on a long-sleeve flannel, in the
middle of a balmy midwestern May, positioned just so, as you
teach yourself, your newly fat self, how to dress in order to hide.
I've got plenty to say. But as I navigate page after page, as I need
to put off finishing until the next day, I can't help but commune
with the dozens of others who have filled out this packet with
immeasurable desperation, not to mention the literally millions
of others who would if only their wealth rivaled their weight. My
answers are short because that's the quickest way to finish, because something on a national scale has gone wrong. And it's not

[11] During a break from the paperwork that night, I spend an hour composing a
rival scale, the BFI (Body Fixation Index): Take the number of times each day you
think about your body and multiply it by the quality of these thoughts (the scale
runs from 5 (very positive) to −5 (very negative), 0 is neutral). High numbers, positive or negative, are significant, representing either narcissism or self-loathing.
Obviously, the scale is far from objective (i.e., How does one quantify the frequency of thinking about something? One man's 4 is another man's 2, etc.). But,
then again, that's the point. My feelings about my body are necessarily, that is tau-
tologically, subjective. If you really hate your body, it doesn't matter if you're actually in a healthy weight range, and here we enter the bottomless pit of eating
disorders, body-image madness; the list goes on, sorry, ad nauseam. And don't
think Will Power isn't on to this. It's only a matter of time until they're "escorting"
millionaire housewives who will do anything to get rid of the negligible amount of
cellulite on their fifty-year-old thighs.

just that now I see how I'm in the middle of it, that I knew, it's that "it" is so vast, and so, so wrong.

VI. WEDNESDAY, OCTOBER 19

10:00 A.M.

My diet escort, Peter informed me over the phone two days ago, will be an Israeli named Ron Bakar. Peter—whose kindness is nearly unbearable, I almost expect him to offer to pay me for my time—says he met Ron during his personal-security days, when Ron was making sure no one got too close to a fellow Israeli high up in the Promised Land's vaunted hi-tech sector. The move into personal security is common enough for Israelis who, like Ron, served in elite units during their three years of compulsory military service. After the army Ron spent some time in South America and West Africa, though Peter declined to elaborate if this was for business or pleasure.[12]

We met, as arranged, at the El Cerrito Plaza BART stop. Ron (in jeans, a plain, snug white T-shirt, and a light leather jacket) is, unlike Peter, of average size. Either he's not truly up to the task of bodyguard, or he is thanks to unconventional abilities (i.e., see Martin Sheen's character in *Apocalypse Now*). He's smoking a cigarette, which both excites and alarms me, since something so

---

[12] Really, Peter. Young Israelis are now famous the world over for their post-army trips abroad. Escaping the claustrophobia of the Arab Middle East, these travelers, in terms of sheer distance covered, have put to shame the 2,000-year-long journey of that less-voluntary original Jewish exile. Ecuador, Nepal, Thailand, Australia, along with the more obvious United States and Europe, are favorites. But West Africa, not as much. In other words, business, not pleasure, and let's just say he wasn't working in the import/export business either, unless training mercenaries is considered an export.

clearly unprofessional in this context portends future displays of poor judgment by Ron. This excites me because I want an enactment or, better yet, enactments, in practice of what's wrong with Will Power in theory. It alarms me, because if Ron's judgment does indeed fail him, I have a good chance of winding up on the business end of things. Ron and I will be together for the next fourteen hours, and starting at 10:00 A.M. tomorrow will do the same.

We chose to begin my treatment schedule at 10:00 A.M. since, according to my paperwork and dietician interview, during the earlier morning hours I suffer from no self-control deficiencies, nor do I make harmful menu choices. That being said, I woke up wired this morning, an hour before my alarm, and spent the next two-plus hours resisting the urge to make chocolate-chip pancakes or run to the supermarket to buy a box of Froot Loops.

From the beginning our dynamics are strained and awkward. I prepared a dozen or so interview questions for Ron, questions I had yet to pose to either Peter or George, in part to make sure that the first half of my newly schizophrenic journalist/client self maintains its dominance. A sample:

Q: Has Will Power ever considered redesigning its program in such a way that all its clients would enlist the company's services for only a finite period of time? That, in other words, the real sign of success would not merely be weight loss, but the internalization of the diet escort's discipline and resolve.

Q: Has any client ever asked his or her diet escort to participate in his/her (psycho)therapy sessions as an active participant?

Q: What is the company's policy regarding romantic relationships between client and diet escort?

Q: Are there any substantive differences in approach the diet escort takes with male versus female clients?

Q: How exactly does Will Power monitor the fieldwork of a diet escort?

Q: How does the addition of a diet escort to one's life typically affect the client's social, familial, and especially romantic relationships?

But repeated efforts to get Ron to discuss his company—on the BART train, on campus, in my apartment—lead nowhere, as I realize Ron speaks what might be called English as a reluctant second language, forcing me to scrap the interview strategy. Still, I clutch a hand-sized spiral notepad at all times, poised to jot down observations about Ron and the company he represents. Yet Ron is here only to respond to my behavior, to observe me, so I have little to do but consider Ron's potential for action, as I jot down moronically overblown observations like: "He is my moon, my personal satellite." Even worse, Ron shows virtually no interest in me, but his physical proximity cramps my contemplative style all the same. If part of his job description involves making small talk to distract the client from reflecting on the ridiculous relationship he's entered into, Ron is not doing his job.

Before we even got to the Berkeley BART stop, I had realized with curious dread that if there was to be any action today, it was up to me to initiate.

10:15 A.M.

Walking to campus from the BART station, past a dense series of cafés and a donut shop,[13] I'm suddenly much less concerned

[13] Donut shop!

with matters of diet than with the dynamics of our ridiculous duo.[14] Why won't Ron talk more? Does he dislike me? What does he want? I catch myself getting stuck in this Roncentric cul-de-sac of concerns and nearly laugh out loud. This isn't about Ron, it's about me, the client, me and my needs. He's here to serve me, to look out for me, to make sure I don't get carried away at lunch. I steal a look at Ron, crossing the Oxford Street border into campus, smoking another cigarette, staring at nothing in particular, and I decide not to worry about Ron's happiness. But I falter almost immediately, unable to free myself, as Ron clearly can, from our interdependence. How can I be at ease alongside, right alongside, nearly touching, this alien presence who may or may not like me, who I may or may not like? In fact, I don't think I like Ron, because he's aloof and uninterested in me, and by extension, in us.

---

[14] Okay, so this isn't entirely true, not at all. I've walked past this donut shop over 150 times since arriving at Berkeley, but I've entered only once, and that was to buy a bottle of water after playing basketball. Donuts are super yummy, in particular the filled variety. Fried food tastes good and sweet food tastes good; therefore fried sweet food tastes very good. This is simply true. But even I, a guy with moderately unhealthy eating habits, figured out there is just never a right time for a donut. Certainly not in the A.M., when the dense sugary grease burrows lethally to the heart of a man's "it's a new day" gumption. And as the hours pass, the donut becomes no more appropriate. The postdinner dessert time slot is really the only potentially appropriate time, but by then donuts tend not to be fresh, and unless you really like donuts or want to make a bold (if trivial) statement problematizing the culturally constructed, and thus contingent and arbitrary, schedule for the consumption of sweets throughout the day (chocolate-chip *pancakes* in the morning okay, but chocolate-chip *cookies* in the morning not okay), why would you bother with the donut when you can have cookies, cake, or (and/or!) ice cream without having your friends think you eccentric? But okay. That being said, walking with, being *escorted* by Ron, my designated "oh no you don't," I wanted a donut, immediately. It's the whole you don't know what you have until it's gone. Robbed of my freedom to eat donuts, I wanted a donut, badly.

11:00 A.M.

Meeting with my adviser. Ron waits outside, having been assured by me that no food is kept in her office.

12:15 P.M.

Lunch. Burritos. Uneventful. The ebb and flow of my fear of Ron is flowing, so I fail to summon the nerve necessary for mealtime provocation, ordering a cowardly regular. In my defense, I know that sticking my body with any more metabolic duties than that will lead to narcoleptic disaster during my upcoming graduate seminar. Ron has no such reservations and eats like a pig, inhaling his foot of lunch in about forty-five seconds. Apparently untrained in the concept of leading by example.

1:10 P.M.

Graduate seminar. English 230—Modernism and the Novel. Joyce writes:

> Mr. Leopold Bloom ate with relish the inner organs of beasts and fowls. He liked thick giblet soup, nutty gizzards, a stuffed roast heart, liver slices fried with crustcrumbs, fried hencod's roes. Most of all he liked grilled mutton kidneys which gave to his palate a fine tang of faintly scented urine.
>
> Kidneys were in his mind as he moved about the kitchen softly, righting her breakfast things on the humpy tray. Gelid light and air were in the kitchen but out of doors

gentle summer morning everywhere. Made him feel a bit peckish.[15]

My reading: no shit. I'm hungry. I say to myself, over and over, that word "peckish." I consider the etymology of the term. Does it, like "gnawing hunger," express the way hunger tirelessly tells you you're hungry? Because I am. I got up too early, I underate at lunch. And I'm bored. Whether Ron likes it or not, I'm getting a snack at the break. A naughty snack.

2:25 P.M.

Break. In the student store I point to a large chocolate-chip cookie half-dipped in thick chocolate. "What do you say?" I ask Ron.

"Get a fruit or nuts and raisins," he responds.

"But I want this," I counter.

"Then get it."

I look at him, amused and surprised. "But, but what about your job?" I ask, fearful that he may take this as an insult.

"I will do my job."

2:32 P.M.

On the way back to class, Ron tries to grab the cookie from me, right out of my hand. "Hey," I laugh, amazed at the simplistic, childish tactic, which nearly does the trick. I stuff the treat deep into the front pant pocket farthest from Ron and jog the rest of the way.

[15] James Joyce, *Ulysses* (New York: Vintage, 1990), 54–55.

2:40 P.M.

Back in class, I put the cookie on display, brazenly laying it on top of its retracted Saran Wrap. Ron sits to my right, so the cookie sits to my left. I begin eating. It tastes good, and the simultaneous defiance of authority produces an almost-sexual pleasure. Ron seems to squirm. He gestures for my notebook and pen, and I pass them to him. He writes, in the bizarre script of the foreign: "You should stop. Think about instead what you will be eating this evening." I read the note and nod in a way that would appear to signal compliance, only to grin obnoxiously and break off a particularly large chunk of chocolate-coated cookie. Ron leans in to me and actually pinches my side, whispering, "Stop." I playfully pinch his thigh and whisper, "I don't want to." When Ron's arm speeds past me, I'm caught off guard. The cookie is purposely beyond arm's reach, so Ron must stand and push my chair over with his hip. This sudden large-scale physical event and the accompanying sound of furniture scraping rouse the class from the semislumber of its flaccid exegesis. Lucky for Ron, who in one motion grabs the remaining cookie and stuffs it into his mouth (stuffs *my* cookie into *his* mouth!), his action is so beyond the scope of anything expected or acceptable for a graduate seminar that outside of a puzzled stare from the by-now-weary professor and a giggle or two from the students, it goes unnoticed. Like farting at a board meeting.

4:15 P.M.

Waiting for the BART train, Ron provides a short explanation of the diet escort's M.O. It's a memorized speech, because outside of the accent, he sounds like he actually speaks English:

Redirection must always be verbal first. The client must be given the opportunity and encouragement to make the right decision on his own. Only when this fails to achieve the necessary results must the escort intervene, and then in such a way that will cause minimum distraction and minimum physical discomfort or harm to the client.

4:45 P.M.

For the rest of the afternoon I hide in my room alone, after Ron checked for snacks, first reading Walter Benjamin and William Faulkner. Then I try editing drafts of the first three sections of this article, or whatever the hell it's become. With the ending of this piece still so uncertain, I have no idea how to represent what's already happened. Early on I visualized my essay being equal parts irony, comedy, and tragedy, hoping that even a sophisticated reader wouldn't know quite what to do with the slant of my report. Yet rereading them with Ron loitering in my living room in complete silence (no TV, no music, not even a phone call) for the last two hours, the nuanced tones of my earlier observations sound vastly off pitch. In fact, it feels like another article entirely from the one I'm *in* right now. I call my editor for advice and support. No answer.

7:15 P.M.

We visit the always-depressing El Cerrito Plaza, a mall that had its heyday for about forty-five minutes in the late 1970s, in order to buy food for dinner. Ron deconstructs my Albertson's grocery store as we stand right inside the entrance: "Everything from, eh, aisle three to aisle eleven is, it is shit. It is process food, and it is like garbage. Only buy fruits and vegetables, good meat, and rice. Not even bread is good." We get salmon, green beans, and potatoes. We stop at the video store and rent a Jackie Chan movie, I figure maybe we'll even bond.

8:00 P.M.

It turns out Ron's not a bad cook, and he shows me a few tricks: the versatility of a lemon, the glory of olive oil, the importance of undercooking vegetables. Ron is relaxed and in the general vicinity of friendly. He interacts with me via a series of what I fear are Will Power slogans:

> If you are a person who loves food, then cook more and eat less.

> Eating out is dangerous, that is why the food tastes good.

> Fast food. Never, never, never. Ever.

I try having an actual conversation with him, by asking him to elaborate on these nuggets of nutritional wisdom, but we get nowhere.

8:20 P.M.

As I'm rising to head back to the stove top to take a little more of everything, Ron raises his hand, "Wait a moment. You ate enough." I smile, nervously. "Five minutes, if you are still hungry, then eat." I wait and don't eat any more.

9:00 P.M.

My hunch about Jackie Chan is right. Ron goes bananas. He's never seen anything quite like *Drunken Master 2,* Mr. Chan's second comedic and violent gloss on one of the grandest forms of overindulgence. As a man who makes his living by hurting people with his bare hands, Ron could hardly ask for anything more. I'm ordered time and again to pause, rewind, and replay in slow motion. Soon my diet escort has moved my coffee table to open up some floor space, and using me as the object of Jackie Chan's unlikely series of blows, a jovial Ron mimics the master himself.

9:30 P.M.

Watching Ron lose himself in such personal pleasure, I get an idea. I head to my room and return with my pipe and some pot. I mean, because if Ron's going to have the time of his life, why shouldn't I at least try? The sight of my contraband clearly, if only briefly, jolts Ron, and I nearly recoil in the face of his latent authority until I realize his jurisdiction does not extend to drugs, except for chocolate.

9:36 P.M.

I smoke.

9:40 P.M.

It's one thing to spend an entire day with a mostly uncommunicative ex-commando who has been assigned to you and no one else in order to ensure that you don't eat too much; it's another thing, near the very end of this unlikely day, to propel oneself into the sporadically perceptive depths of a marijuana high. Because not only is Ron in my apartment at the expense of my privacy, but it's like both a spatial and a bodily violation. I mean he's in my apartment, and I don't feel like I invited him, not in the way I invite other people into my apartment. And then there's the whole ridiculous business of his menacing presence, which is that if I do the wrong thing, wrong along the lines of *eating* too much, according to him nonetheless, then he'll intervene. Intervene in *my* home by doing something to *my* body. I'm so influenced—frozen—by the feedback loop of my emotional sound track that suddenly I can't even look at scary Ron, he's way too much of an ominous alien presence. I watch Jackie Chan sit in an abandoned restaurant which is about to be attacked by one hundred men with hatchets. My jaw is absolutely clenched; otherwise I'd tell Ron, "This is where things get out of control."

9:43 P.M.

I have to eat. I simply must eat something. Did I consider this likely development when I retreated to my bedroom? Hard to say. I know, the munchies, of course you were going to get the munchies. But truth is, I usually don't get them. I used to, but not anymore. What really happened is that I didn't eat enough dinner, this following an interrupted snack, a snack initiated because I didn't eat enough lunch or breakfast. I'm genuinely hungry. It's not the munchies, it's a sincere reading of my digestive system. But I do fear Ron.

"Ron"—I pause the VCR—"I'm a bit hungry." I'm trying so

hard to sound like this is all no big deal. "How about some suggestions from a professional?" Ron just stares, confused. "Ron, what should I eat? I'm so hungry."

"Do you have any fruit?"

"Hmm." The gravity of his question is beyond measure. "I think there's an old orange on top of the fridge."

"Then eat that." He turns back to the TV, trying to end the conversation.

"Ron"—I struggle for a steady intonation—"is any amount of ice cream acceptable?"

"When did you last eat ice cream?"

Normally I would lie, but I'm trapped in the clutches of my narcotic truth serum. "Yesterday."

"You should have none today."

"But I don't want fruit."

"Do you have raisins or other dried fruit?"

"No."

"Then it is the orange for you."

I actually say "fuck," like I just heard my flight's been delayed indefinitely. I give Ron back his Jackie Chan and go to the kitchen.

9:47 P.M.

Ron can't see me in the kitchen.

9:52 P.M.

By the time Ron remembers he's still on duty, I'm almost into Act III of my one-man show entitled "All the Ice Cream in the World." The script has no spoken lines as such, just a single stage direction: "Shovel." There's a semiconscious quality to surrendering so completely to one's sense of taste. I'm in the moment. My entire being works in unison to get as much ice cream[16] in my mouth as quickly as possible, because it figures, to the extent that any figuring is going on, that if a little is good, then a lot is much gooder, much, much gooder. Hovering above the self-contained ontology of my gluttony is a single fuzzy thought, an ominous notion which doesn't ever come together, but is instead the strange humming resonance of two distinct, well, things. One is this sensation—this pure, straight-to-the-id thump of biochemical pleasure and satisfaction—that at this moment I can do nothing but obey. The other is as abstract as the first is concrete. It has something to do with Late Capitalism, with the polarization of the private and public spheres, with the utter and complete breakdown of all traditional social frameworks. Not the kind of thing worth transcribing in all its brilliant fragmentation. Let's just say it made perfect sense at the time. As Ron seizes the pint of insubordination from me, as I tell him to "fuck off and leave me the fuck alone," as Ron then does something to my wrist which first causes me to instantly rematerialize in my living room (my lonely spoon clanking behind me on the kitchen tiling), and then to collapse face-first on my far from clean carpeting, with Ron applying more than adequate pressure to my general back region, I finally understand.

I was foolish to smoke pot; I realize that now. My always-strained relationship with Ron put me on edge, and though that's when many people choose to smoke, it never bodes well for me. And though it led to the scene just described, and a sore wrist for

---

[16] Ben & Jerry's superlative New York Super Fudge Chunk—why pussyfoot around?

over two weeks after, only with Ron actively restraining and indeed dominating me, influencing me not with words or ideas or any collective affiliations, but through the preverbal language of his physical force, only then was it clear to me that Will Power needs to exist. Not that it should or ought to exist, but that it must exist, that of course it *has to be* as a function of all the other conditions which *are the case* at this moment in the history of our nation.

Were I to have been an actual paying customer of Will Power, I would have been paying around $100 per hour for hour after uneventful hour of service, all so that when I lost myself in indulgence someone like Ron could, more or less, kick my ass. Though I could feel the unhappy harmony of squeals coming from the bones, muscles, and ligaments of my shoulder region as Ron tugged some more, and, I think, cursed me in some Semitic tongue,[17] I was entirely cognizant of the fact that, in theory at least, Ron was my *employee*. He was working for me. He was relying on me for his livelihood. This, again theoretically, was what I wanted, what I was paying not good, but excellent, money for. Things like this don't just happen. Maybe I'm getting cause and effect mixed up here, but if a service as severe as this one actually exists, then the need for it must be ineffably great. If you have termites, you hire an exterminator; if your pipes are clogged, you hire a plumber; if your marriage is stuck, you hire a marriage counselor; and if you're exceedingly obese and equally wealthy, you hire Will Power. They'll take it from there.

---

[17] Meanwhile, nothing could keep the sound production team of *Drunken Master 2* from delivering one over-the-top "THWACK" after another. And because the movie was subtitled and not dubbed, the sound scape of my intervention included, as its final ingredient, people provoking one another in a rather emotive Cantonese.

VII. *GLADIATOR*

I'm sitting in a nearly empty movie theater, fifteen minutes before showtime, a good place to collect one's thoughts. My watch says 11:50 A.M. and I'm surrounded by a large popcorn, large Coke, and $3 box of Junior Mints. I woke up early, sore and upset. After limping through my morning self-care routine, unable to wash myself or even brush my teeth in normal fashion due to strained left shoulder and wrist, I rushed to BART and headed to the city, ditching, or more precisely, fleeing from Ron. There are only eleven other people in the theater, but I'm sitting in the crappy seats near the emergency exit in the far back corner, just in case Ron tracks me down.

In a few minutes Russell Crowe will help people lose weight the old-fashioned way, via dismemberment: a fifteen-pound arm, a thirty-pound leg, a ten-pound head. I, meanwhile, will embark on a self-destructive journey of defiant consumption, ingesting some fifteen hundred empty calories in the time it takes the strapping Australian actor to avenge the brutal murder of his fictional wife and child. As the credits roll, I belch a hideous echo of my concessions, which tastes like an Altoid-flavored hot-fudge sundae.

VIII. JUST A LITTLE MORE

Over the past six weeks I've gained fifteen pounds.[18] Only one pair of pants still fits. Mirrors have never been so cruel. Yet

---

[18] Pushing my BMI, unless I've somehow grown taller as well, up to a dangerously close-to-obese 28.1.

every time I try to curb my bingeing, a literally self-defiant reflex impels me to perform, pigheaded, my independence from our culture of dieting. Against my most rational wishes, my body has enacted an alliance with the ever-growing Fat Pride movement.[19] My one-man army is staging a guerrilla resistance campaign against America's War on Fat. My run-in with Will Power didn't expose to me the poverty of my own self-control; instead, through a collision of forces I didn't know existed, my bodily intentions were realigned in reverse. I'm one spiteful glutton, determined even when full.

Peter and I have exchanged a dozen e-mails since my day with Ron. Turns out that "Ron and Will Power have elected to go their separate ways." The language of our correspondence reflects the defensive mistrust of prelitigious relationships, no one accuses anyone of guilt or even bad intentions, but no one exactly apologizes, either. Peter repeatedly invokes words like "unfortunate" and "unforeseen" in his reconstructions of October 19. There's no question that Will Power's lawyers are previewing Peter's e-mails. I'm surprised the savvier George hasn't taken over these communications entirely. I have no intention of hiring a lawyer, but Will Power's paranoia is well founded. Only time will tell what their impact will be like on the American diet industry, but I have no doubt that before they're done they'll break new ground in litigation and insurance defense, the only sectors of our nation more bloated than the national body itself.

---

[19] Largely a movement of and for women, the Fat Pride or Fat Acceptance philosophy takes dead aim at the endless dissemination of images that essentially conflate anorexia and beauty in our deeply visual culture. Stressing a love for one's body, regardless of its size, the Fat Pride movement argues that sexy, healthy, and heavy are far from mutually exclusive categories. I support them, I suppose, but truth be told, I still feel like shit.

As for me, I plan to seize control of my appetite any day now. The New Year is approaching and, sadly, I may need to make a resolution this time. Either that or transfer to the business school. Because if I can't do this on my own, I'm going to need a fortune to hire the guys who can do it for me.

THE END OF LARRY'S WALLET

Just before the world came to an end once and for all, Larry lost his wallet. Lost it or misplaced it. In short, Larry could not find his wallet, but had yet to arrive at the moment in which it could be said that Larry did not find his wallet. He was still looking. Larry—who, were we to take a long-term perspective, was never doing great—was stuck somewhere in a particularly rough stretch. It's hard to say where he was in the stretch, since it's hard to say just how long the stretch was going to be. He was, in terms of external time, about five weeks into a real crappy period, this following a real lousy eighteen-month stretch. The thing that was killing him—this prior to misplacing/losing his wallet, which obviously did nothing to improve matters—was that he already felt like he was just at the edge of what he could handle. He had begun visualizing his condition as one of "red-lining": that some needle in some internal meter or gauge was getting dangerously close to entering the red part of said meter or gauge. And numerous aspects of this red-lining were worrisome: (1) Would the needle eventually enter the red? (2) What type of damage would be wrought by the needle spending so much time just on this side of red (which was often colored orange)? (3) Was this now normal for him (being nearly in the red)? (4) Can dangerous be normal or does that make it abnormal? And so, then being already in a really rotten state, just on this side of overheating and breaking down, just barely being able to get up in the morning, constantly anxious or depressed or both, and then not being able to find one's wallet, how was Larry to get through this?

The world, ontologically speaking, did not actually come to an end once and for all. That would be more than just an overstatement, it would be inaccurate altogether. The world, as in the planet Earth, didn't just disappear, didn't get blown into a million tiny pieces. It wasn't quite that bad. What did happen was a significant nuclear exchange between two nation-states. Actually, it hadn't happened yet, in relation to the time during which Larry had lost/misplaced/couldn't find his wallet. But it was going to happen. We know now, in fact, that it did. When it did happen, huge numbers of people were to die. Between ten and fifteen million, at least. And that was immediately, there were certainly many whose deaths would soon follow. And so such a horrific, massive, almost instantaneous conflagration, killing, eventually, more than half the people who died around the world during the six long and horrible years of the Second World War, this changed the world. And not the way 9/11 changed the world, or the way the fall of the Berlin Wall changed the world. We're not talking just geopolitics or even global economics. It was that, but it was a lot more. At the time, people didn't have the conceptual vocabulary to put their finger on it. At least the cable news people didn't.

Larry had been looking for his wallet for fourteen minutes. This is the amount of time during a search for an object like a wallet (the other main object "like a wallet" being a set of keys) that one enters Phase Three of the search. Phase One consists of a brief survey of the object's typical resting places. Though mildly annoying, the Phase One experience rarely includes self-conscious worrying. One tends not to think sentences such as "I have lost my keys" or even "I may have lost my wallet." Anxiety levels rise only slightly, unless one is running late, but Larry was not. Yet Phase One cannot last, reasonably, more than ninety seconds. At the end of ninety seconds, Phase Two begins. The transition from Phase One to Phase Two consists of a brief cessation of searching efforts, a sigh or other breathing-related event, and a clear and conscious utterance (at times merely internalized) that the searching "I" has not found the object, and that this is bad, and that where is it? The searching subject, who during Phase One was still picturing, however passively, the story of his or her life as it was expected to unfold immediately after finding the object, is forced to stop this visualization, and instead must now accept that until the object is discovered, his or her life story, for better or for worse, is now on hold, and may, if the object is never found, take a slightly different course altogether. Phase Two, in contrast to Phase One, is unequivocally sucky. Anxiety levels noticeably escalate. The searching subject's ability to maintain rational thought is compromised, this in response to the upsetting of a rational, normal world order, itself manifested in the failure of the object to be located in any of its typical, normal resting places. Depending on the size of one's dwelling, the number of second-tier potential resting sites, and the contours of one's patience-anxiety-faith algorithm, Phase Two can last just over eleven minutes. At which point one enters Phase Three, a bad phase if there ever was one.

The nuclear exchange was in and around the Indian subcontinent. Between India and Pakistan, to be exact. In total, seven nuclear missiles were launched, six of which detonated successfully: four Indian, two Pakistani (the dud warhead was Indian). The Indian missiles contained warheads, it was later estimated, in the area of 1.2 megatons, while the Pakistani warheads were each just below one megaton. India, it is almost certain, launched the first, single missile, though their accounts suggest that they believed they had in fact only launched the second. Pakistan responded with two missiles, to which India responded with four (including the dud). Pakistan did not respond with any additional missiles, ending the exchange. In total, from the launching of the first missile to the landing of the last missile, sixty-four minutes passed. The missiles destroyed, quite extensively, the following cities: Bangalore, India; Hyderabad, India; Rawalpindi, Pakistan; Faisalabad, Pakistan (two missiles); and, coincidentally, Hyderabad, Pakistan. Except for the second missile to land in Faisalabad, each weapon detonated, as planned, some two to three thousand meters above the earth's surface, thereby maximizing the magnitude of the initial blast over the outlying area. Of the six missiles which detonated, five landed within a kilometer of their target. The Pakistani missile which landed near Bangalore was actually aimed at Madurai, some 450 kilometers to the south. Due to India's well-known high-population densities, however, this did little to lessen human casualties.

Larry entered Phase Three in the moment he decided to go down and check his car. He left apartment #1207, walked down the plain hallway, waited for the slow, plain elevator, and rode it down to the plain, melancholy basement parking garage, surrounded, absolutely, by the concentric circles of his immediate despair and, moving outwards, his now-typical sorrow until, finally, he reached the rigid, alien outer shell of who he had most certainly now become. He rushed, reluctantly, toward his fading Volvo, hoping and pessimistic. This, this parking garage and this elevator and that hallway and most of all apartment #1207 were not Larry's. Because if this happened only three months ago, he wouldn't have had to walk down a plain hallway to check his car for a goddamn lost wallet, or wait endlessly for some shitty elevator, or ride it with some sad-sack tenant from some higher floor, or pass in the miserable, cruel light of the parking garage near-strangers who, like him, slept alone. Only recently did all this become his setting, when he and Karen, after nine years, gave up. He left and she stayed.

The moment he opens the car door, he knows it isn't there. He knows because the single best improvement, and perhaps the only improvement at all, is the current spotlessness of his car. The twin forces of chaos and entropy, which transformed his sedan into a combination dumpster/locker room, simply expired when he left, and now he huddles up to the faint warmth of the control he wields over his car. No refuse, no disorder, no anything. Even the umbrella stays in the trunk. He skins his forearm checking under the seat, kneeling on the cold, oddly smooth cement. Nothing. And now Phase Three, horrible enough when almost mitigated by continuous, around the clock rummaging, suffocates Larry in his return to #1207, as he waits for the lazy elevator, as he jogs over the cheap carpeting of the long, long hallway.

Three months ago, he could have asked Karen, who, okay, probably would have less helped or even expressed concern than simply tucked his absentmindedness into the overflowing, unorganized mound of mental evidence she collected against her once-beloved. But he could have asked her, and maybe she would have known, and if not, he could have asked Lucy. Lucy wouldn't have helped—she probably wouldn't have even understood—but he could have persuaded her, or simply told her to join him in his quest to find his wallet. Her distraction would have been instantaneous. She would have interpreted the trip to the car as an opportunity to recruit him for a spontaneous plan of her own, one she devised as she spoke it aloud to him: ice cream, the park, Zoe's, the mall. If he was lucky, she would turn on the hazard lights and not climb on him; she would foolishly try to buckle herself into her car seat and not lock and unlock and lock and unlock and lock and unlock the doors; she would giggle idiotically and not complain of pain in her ears.

The sudden obliteration of a couple dozen million people confronted the remainder of the earth's population with the following bind: You must respond to this somehow, there is no way to respond to this. There was nothing to do, there was nothing to say; in fact, many people, around the world, years later, would recall that there was nothing to think. There was, of course, a great deal to think, not to mention say and even do, but too much, really, and so minds simply shut down, ground to a halt. People, masses of people, people in Chile and Nebraska and Zanzibar, sat and stared dumbfounded, silent in their mother tongue.

The news shows, of course, took over, or tried to, but even they were stymied. There was nothing to show as such. Unlucky local correspondents, like anyone else in the area, were dead, dying, or at best incapacitated, while the fallout, firestorms, and widespread destruction of infrastructure precluded the arrival of any replacements. Satellite feeds, due to atmospheric debris and electromagnetic pulses, were largely worthless, at least to the average viewer. Without images of the real thing to show, the cable and network news people were at first stuck with a host of second-string images: archival footage of Hiroshima and Nagasaki (which they were quick to point out were nothing compared to what was believed to have occurred in this case), recent shots of the now-destroyed cities, maps (municipal, regional, national, global), disarmingly sterile military/corporate videos of the missiles used or missiles like them or missile tests, still shots, or stock footage of the leaders believed to be responsible, and sites at the outer rim of the disaster: Karachi, Calcutta, European embassies, international airports, and community centers throughout the Pakistani and Indian diasporas.

In the time it took for the various networks and cable-news stations to verify the nuclear exchange, they had all switched to what is called in the trade "Block Mode," in which all resources and programming are focused on one event, one unfolding story. The cable stations had taken to entering Block Mode with great regularity in recent years, since the urgency implied by Block Mode, research indicated, increases the duration of the typical viewing session from eighteen to twenty-four minutes. And, the various network heads and news producers had concluded, Block Mode could be invoked for periods as short as two hours in the case of remote earthquakes, odd kidnappings, police standoffs, and premature celebrity deaths. Yet it was the truly large stories—the Gulf Wars, 9/11, the 2000 presidential election—where Block Mode found its raison d'être. And as much as the folks over at CNN, Fox, and MSNBC regretted the deaths often needed to motivate a weeklong Block Mode, no one involved, in the privacy of their own thoughts, denied themselves the satisfaction of Block Mode, which was, after all, their time.

Because the thing about Phase Three is this: It causes your life to stall, and that's bad enough, but depending on its duration, and the state of the individual passing through it, the slightest dread and weariness turn it straight into Phase Four. Phase Four is an existential inversion or abbreviation of Three: Your life *is* stalled. Independent of the absent wallet, prior to the keys seeking refuge under your couch or in the coatroom of last night's restaurant, your life was already stuck, broken, out of joint, and this is but one sign, the official announcement of something you knew all along. Larry feels it. Of course his wallet is missing. How could it not be missing?

Larry's wallet contained: two heavily leaned upon credit cards, an Illinois driver's license, a Cook County library card, a Supercuts frequent-haircut card (marked with seven of the ten stamps required for a complimentary trim), two pictures of Lucy (one from last year's Halloween—fairy—and the other from her third birthday, candid and perfect), sixty dollars (the previous evening during his interface with the cash machine he had wavered for forty painful seconds trying to choose between sixty and eighty, unable to decide how much to withdraw, until, wisely but only sort of, he now concludes, choosing the lesser amount), a Blockbuster card, two Jiffy Lube cards (each marked with only one of the eight stamps needed for a free oil change), seven business cards of his own ("Larry Specter, President, Mediocre Foods"), six business cards of other people, three scraps of paper with random ideas ("Retro graphics?" "Call Steve Powers at Jewel," "Ketchup or Mayo, which is king?"), and receipts from three grocery stores, four restaurants, one movie theater, two video rental shops, and four gas stations. The wallet was brown leather. Karen bought it for him as a present, or they bought it together, or both. He didn't care for it all that much. He felt, in terms of design, that it was someone else's wallet that perhaps he was supposed to but was unable to grow into, and so he experienced a pinch of self-alienation every time he reached for it. Along with this figurative pinch was a very literal prick supplied by some mystifying bit of hard sharpened plastic reinforcement that had broken through the leather at two of the wallet's corners. Larry had spent some twenty frustrating minutes divided over three pointless sessions—equipped with pliers, scissors, and nail file—trying to remove or blunt the invincible, jagged plastic spikes. Indeed, Larry had intended for some time now to buy another wallet altogether—a more Larryish wallet free of dangerous corners that seemed to poke him with alarming regularity—but he was not exactly the kind of guy who goes wallet shopping. Larry, to sum up, hated his wallet. But he wanted it now, obviously.

Initially, an impressive team of executives from New York and D.C. steadied themselves and inhaled deeply, as they realized that all eyes would be on them, that it was their responsibility to lead America and the world through this story: to report, clarify, interpret, illuminate. Cameramen, scriptwriters, and makeup artists hunkered down with fresh coffee, grounded in the solemn air of destiny and duty, while authority figures at every level at every studio said things like "Now's our time," "Be sharp," and "Let's go, people."

The intensity of the first hour precluded self-reflection. Curiosity, dread, and habit found the media busy sketching out the basic shape of the event. Forty minutes were devoted to the telecast of a confused Pentagon briefing. After testing a few possible directions (description of targets hit, exact times of each strike, fine details of the weapons likely used), the press conference inevitably settled on the topic that would sit stubbornly, awesome and impenetrable, at the center of everyone's attention for the foreseeable future:

Q: Can you give us any idea about the number of civilian casualties?

A: At this time it is impossible to specify, but we fear they are significant.

Q: Can you be more specific? Thousands? Tens of thousands?

A: Preliminary intelligence, and I repeat this is only the most preliminary estimate, suggests a possible range from five to twenty to perhaps even forty million.

And it was then, in the wake of the jolt of this information, that the television media began to falter. Thirty-odd Pentagon correspondents stared into space, while the chief military spokesman began chewing his lip and rubbing his left eye frantically, a nervous habit he picked up in Vietnam and was able to overcome only after months of private therapy and treatments.

Inside his apartment, Larry got intimate with Phase Four. He attacked his new couch, demanding, aloud, where it put Larry's wallet. He hurled its pillows across the living room—toward the new television, at an empty bookshelf, up to the bare white ceiling. The couch was accused of being a piece of shit, a motherfucker, and a motherfucking piece of shit. The catastrophic flavor of Phase Four—the unrelenting sense of helplessness, of cruel injustice, of debilitating confusion—does create opportunities for catharsis. Larry's relationship with his couch was in its infancy, as the couch had only entered his life the weekend after moving out, when he purchased it at an IKEA. Yet Larry had already harbored suspicions toward this couch even before he bought it, even before the moment he tried out an exact replica of this couch in an IKEA showroom. During his one previous visit to the superstore, with Karen, Larry already mistrusted IKEA. Its irresistible appeal, its low prices, massive selection, Swedish mystique, and the largely unironic approval of their social caste, it all rubbed Larry the wrong way. He couldn't formulate his opposition, but sensed it nonetheless. And then only a few months later, banished and wildly concerned with insolvency and paternal impotency, with no time and less energy to consider what type of aesthetic he might try to capture in his new dwelling, all this bad news manifested itself in his immediate fate: You must go to IKEA and buy a couch. So he bore the red couch like a curse, and thus never truly welcomed it into his home (a similar domestic cold shoulder having been given to the IKEA bookshelf, TV stand, coffee table, kitchen table, and kitchen chairs). And so now he let the couch have it. After the opening volley of curses, he pushed it out from the wall, kicked it, hard, turned it over, and asked again, threateningly, where it had hidden his wallet. No question about it—the couch was to blame.

And so what was there to do? What additional information did anyone need? While there arose an instant urge to know exactly, or even more or less, how many died, this was an urge fated to be unfulfilled. First off, no one could ever know, since entire extended families, whole civic centers and their bureaucracies, thick buildings of public records, of remarkable digital memory, were vaporized. A circle, some ten kilometers in diameter, had spread around each target. Inside, nothing would be known. Which meant estimates, very general estimates. Between a million and a million and a half here, two to three million there, somewhere in the range of twelve to sixteen million overall, approximately. Numerous efforts were made to narrow this down. In Karachi and Calcutta, a host of government databases were scoured: birth records, census results, high school matriculation exams, military recruitment logs, voting rosters, income-tax spreadsheets. Leading demographers, tenured sociologists, internationally renowned statisticians, high-ranking public-health officials, cutting-edge urban anthropologists, and economists with global reputations attempted to update the data, extrapolate, speculate, basing their figures on the latest birth and infant-mortality rates, recent trends in urbanization, emigration, and immigration. Eccentric mathematicians were enlisted in the effort to produce and calibrate the proper formulas that might fill in the doubt concerning population shifts in the last six to twelve months. Within a week, a handful of very specific estimates were produced: The Pakistani health ministry announced 6.4 million casualties, the Indian social security offices, 9.1 million, the respective tax departments, 7 and 8.5 million, respectively. The average of the so-called authoritative estimates came out to 7.2 million Pakistani deaths, 9 million Indian deaths, all this with a 500,000- to 1 million–person margin of error in either direction. So, confidently it could be said that overall between 14 and 18 million who were alive on Tuesday morning were now gone. A range of 4 million people.

The phone rang a few moments later—catching Larry off guard as he lay spent across the hard edge of the couch's bottom wooden frame, which at this moment pointed to the ceiling. For two rings he debated answering the call, instinctively weighing the evenly matched pros and cons of putting Phase Four on hold.

"Hello," he announced, short of breath.

"Hey, Larry, this is Steve Powers over at Jewel."

"Hey, Steve, good to hear from you. I've been meaning to call." Larry's enthusiasm was sincere, and the accompanying up-surge in energy almost helped him put things into perspective. He tried to find a position near the phone which would feel natural and normal, but would not permit him any view of the ravaged living room. This was difficult.

"Larry, I've got the winter meeting with Purchasing on Monday, and I'm thinking real seriously about putting in a big push for Mediocre Foods, but, well, I think I need a bit more convincing."

One of the many problems with these numbers, and there were many to be sure, was that they necessarily disregarded the thousands and possibly millions who were dying as they were being tabulated, along with the millions who would die in the weeks, months, and years to come from untreated injuries, fallout, and the long-term contamination of water and soil. Indeed, two days after the last numbers were announced, a well-known nuclear physicist and longtime public spokesperson for the movement for global disarmament claimed, with equal degrees of outrage and grief, that the numbers, whatever they were that Tuesday morning, were now at least a half million to a million higher. Removing his thick glasses and appearing to just about pull out a chunk of his unruly hair, the physicist delivered a gruesome list of causes for this second, ongoing wave of fatalities: massive third-degree burns left untreated, collapsed buildings trapping survivors, intense short-term fallout radiation ten to fifteen kilometers from ground zero, the firestorm in Bangalore, the conflagration in Rawalpindi, mechanical injuries caused by victims being blown into wood, glass, and cement obstructions (and vice versa). After catching his breath and returning his glasses to his face, the physicist next elaborated on so-called synergistic effects, of combined injuries, of the effect of radiation on burn victims, of the way blood damage—caused by exposure to three hundred reins or more—significantly limits a body's ability to stave off infection around open wounds, of any and all injuries exacerbated by the severe environmental damage and poor sanitation in the targeted areas. Finally, the physicist concluded, looking away from the camera, that the initial number of injured was approximately equal to the initial number of dead, and that a third to a half of the injured were likely to die during the coming three months. Looking back at the camera, he added, "And then there's the long-term effects, which will reach well beyond the Indian subcontinent."

This incident, along with others like it, prompted daily efforts to extrapolate and re-extrapolate, to update, almost hourly, the latest estimated number dead. But the real problem emerged while all this research and number crunching was under way, while small groups of once-scattered world experts came together to quantify the unquantifiable, as very simple, quite uneducated people arrived quickly at a most simple conclusion: It (the exact number) didn't much matter. Even if the best-case scenario was, six days after the exchange, in fact a wild overestimate, even if the true figure was, say, only eleven million, well, then, only eleven million people died, a phrase which means nothing at all to anyone. Maybe only eleven million people died.

———

Larry's second wind had already ebbed, and Phase Four, like a fucking bear, was not about to go away so easily. Larry wiped his brow and tried hard to imagine what a confident, charismatic person might sound like. "Sure, Steve, no problem at all. What exactly are you looking for? Numbers, references, projections, investor information?" The tone was reasonable, but the phrasing concerned him. He fought off Phase Four, the doubt, the anxiety, the fury, because he knew this was his to sell. A big check, a giant account like this would make canceling all his credit cards and asking Karen for new pictures of Lucy tolerable.

"No, it's none of that, Larry. I know that if we get it in the stores it'll sell. That you've convinced me of. I had my doubts, but you've put them to rest."

"Well—"

"—it's just that the fellas over in Purchasing, they don't like to go out on a limb. You know, they feel comfortable ordering a quarter-million liters of Coke and a hundred thousand bags of potato chips a few times a year. Getting them to agree to hummus a few years back was a major undertaking. Men who wind up in Purchasing are not the adventurous type. They like organized spreadsheets, strong coffee, and prime rib—you know what I'm getting at here?"

"Sure, I—"

"Because what I'm having trouble wrapping my head around is delivering the following pitch to these men: 'Gentlemen, I want to introduce a new line I think we should try out: Mediocre Foods. The concept behind the line is this: Buy generic foods—ketchup, salad dressing, tomato paste, mayonnaise, and the like—directly from the generic-foods distributor, repackage them in these eye-catching bottles, cans, jars, and labels with highly ironic names that the eighteen-to-thirty-four-year-old educated, urban middle class will be unable to resist. Names like: "Subpar Mustard," "Slightly Disappointing BBQ Sauce," "Nothing to Write Home About Mac 'n' Cheese." A bit marked up from the generic line itself, Mediocre Foods still comes in at 10 to 20 percent below brand-name lines. And, as we all know, they taste fine. Trials in Bucktown and the Ukrainian Village were a huge success. I've got the numbers if anyone is interested in taking a look. Jewel could make a killing with Mediocre Foods.' Saying it to you right now, Larry, it's great stuff, but truthfully, I just don't know if I can survive that pitch in front of the guys from Purchasing. I know, I know that it can be done, but these guys are serious old school. They're not open-minded like me, Larry. I spent a semester in Paris, Larry, you know, I listen to jazz sometimes, I've inhaled, if you know what I mean. But these guys—"

"Would you like me there, Steve? Because I'd be happy to make a presentation, believe me." Larry knew all he could do right now was somehow transfuse to Steve a large dose of unwavering optimism that he himself lacked. Please, Steve, please. That's what he thought.

"No, Larry, that wouldn't be possible, I just—a—"

Call waiting.

At first the executives of all the major media outlets, however regrettably and secretly, savored the opportunity presented to them. The newspapers published massive special sections devoted to the disaster. Trying to cover every angle, they produced lengthy articles about the two countries, their history, their politics, culture, and religion. In concert with the local and foreign intelligence communities in the military and various state departments, the press meticulously reconstructed, as best they could, the weeklong hostilities that had so suddenly escalated into the exchange. Readers were given every bit of declassified information, every nugget of scientific knowledge concerning nuclear-weapons programs, from the Manhattan Project to the present, with special attention, naturally, given to the Pakistani and Indian programs, concerning which, unfortunately, numerous mysteries remained. Rather quickly terms like "overpressure" and "roentgens" became as commonplace as "NASDAQ" and "windchill" in American kitchens and middle-school classrooms. For the first few days, the papers, sharing content at unprecedented levels, published issues of record size. The first Sunday *New York Times* after the events threatened a thousand pages and weighed over four pounds. Editors at every level, there in those first few days, found everything relevant. Such was their sense of duty.

But after a week, there were problems. There was no formula for this. First, what about the other sections of the paper? Was it ethical to print the box score for the Clippers-Warriors basketball game? Was anyone truly interested in the ongoing scandal involving the local comptroller? The investigatory piece on antifreeze, did anyone really care? What kind of warped view of reality was required for someone to assert, "The investigatory piece on antifreeze matters"? And comics? Showtimes? Celebrity gossip? They were all out for the first week, out of necessity, as all resources were mobilized for this singular event. Personal-technology columnists were put to editing narratives on the dispute over Kashmir. Photographers, with little to photograph, were instructed to call upon their expertise in the finer points of visual composition in order to contemplate the layout of page after page of dense text. But at some point, somewhere, in the business staff, there were murmurings. What? The markets are going to stay closed forever? They're slated to reopen on the eighteenth—aren't we going to cover it? People need to laugh, the comics editor suggested, discreetly, to the managing editor. We need to keep the pressure on the comptroller, or he's going to get off. I know it doesn't matter much, but, look, it matters.

Can't take it. Must take it. Want to take it. Should take it? "Steve, can you hold just a moment."

"Sure."

Flash. "Hello."

"It's Karen."

"Hi. Hey. Um, I'm on the other line, I—a—"

"I spoke to Lucy's doctor, he said that—"

"Hold on a sec, let me get off the other line."

Flash. "Steve. It's my, my wife, we've got a little family… thing happening. I, I got to, uh…"

"No problem, Lar, I'll call again tomorrow."

"Could I come by? I'd really like to do that."

"Call me. We'll see. Take care."

Flash. "Sorry." And he turned around. It was the proper thing to do. To get his mind into the new call and out of the last one. To change the backdrop. It would help him pay attention to Karen, something that was oddly difficult at times. "I just got off the phone with Dr. Rojas." A difficulty compounded by his tendency to disengage when Lucy's medical complications were being discussed. "X-ray of the mastoid." But here was the couch, and one of his shoes, and here she was on the other line, already talking ("a procedure to control dizziness"), the cause of this couch, and possibly, thanks to the logic of Phase Four, somehow responsible for the wallet as well.

"—and Dr. Rojas thinks that we need to do a CAT scan first, he's not so sure that reconstruction will be possible. But I don't know, Larry, could you call Michael Feldman and ask him to talk to his friend first?"

"Why, exactly?"

"Why? What do you mean 'why'?"

"I, uh, I think I'm following you"—perhaps she wasn't on to him—"but if—"

"If?—"

"If I'm going to call Mike, I want to be sure I can explain this."

Not that there wasn't plenty to report on the story itself. There were the immediate border skirmishes and the intense debates held at the UN and the impromptu G-8 Summit, where diplomats weighed sending buffer forces and humanitarian aid. Daily readings, taken, somehow, from satellites, measured fallout and threatening weather patterns. Never in the history of the world had wind patterns garnered so much interest, wind patterns that proved virtually impossible to predict more than a day or two in advance. Then there were the stories of the hundreds of thousands of mostly doomed, often contaminated refugees—hair falling out, skin falling off—who abandoned their mostly destroyed, often smoldering homes and villages and walked straight toward the wind, not knowing, in one case, that they were headed directly into a different radioactive plume. These stories, and others like it, were captured by daredevil, freelance reporters, some with moon suits, some crazy ones without, who headed, insanely, to the devastation. And then there were the memorials. The endless memorials. Everywhere, all the time. The flowers and the vigils and the services. Around the world.

But how was this all to be brought together? How were they to strike a balance, an impossible balance between this ever-swelling story and everything else? People had a right to know about the latest unemployment figures, but could it be put in the same section as the story, or did the story need its own section, which would obviously need to be the first section, indefinitely? And to what extent was the story about the initial nuclear attacks and to what extent did it revolve around the fallout, both literal and figurative? And what to call the story in the first place? "The Exchange"? "Nuclear Holocaust"? Some thought the date would do, but unlike 9/11, 12/9 just didn't sound right, and anyway, it was still 12/8 in the United States when it happened, so it wasn't really 12/9, at least that's not how people thought of it.

And so Karen began her explanation again, while Larry, largely conscious of the self-loathing to follow, couldn't stop reflecting on his inability to grasp, ever, the details of Lucy's complications. At first she was just one of those kids who got a lot of ear infections. An ear rubber from about six months on. They used to joke about it, giving her all sorts of moronic nicknames based on the words and sounds: Rubby, Rubby the Ear Rubber, Rubby von Rub-Rub, Dr. Rubbenstein, etc. Until at some point Karen decided something was wrong. And so started the trips to the doctor, and the antibiotics, and the drops, and the need to re-member to give the antibiotics and the drops. And then the re-mission, and then back to the doctor, and then more antibiotics and more drops. Somewhere, not long before her second birth-day, when he began smelling the beginning of the end both at work and in his marriage, the full force of Larry's discomfort with his life was suddenly translated into a reliable incapacity to function at all in the face of Lucy's conditions. He would take her to the doctor when it was his turn. He would try to listen to the doctor and try to ask the questions that Karen told him to ask, which, if he was the least bit smart and honest with himself in the hours before the appointment, he would write down so as not to forget. And there, in front of the doctor, forcing his eyes to appear interested, naturally, and concerned, properly, Larry would likewise jot down notes, notes that were largely useless since the rest barely even went in one ear to begin with. The moment they left the office he would forget about it entirely, more than once driving straight home and forgetting to get the prescription filled.

But soon, the people decided. The delivery-truck drivers who emptied and refilled the newsstands noticed it first. After a weeklong unprecedented spike in nonsubscriber readership, with newsstands emptied by 9:30 A.M., with afternoon editions gobbled up instantly, things suddenly dropped off. After a week, no one was interested in the afternoon paper. Pretty soon they were picking up as many unread papers as they were dropping off new ones each morning. At ten days, circulation noticed it, too. Virtually no one was renewing their subscription. Not many cancellations, just a bunch of longtime subscribers passively letting theirs run out. And according to the early morning drivers who rode through the bedroom communities, tossing papers expertly out their passenger windows, few people were bothering to bring in the already paid for morning paper. Small mounds of uncollected, unwanted editions formed up and down the suburban streets. Everyone, it appeared, was on vacation, though the travel industry, alarmed but unsurprised by their own suddenly empty airplanes and hotels, knew this to be untrue.

He did care about Lucy, though. He would ask her how she was feeling, and he would hold her, and rock her, and help her fall asleep sitting up, so it would hurt less. But even this would end in his visual, nearly abstract contemplation of her right ear. Larry would admire its folds, her miniature lobe, and the way all that delicate flesh funneled into an orifice leading to all the trouble. Eventually Karen caught on. It only took her so long because she was rightly focused on Lucy, not Larry. Right there, either the week before or the week after he moved out, it was impossible to reconstruct it now, she called him out on it. You don't care, really, you just want it to go away. That's bullshit and you know it. Sure, I want it to go away, but that doesn't mean I don't care. And then she weighed in with her evidence, which was irrefutable. He tried, sort of, to explain this syndrome of his, but he barely understood it, and, in truth, there was no way to buy any sympathy with it no matter how well presented. And, moreover, this coming either right before or right after the separation, either the last straw or vindication or a bit of postconjugal pus, all was already lost. She had already caught him spacing out as he considered the colored ear chart, wondering who was first responsible for creating the *Gray's Anatomy* aesthetic, wondering how, if at all, it could be harnessed for a magazine ad. Not because he was unconcerned, not because he didn't recognize the urgency that accompanied a word like "cholesteatoma."

People were, however, still watching television. On that first Tuesday, everyone had it on, because that's what you did when Block Mode, a real, 100 percent legitimate, genuine, necessary Block Mode, surfaced. But the lack of available images combined with the immeasurable and unimaginable horror of the events compelled even the most text-averse American to consult the newspaper. The meditative silence and prayerlike solitude of reading, the sobering experience of all at once grasping the un-bridgeable gap between word and thing, the newspaper provided these necessities in abundance. That and there was only so much information the visual media could cram into an hour. The newspaper publishers assumed no one was reading everything, but they suspected everything was being read by someone. Some readers were interested in Indian history, some wanted compar-isons with Hiroshima, while others hoped to understand the finer points of nuclear fusion. TV had to decide what everyone was going to see at the same time. Truthfully, they just didn't know. And their mock-solemn tone, the kind of crap they used to summon effortlessly and habitually to describe a tragically botched bank robbery, it just didn't fly fifteen million dead later. The patently and inherently superficial core of television news was mostly crushed, at least at first, by this story. The average news anchor's persona was involuntarily shed, and what was left underneath was not fit for television. Most female newscast-ers—and more than a few male ones—cried horribly in the middle of a report. The men, on the whole, disassociated and/or stammered, while the guy from Fox simply cursed. Few were callous enough to call it an embarrassment, to draw atten-tion to it in any way as a thing that could possibly matter, but that's what it was: a trivial embarrassment.

Lucy stayed over at his place for the first time four weeks ago. They had pizza and rented *Toy Story* and ate a remarkable amount of crap. She passed out not three minutes after a sugar-induced hula-hoop mini-marathon, her chin shiny with drool. Larry moved her into the sterile second bedroom, the few stuffed animals assembled to create atmosphere only accentuating his failure. The rest of the evening, wasted in front of cable television, hurt. With his only child asleep not far away, Larry was stunned to realize how great his loneliness had become. He didn't stand a chance without Karen. Not with Lucy, and not, really, with himself. Having her here, having a little feeling of family and togetherness made clear that it would only ever be a small fraction of what once was. Karen brought energy and created order; she knew, effortlessly, how to pilot Lucy. Larry was merely responsible for punctuated moments of idiocy in order to keep things interesting. He decided, as he watched an insubordinate homicide detective rightfully cut short another man's life, that he was determined to make this work. He was unable to convince himself that he could sustain his determination.

Only a few hours later, roused from an already evaporated dream, Larry heard Lucy moaning and crying, "My ear, my ear." He'd heard it hundreds of times. So he lifted her up and hugged her heft, asking, as was their routine, if he should take a look. There was never anything to see, since the problems were all inside, but she didn't know this, and she still believed in her father. But the stench had already filled the room. When he looked, for the first time he did in fact see something. Mostly clear, but not entirely, just some fluid. And the smell, the horrible smell. He brought his nose close and inhaled with paralyzed loving calm, ingesting the smell of something that wanted so badly to get out, something that should have never been inside in the first place.

But about five days into it, things began to turn around. The recently absent viewing public had just about gotten their fill of the written word, while the big-time TV producers and directors

were finding their footing. A new minimalist, understated an-
choring strategy had emerged, one aptly suited to accompany
the shocking images now pouring in. A hastily produced ninety-
minute documentary on India and Pakistan (*A World Lost*) was
shown daily on all channels. Nuclear scientists, historians, political analysts, retired generals, diplomats, spiritual leaders,
filmmakers, novelists, poets, and philosophers made regular
appearances, offering generously their insufficient wisdom.
Multiple appendages of the American government—Pentagon,
NSA, the Senate Armed Services Committee—held numerous
press conferences daily, answering the latest questions with the
latest answers. Television was back and fully in charge.

Yet hastily arranged phone surveys by the major news outlets—set up less for the benefit of their sponsors (who had
stopped running commercials—every last one of which, from
the sentimental to the comical, now came off as utterly asinine—and were instead merely "presenting this hour of...")
than to satisfy their own curiosity concerning the viewing public's interests—revealed an insatiable demand for what came to
be called the "mourning/commemoration" angle. To be sure,
people wanted to know what had happened and what was still
happening "over there," but they just as strongly expressed a
need to work through their own trauma. This was, it turned out
after all, an American story, too. Just being alive and knowing
about this, whether in Cleveland or Bozeman, swallowing portions of sadness, guilt, gratitude, and impotence, this was an
event, too, and was in many ways the only event most Americans
could comprehend. So news crews, both local and national, regularly hunted down and covered memorials, however spontaneous and limited. On the second Sunday following the
exchange, a dozen or more massive memorials were held across

the globe, from New York to Tokyo, where presidents, premiers, Nobel laureates of all stripes, and aging survivors of Nagasaki called for remembrance and demanded global disarmament. Tens of millions attended, marching somberly, emptying the world's flower shops, constructing ad hoc mountains of roses and tulips. But despite the speeches and the placards, despite the well-framed shots of fully grown white men holding hands and crying inconsolably, Sunday was not enough.

What everyone wanted was a survivor's story, but there weren't any, any survivors or stories, at least not the kind Americans could digest. A few suicidal foreign correspondents entered the radioactive zones to interview Pakistani and Indian survivors, right there on the side of a dirt road packed with refugees or in a poorly lit, crowded hospital ward, but the obliterated world of these survivors simply didn't translate. A little, but not really. The vast barren landscapes they attempted to describe, their effort to give an account of what they had seen, it was all much too much. Americans tried to meet their testimony halfway, but the empathy required to connect with these foreign, indeed alien, stories left the typical viewer emotionally exposed and exhausted. It soon became clear that Americans wanted to hear from single family members living abroad: students, computer programmers, radiologists, mathematicians, and importer/exporters. These were tracked down in steady numbers, but they, quite honestly, tended to disappoint. Either they refused to appear—something which occurred in surprisingly large numbers—or they had little to say. Everyone's English was fine—that wasn't the problem—it was just the interviews never went anywhere. In nine out of ten cases the interview got stuck in the realm of empty clichés, and when the exchange got specific it quickly deteriorated into demonstrations of uncontrollable sorrow. It wasn't, simply put, good television. What was needed was one of these sudden orphans, but one who could formulate properly his new identity, measured against, indeed drawn out from, the inexpressible magnitude of his loss. Such a person was Naren Joshi.

It took a few tries to remember how to pronounce "cholesteatoma," and he still hasn't entirely come to understand what it is. All its ingredients are known to him—skin growth, middle ear, eustachian tube, sac, cyst—but he simply cannot learn how they come together, he can't really construct a single viable narrative from etiology to the present, not even a hypothetical version. In conversation with his futile parents he tried to inform them, to update them, to alarm them. He told his two friends, who, thankfully, sort of, didn't really want to hear about it, though they did care. Karen, he could tell, was by now a true expert, utterly fluent in terminology and treatments. She had assembled a network of informal advisers and consultants, unearthing any ear, nose, and throat specialist connected in any way to anyone she ever knew. Two otolaryngologist–head-and-neck surgeons, one with pediatric expertise, had even been located. The problem was that Lucy's case had been detected late, and now Karen began peppering her reports with the vocabulary of complications: He's almost certain he's heard her say things like "hearing loss," "facial nerve damage," "bone erosion," and "muscle paralysis." Only he couldn't ever seem to establish what had happened and what only might happen, and he was terrified to ask any question specific enough to find out, for fear of exposing to Karen the full extent of his ignorance. And try as he might, when the subject came up, as it did almost daily, with ever-crescendoing urgency, something inside him, probably not all that far from his own perfectly functioning ears, shut down, making him worth-less.

I remember the movie *Independence Day*. I saw it. I didn't want to see it. The premise from the previews struck me as ridiculous. But then the movie became a huge hit, the runaway hit of the summer, whatever summer that was. So I broke down and saw it. With a not-so-slight sense of irony, my wife and I decided to see it. That's how we bought the ticket, the way you buy junk food or sit down to watch bad television. You're giving in to something you'll later regret, and this is bad, but maybe only a little, and really, what's the big deal? It feels good at the time, and there are health benefits to be had from such easy, immediate pleasure. And so I'm watching the beginning of the movie with a semi-embarrassed grin, but really I'm waiting, because I know what's coming, everyone does. About a third of the way into the movie, there are going to be some events represented that have never as such been represented in film: the sudden and complete obliter-ation of national icons. A bright beam and then instantly, boom, the White House, the Empire State Building, a Southern California skyscraper, all gone. Some of these images we had seen in the previews. At the time, out of context, it was funny. My limited fascination during the previews stemmed from wish fulfillment, from agreement, yes, please let's pretend that power-ful, hostile aliens come to Earth and for no reason destroy the White House, because if they don't have it coming, then I don't know who does. During the previews, in no way did I identify with the victims of these special effects. I identified solely with myself, the spectator.

Naren Joshi was discovered by an ambitious assistant producer in the Orange Country Indian Community Center about ten days after the exchange. The assistant producer, a fourth-generation American of Polish descent, came to the community center to, more or less, scout for talent. She found Naren at the perimeter of a large gathering in the main hall of the community center, a gathering that had formed nine days earlier and had yet to disassemble. Naren, dressed in a beautiful, if extremely wrinkled, silk shirt, sat mostly silent, drinking his strong coffee. Occasionally he joined in the singing that broke out among the group. The assistant producer was immediately drawn to him, such was his involuntary charisma. She sat down next to him, asking if this was okay. Naren, polite and gracious, welcomed her. And they spoke for three hours. Precocious, confident, and almost unbearably handsome, Naren Joshi came to the United States from his hometown of Bangalore, India, three days before his nineteenth birthday to study computer science at Stanford University. Secretly hating the sciences and longing to fulfill his lifelong ambition of becoming an actor, Naren transferred to UCLA with the sole intention of breaking into film. Armed only with his shocking good looks and a preternatural sense of what was involved in pretending to be someone else, Naren found bit parts quickly, benefiting from the latest Hollywood trend of casting the more obscure minorities (Korean Americans, South American immigrants, Indians, etc.) as supporting players in mainstream movies about regular, white Americans.

"So when do you think you can call Michael about his friend, since I'd like to get back to Dr. Rojas by tomorrow morning at the latest. Last time you said you'd call him right away, but it took you nearly a week, because I need to know—"

"Karen."

"It's just we're at a really crucial moment here, and we might have to make some very difficult decisions, and I—"

"Karen."

"What?"

"I can't find my wallet."

"What?"

"I can't find my wallet. I don't know where I put it."

"Larry." Silence. "Larry, I don't... How long have you been looking for it?"

"I don't know. Twenty minutes, maybe a half hour."

"Lar, I'm sorry, I just don't have time for this right now."

"There's just not that many places it could be. It's a new place. I don't have that much clutter, and not much furniture either. Back at home there was the chest and the hutch and the hook thing and that old tray and all of Lucy's stuff and all the mail we used to leave lying around, I barely get any mail here."

Pause.

"You'll find it."

"You think so?"

"If it's there, you'll find it."

"Do you think it's here?"

"Larry? Are you going to call Michael or not?"

"Because if it's not here, man, I'd just like to know. In fact, if I had to choose between it not being here and gone forever, on the one hand, and it being here but impossible to locate, I'd choose gone."

"Larry, I'll wait until tomorrow at noon, and then I'm going to give Dr. Rojas my decision."

"I really don't like Michael."

"You really don't like Michael. Larry, I don't give a shit if you don't like Michael. Please call him."

"This is Lucy we're talking about."

"What?"

"This is Lucy we're talking about. It was coming. I know. You're right. I'll call him. Sorry. Even if he's an asshole."

"Good."

"Are you worried?"

"About Lucy?"

"Yeah. Yeah, about Lucy."

"Yes. I'm pretty terrified."

"Me too."

"Alright, so we'll talk—"

"Karen, if I don't find my wallet, I don't know what I'm going to do."

"What do you mean, Lar, you do what everyone else does when they lose their wallet. Cancel your credit cards, go get a new driver's license, and buy a new wallet. What's the big deal?"

"It's not that. I just don't know what I'm going to do."

"Larry, I've really got to go."

"I mean, where is the fucking thing?"

"Call Michael."

"Will you come here and help me look if I call?"

"'Bye, Larry."

"Please."

Nothing.

Yet one of the great accomplishments of *Independence Day* was that during the total-annihilation sequence, and it was most certainly a sequence—five straight minutes of nothing but massive explosions and related chaos—during that time it was just too intense to laugh at. Visually, it was pretty awesome (in the "Shock and Awe" sense of the word), but the sound, the unabating, visceral sound, was the key. The year was 1996 (I looked it up), only a few summers after *Jurassic Park* (1993), after a new generation of surround sound, subwoofers, and digital audio postproduction had enabled some very loud and complicated things to be heard. The volume, the abrasive, thundering blasts, masterfully orchestrated, overwhelmed me, until I couldn't laugh, until I had to, physiologically and neurologically, take the literally inhuman scope of the aliens' brutal attack seriously. Those bastards, they just blew up the White House.

It was a sobering moment on two levels. First, as just mentioned, on the level of plot. Spectacle, for sure, yet a bit of horror, too. But second, and more important, as a self-aware cultural-critic moviegoer, I had just been beaten down to the point that I was unable to resist watching the movie as those who created the movie wanted me to watch it. And I really didn't want to watch it their way. This was something I read about later, this reluctant admission that *Independence Day,* against all odds, succeeded in commanding, unironically, our ever more difficult to command, indeed even locate, unironic attention. From a now-safe, if humbled, distance, the critics conceded (and I had to agree) that at first glance the movie begged a campy reading (and unless you have an impressive home-theater system, that's how it's watched today on video and DVD), but once you were strapped into your theater seat, it worked. And how did it work? By raising the volume—and the stakes, and violence, and the body count—in every which way. By forcing us to imagine at length, and with a great deal of assistance on their part, the death of millions of people, all at once.

The assistant producer, sometime later that evening, driving home in her daze, would realize that she fell in love with Naren within the first twenty minutes. But at the time she was too spellbound to notice. Their encounter, she would tell the head producer the next morning, was a mix between the perfect date and the world's best therapy session. Natural, calming, engaging, healing. Naren's speech was effortless, his accent simply magnificent, and he opened up with gradual elegance, telling the assistant producer lively anecdotes about his childhood and early adolescence. He wistfully reproduced the smells and sounds of Bangalore, the voice of his grandmother, and the way his schoolmaster would reprimand him for disobeying his teacher. Patiently and with great care he reconstructed his entire family tree, sketching it out carefully on the back of a computer printout containing the assistant producer's directions to the community center. His hand did not shake, and when he cried as he wrote out the name of his youngest sister, Mahima, he maintained his self-control, laughing at himself and wiping away the tear with the back of his beautiful caramel-colored hand.

The concept that became "Mediocre Foods" was born at Joel and Kate's, after a bottle and a half of wine, after the girls had been plugged into a video. Kate, ever frenetic, her frizzy hair uncharacteristically pulled up in response to the heat of their small kitchen, her neck splotched in red, decided as she put together yet another dinner for the six of them revolving around tomatoes, butter, and garlic, that using all the sausages in the dish would ruin it, but that all the sausages had to be cooked, lest they go bad. Which meant a sausage appetizer, a single cooked sausage cut into disks on a white plate and placed on the table. It needed something more. Larry went to their fridge, such was their intimacy, and looked inside. Then:

"My Lord, Kate, you have like sixteen different kinds of mustards!"

"What are you talking about, sixteen?" Larry had strongly

mixed opinions about Kate, and her inability to detect hyperbole was on the negative side of the ledger.

"Karen, come take a look at this." Karen came over, a slight smile rising on her face, taking pleasure in what she recognized immediately as the duty to play along.

"This is troubling," she announced gravely after surveying the inside door of the fridge. "Extremely troubling."

"What are you doing in our fridge over there?" Joel finally chimed in, not quite finding the proper tone for his comment, but communicating nevertheless that something was afoot that required cooperation cloaked in feigned resistance.

"An intervention," Larry declared. "As your friends, we must."

Karen began removing containers of varying size, most glass, all colored or filled with something along the spectrum between yellow and brown. As she placed them on the counter Larry counted aloud, each number more accusatory than the next, all the way to the number nine. "Nine. Nine types of mustard. Do you even like mustard?"

Kate and Joel looked at each other, raised eyebrows, shrugged shoulders.

"On a hot dog."

"You need a sweet brown mustard for grilled cheese."

"Samantha only eats French's."

"And then there's Gulden's."

"And Grey Poupon."

"It's not like those two were up to our discretion."

"And that little one"—Joel pointed to an inch-high jar—"I mean, that doesn't count. We bought it in Wisconsin at a fair years back. Throw it out."

Karen tossed it in the garbage.

"Eight. You have eight types of mustard." Larry continued. "That is simply not normal. I won't get into the societal ramifications here, but I could, you all know I could."

"Yeah, that we know," Kate said without turning back from the stove.

Grins were on everyone's faces, and it looked like they were going to let it go at that. Karen began returning the containers to the fridge, asking Joel if they in fact wanted to hold on to all of them. "Does mustard go bad?" he asked. No one could confidently answer, so back inside they all went.

Larry returned to the kitchen table, satisfied that the evening had been injected with some life, since evenings at Joel and Kate's, however pleasant they might be and however great their girls got along, were often boring.

Five minutes passed before it struck Larry: "What if it isn't abnormal?" he asked urgently.

"Huh?"

"What if it isn't abnormal to have a lot of types of mustard?" No one responded. "Karen, c'mon, think, how many types of mustard do we have?"

"I don't know." She started counting on her fingers as the two of them listed them from memory. Joel and Kate seized the opportunity for some role reversal, but by the time they reached six, Larry cut them off, stunned by his conclusions.

"How did they get us to buy so much fucking mustard? It's not like we consider ourselves mustard connoisseurs. People don't have mustard cellars, but between the two couples here, we're averaging at least seven-and-a-half types of mustards per household. Can that be a fluke?"

"I doubt it," Joel said.

"Karen, call the Sterns."

"What?"

"Call the Sterns, see what their mustard count is."

" '*Mustard count*'? Larry, no, I'm not calling the Sterns to ask them how much mustard they have."

"What's their number? I'll call them myself." He rose and headed to a phone.

"Lar, spazoid, stop it." Karen invoked her authority. "What does it matter?"

"I'm not sure, but it's big. Think about it. How did they get us to buy so much?" And before anyone could respond, he found his next move. "Open the fridge. Karen, open the god-damn fridge!"

She didn't budge so he did it himself. He inspected it. "As I thought. Only one type of ketchup. Nine to one—"

"Eight to one—"

"Fine. Eight to one. What kind of insane ratio is that? And you probably prefer ketchup, as a category, as a generic condi-ment, over mustard."

"True," Joel concurred.

"Not me, just for french fries, but not even all the time," Kate said, shaking her head.

Larry hollered into the next room, "Girls, mustard or ketchup, which do you like most?"

No answer. He went into the next room. Asked again. No answer. He paused the video. The girls stared at him confused and impatient. He asked a third time.

Lucy: "Dada, I want a hot dog."

Samantha: "Me too, and Jell-O."

His: "Green Jell-O, green Jell-O, green Jell-O."

Theirs: "And ice cream. When Lucy has ice cream, she gets lots."

"Girls, girls, whoa. What do you want on your hot dog? Mustard or ketchup?"

"Ketchup," Lucy finally answered.

"Mustard," Samantha replied. "And ketchup."

"Thank you. I now return you to your regularly scheduled nonsense."

Back in the kitchen. "Two ketchups, one mustard. At best it's even."

Kate, whose patience for Larry's frequent epiphanies and rants typically ran out first, interrupted. "Larry, please stop talking about mustard and ketchup. I'm losing my appetite."

Sensitive to socially disagreeable behavior on her husband's part, Karen agreed. "Yeah, Lar, enough already, I promise, we can talk about it on the way home."

"Impatience and a patronizing tone, that's what I get. I'm on the cusp of an entrepreneurial gem, of discovering a potentially massive untapped market, and I'm getting pressured to clam up. No way. Please, just follow me here for a moment." Wisely, he didn't stop to check his audience's mood. "We like ketchup more than mustard. But we buy only about 10 percent as much ketchup as we do mustard."

"I've got to disagree with you there, Specter. Think about it. We buy Heinz pretty regularly. About a half-dozen times a year. Some of those mustards are from the early Clinton years."

"Fair enough. Still. Still. You're not buying ketchup at some country inn over in Door County. You're not buying a particular ketchup solely for the construction of a single sandwich." He paused, as it struck him. He savored it briefly before sharing it with his wife and friends. "I see our future, gang, one of wealth and comfort. And its name is Yuppie Ketchup. Yuppie Ketchup." He smiled and fought off the urge to bow. "If we can get people, normal people like us, to buy, on average, even half as many types of ketchup as they do mustard, we'll be rich beyond our wildest fantasies. But we've got to dress it up. Yuppie Ketchup."

"Isn't salsa yuppie ketchup?" Joel asked, sincerely.

"Shut up, Joel, just shut up."

Later in the movie, when those in charge of maintaining dramatic tension in the last few minutes before the Jew and the black guy save the planet, they actually allow themselves—both the writers and the fictional president—to fire a nuclear weapon at Houston, Texas (I'm pretty sure it was Houston). The idea, of course, was, wow, this is one hell of an adversary, and we've really run out of options here, sir, and what more do we have to lose other than the million people who will die in a moment, but look, people, this is what we're dealing with, dammit, we've got no choice. And by this point, or right after this point, when the dust clears, and the dumbfounded helmeted soldier from inside the heavily armored mobile unit that fired the nuclear weapon from some safe number of miles away reports to a really stressed-out, sleep-deprived general in his underground bunker that, sir, I don't believe this but it's still there (the massive garbage-can-lid–shaped spaceship), at that point even I had trouble swallowing my saliva, because, damn, that is some serious shit, and how can you resist an imagination that's willing to pretend to destroy that much of our country and kill that many people just to get people to pay $7.50 to see it all happen? In general, culturally speaking, it's not a good sign. In general, it's the kind of thing the future will look back on with something less than approval. And as a result of three things—(1) my failure to laugh off the unprecedented, previously unimaginable devastation of the plot, (2) my inability to ignore the fact that said plot required a remarkable amount of premeditated and coordinated effort on the part of actors, the director, producers, special-effects wizards, studio heads, and a support crew of thousands, and (3) feeling rotten and implicated by the fact that we the people gave the whole catastrophe an enormous thumbs up by paying top dollar to place our asses, by the millions, in these movie-house seats—I watched the rest of the movie, eating my crappy, overpriced popcorn, with great consternation.

The assistant producer called her boss early the following morning, eleven minutes before she felt it was appropriate to call. In her excitement she did a poor job expressing the urgency of the Naren Joshi angle, until after a quarter hour she said over and over, "Trust me, Bill, just trust me." Naren met with the seasoned, cynical head producer the next afternoon. After their meeting, the producer excused himself and sat weeping in his private bathroom, feeling that he had for the first time understood, however incompletely, the loss. He made a call to an executive producer, leading to another meeting, leading to another epiphany. And so the calls and meetings went, for another six days, each caller driven by an inexpressible obligation to convey the magnitude of his or her encounter with Naren Joshi. Like the best movie you've ever seen, or the best book you've ever read, or, hell, the best sex you've ever had. It was qualitatively different, the studio president told the agent of the now-retired news anchor, the one who had changed television news forever. It hurt, to be certain, but there was a certain pleasure involved, because it all was so perfect. The studio president, hunched over his $7,000 desk, begged the agent to do whatever it took to lure the retired news anchor out of retirement, just this once. The retired news anchor had done only a half-dozen interviews during his thirty-plus years; he found them petty, so he wrote in his memoirs. All the same, everyone in the business regarded them as classics: focused, natural, powerful, informative. The agent said he'd see what he could do. The studio president put it like this: Spare yourself no hyperbole. Anything you can imagine, this is bigger.

Over the course of the next few days, Larry can't leave it alone. Ketchup, types of ketchup. He has a legal pad in the living room waiting for entries, but seventy-two hours later, all he's got is:

THE FUTURE OF KETCHUP
- Sun-dried tomato
- Spicy
- Heirloom
- Garlic

Which isn't a bad start, but it isn't taking off as he's hoped. Karen, for her part, is less than enthusiastic about the whole enterprise, seeing it as another instance of Larry's short attention span, a short attention span often manifested in various get-rich-quick schemes. Within the various future narratives describing the end of their marriage, Larry's fondness for such schemes in general, and yuppie ketchup in particular, will alternate, regularly, depending on whom you ask, between cause and symptom. But whatever the case, it was in there somewhere. The following fight, then, being either cause or symptom:

"Karen, c'mon, help me think up kinds of ketchup."
"Larry. Please. No."
"What's the big deal? You said you would."

"That's untrue."

"Bullshit. You said, and I quote, 'Larry, another time. Ple-ease.'"

"I was not volunteering to help you another time, I was asking you to stop talking about it around me."

"Why do you hate yuppie ketchup?"

"I don't. Lar, it's not the point, I—"

"But you do"—allowing himself a small smile, thinking himself cute—"you hate yuppie ketchup!"

"Larry"—smiling, too, a bit, but mostly exasperated, and the little part of her that does find him cute is in fact accessible only after burrowing through a few layers of longing and exasperation—"Larry, I don't hate yuppie ketchup. There is no such thing as yuppie ketchup—"

"That's the point. We're going to invent it. Me and you."

"No we're not. No we're not, and you know it. We're not because I don't give a shit about ketchup and because you're not going to spend time 'inventing' yuppie ketchup when you should be revising your résumé and making calls."

"What? The two are mutually exclusive? You expect me to spend eight hours a day, five days a week playing around with fonts and calling friends of associates of my father's acquaintances? Is yuppie ketchup that threatening?"

"No, it's not. Fine. Here are my suggestions: 'Ketchup that ruins your marriage,' 'Ketchup not worth spending so much time talking about,' 'Ketchup that is just that and absolutely nothing more,' 'This is ketchup, so don't get your hopes up; it won't change your life for the better,' 'Ketchup, fucking, shitty ketchup.'" Karen was on a roll, but she got hold of herself and left the room, feeling that such displays of self-control needed to be introduced into their home as often as possible.

Seven long seconds later, Larry screamed after her. "Karen! Karen! You're a genius! You're going to make us rich!"

And so what am I getting at? Just this: Am I doing the same thing here in "The End of Larry's Wallet"? Because though I was thoroughly entertained by *Independence Day,* in the sense of captivated and very much not bored, it was hard, not minutes after the movie was over, and probably during a few lulls during the second half, not to sense, in a gross, regretful, taken-advantage-of way, that I'd been manipulated. That they got me not only to voluntarily exchange my money for access to a creative project of dubious value—something far too common at this moment in our history to get worked up about it all on its own—but worse, that they got me to give a shit, to be affected emotionally and psychically by imagining devastation on a scale never before brought to life so vividly. It was cheap, not budget-wise, but as a strategy, as an aesthetic strategy and even cultural philosophy. And so here I am, wanting to write a short story that will engage and even move some ideal reader, by jarring him or her (my ideal reader needing no particular gender), and suddenly I find myself starting out with the phrase "Just before the world came to an end once and for all," this, in fact, being the phrase and idea through which the story first emerged. Is that just my transcription of an *Independence Day* narrative strategy? I really want to believe it's not, but I am scared it will be read that way, as cheap, callous, arrogant, and worst of all, lazy. So much so, that here it is, a self-conscious aside, motivated truly and really by my urge to communicate to you the reader that I realize this whole story is pretty questionable.

And what I'm worried about is this (and, okay, even my (or especially my) worst-case scenario affords me a certain amount

of success): I'm picturing the story getting finished and published and read and talked about to the extent that some possibly
self-promoting, but overall truly concerned, member of the either Pakistani- or Indian-American community, some president
or executive director of some acronymed body, starts making a
stink. To the point that a *Nightline*-type program does a show on
it. Now granted, this is absolute nonsense, since we're talking
about a short story here, and when was the last time a short story
did anything but get read; but still, I need to exaggerate the scenario in order to make my general point. So the aforementioned
immigrant community leader, who is pretty sharp and not bad-
looking and well-educated and a tad bit arrogant (this mostly
stemming from his—no, her—deep belief in the validity of her
opposition and outrage, which is cultivated actively and expertly
by Ted Koppel's head writer, this Gayatri somebody, she is
coached, and even rehearses her opening diatribe a little bit,
since, after all, that's a key element in the show's tried-and-
true formula). She's going to build a really strong case—right
after the opening ninety-second segment setting the stage
(which shows (multiple copies of) the cover of my book (my
book!) in impressive bookstore window displays, maybe some
positive reviews, too, hell, it's been nominated for one of the big
awards, thus showing that this isn't the only aspect of the collection people are talking about and indeed raising the stakes of the
controversy altogether)—about this writer (me) casually deciding to liquidate tens of millions of Indians and Pakistanis in a
story that's really about a guy losing his wallet. And she'll even
suggest, or maybe Ted himself will subtly toss it out there, that
do you think the author, who is a white American—all sides will
agree, for now, to keep my Jewishness out of it, though it will
come up later—would have written the same story switching,

say, France and England for India and Pakistan? And with feigned awkwardness she will respond slowly, "I don't know," her mouth closing into a nasty smile, because of course she knows that I wouldn't, whatever that means. And so, Dr. Hasak-Lowy (that's right, Todd Hasak-Lowy, Doctor of Philosophy), how do you justify this?

The retired news anchor, W, met Naren at the former's modest country home outside Santa Barbara. They were left alone. Naren, though either not yet alive or in India for the duration of W's career, knew his reputation well, and was, to the extent he could, which was comparatively not much at all, a bit intimidated at first. W was arguably the most respected American of the post–WWII era. A largely secularized populace, disillusioned with Watergate, Vietnam, and all the sundry embarrassments to follow, looked to W with nothing short of reverence. He could have won the presidency, running for either party on nearly any platform, such was the conventional wisdom of the last quarter century. In an age where one's ability to communicate on television was beyond paramount, W had no peers, since W was, more or less, responsible for this becoming the case. His voice and well-known stylized idiom, his preference for the adverb over the adjective, the way he stressed the final word of any sentence, and, of course, his calm baritone, all this had become the measure of authority here in the American age of television.

So he and Naren sat together, sizing each other up, two titans of charisma and composure, each forced to steady himself in the bright light of the other's radiant dynamism. Naren understood where he and his story had taken him, to the feet of the last American wise man, and Naren surrendered himself to the role of the prodigy. He found himself, effortlessly, transforming into exactly who he needed to become, this his ultimate role, as he and W improvised the most pointed and enlightening conversation which was ever to be held on the matter of the nuclear exchange between India and Pakistan. W conducted Naren through a series of poignant, devastating monologues, interrupting him only enough to distill, briefly, an elusive notion or to rephrase a particularly potent idea. W instantly understood the power of Naren's English accent, and with little more than a slight turn of his head or the raising of an eyebrow, directed the young immigrant toward words containing the long "a" or ending in a hard "t." But mostly W nodded, the way a laser or a mountain would nod if they could. It all was lost to the air, their first conversation, and they knew it. They knew this should be documented, but somehow its evanescence prodded them further yet, until after ninety minutes both men fell into a deep, profound silence, too moved even to maintain eye contact. This mutual retreat into solitary contemplation marking the end of their first conversation.

When the phone rang again, Larry stared at the device with resentment, wishing it would stop for once. He couldn't, to the extent that he was trying, think up a single good reason to answer or not answer the call. His wallet, after all, couldn't dial his number, and even if it could, it certainly wouldn't speak. He turned his back to the noise, attempting to review his searching strategy up to this moment, in order to formulate an updated approach, one pointed optimistically toward the future. Of course, a person with his wallet could call, of course. But the answering machine, clicking and beeping, had already intervened, saying things like:

Hello, you've reached Larry Specter and the offices of Mediocre Foods, please leave a message. You have only a minute. Thanks.

And then:

Lar, it's Karen. Maybe you're out. Look, you've got to call Michael. This is serious. We need to decide very, very soon.

Larry continued to watch the machine, stuck halfway between biting his nails and eating the tip of his thumb.

Look, Larry, I know you're going through a tough time, we all are. I'm sorry your wallet's gone—

"Gone?!" He spit out, "Misplaced, not gone."

—but this can't be about you right now. You've been flaking too much lately, even for you, but…

Larry waited, wearing an expression of curiosity, impatience, and good-natured despair.

…but here it is. If it comes down to it, and this doesn't work out and we get into custody and you keep dropping the ball, and well—

And that was it, the machine decided. Her minute had ended. Larry watched the newly blinking light on the answering machine for a few beats. He exhaled and, searching for temporary shelter in a clever understatement, said aloud, "Well, that was an unfortunate development." And then he stood there.

My problem, right from the beginning of my appearance on *Nightline,* is that I'm much too willing to consider that there is indeed something wrong, misguided, or even immoral with the very premise of this piece. My agent and publisher (publicly concerned and privately tickled by the controversy) have drenched me in advice and coaching, but all I manage to say during my initial response is that I wanted to explore it, because I had this vague sense that it was worth exploring. And the woman (who is, simply put, winning, and who is good at winning and who, despite her best intentions, knows, if only because she's smart, that a good showing here will certainly open doors for her, doors leading up and away from the immigrant community she represents) can't help but mock my repeated use of "exploring," and asks, rhetorically and sarcastically, "Dr. Hasak-Lowy (she pronounces my name flawlessly, which really fucks me up), might there be other things worth exploring that don't require cheapening the lives of millions of other people you really know nothing about?"

Naren and W met twice more during the next thirty-six hours as an unprecedented alliance of studio executives, producers, and media moguls emerged to arrange the details of Naren and W's televised interview. Naren and W, each for different reasons, demanded it be broadcast live with an absolutely minimal human presence in the interview room throughout the proceedings. In the end, only the top cameraman from ABC was present, cloaked entirely in black. Other than the three men, the room was subtly cluttered with a host of remote-controlled cameras, microphones, and lights, directed from the next room by three of the most skilled technicians in television.

Larry hadn't cried in eleven years. And even then, three days after his father's sudden death, it was an abortive affair: quick, unexpected, clumsy. Karen, for her part, was a champion crier, always ready and able, if not necessarily willing. During their six, to his mind, now-canonized separation fights, Karen had gone through two and a half boxes of Kleenex, as the floor or the nightstand or the couch or the dashboard or the kitchen counter was buried under the crumpled-up, mostly dry white balls. Larry raised his voice and shouted during the second talk, and he thought about crying during the fifth, this at the moment when he realized two separate camps had fully formed, that "we" only had use now as a tinny, formal term relevant for material and legal purposes. An end had been reached. Karen's outburst caught it appropriately. But he didn't know how to do it, so he just kept on smoldering meekly, stewing in his regret and disappointment.

And this is my in, or at least the thing I latch on to, her assertion that I "really know nothing about" these "other" people. I pretend, uncharacteristically, that I have a firm opinion on something and respond:

> Whether or not I am an expert about India, Pakistan, or its peoples is secondary to the premise of the piece, which required that I write on the destruction of a place whose inhabitants would be considered foreign and even "other" by an average American, both an average American as represented *in* the story and an average American reader *of* the story. It was important to me that the site of the exchange be distant from the American imagination because I wanted the story to investigate the complex and essential

inaccessibility of such an event here in America, and this distance, both real and imagined, between the United States and India/Pakistan helped to intensify this inaccessibility.

Talking on TV, I discover, is exhilarating and frightening.

Naren killed himself during the interview. He had wanted to kill himself from the first moment he heard of the nuclear exchange, and had decided he would do so during his interview with W some five minutes into his second conversation with the legendary news anchor. Despite his intelligence and eloquence, he never fully understood why this was necessary, he just knew that it was. He came to terms with this decision less than thirty seconds after he finally settled on it, his voice faltering uncharacteristically during the interim. It was a necessary gesture, an unavoidable sacrifice he had to make, and making it public would amplify his words, would seal his message. The only remaining matter to resolve was the method. He was reluctant to use a gun, wanting his death to be free of the vivid, shocking violence he was sent to describe. The most attractive method was pills or poison, but he had no idea how to ingest pills prior to the interview without likewise killing himself prior to the interview, and similarly he had no idea how to procure an effective poison on such short notice. His always paranoid father, however, on his one brief visit to his son, had decided that Naren, living among violent Americans in the violent city of Los Angeles, needed a weapon. Naren protested and had never touched the gun his father presented to him, with some ceremony, on the final morning of their final meeting. It remained hidden deep in the back of a desk drawer until the morning of the interview, but Naren knew it would work, his father's paranoia matched only by his compulsive attention to detail.

Larry had now held the same expression for the last ten seconds, his eyes fixed on a bare, off-white patch of kitchen/dining-space wall a foot and a half down and to the right from the answering machine. He was concentrating, trying to make sense of his new reality, both in conjunction with and independent of his still-missing wallet. It was tough, really tough, accepting the not-so-subtle implications of Karen's message, assessing what her threat meant in real terms, wondering and dreading just what may be happening to Lucy, keeping his mind off his wallet while mentally cataloging still unsearched places, shouldering the approaching doom of his immediate financial future, and simply breathing. It was a lot to stay on top of all at once, and Larry was failing, with his breath going first. Its rhythm broke apart, so he gasped a bit. And into this crisis, with most of his resources mobilized for holding on to the ever-lengthening name of his loss, his crying crept. He fought it, instinctively, trying to regain control of his breath, while simultaneously sensing the odd, painful way it illuminated this thing that so required illumination.

I look into her monitor to see if any of this is moving her, and her eyes do relax briefly, but she can't allow herself to ask aloud if this premise might have any value. Instead, she takes me to task for my assumptions about Indian otherness.

> Dr. Hasak-Lowy [again with the flawless pronunciation], are you aware that there are as many as one and three-quarter million Indian Americans living in the United

States? And that there are over two hundred thousand Pakistani Americans here as well? This does not include the sizable number of Indian and Pakistani nationals working in high-tech and medical professions across the United States. The Indian American population grew by over 100 percent in the nineties, and is now the third-largest Asian American community in the United States, behind only Chinese and Filipino Americans. We pay taxes, serve in the armed forces, and attend the nation's top colleges and universities in significant numbers. Despite this, in the eyes of many Americans we remain "other" [fingers up for quotation marks] and un-American, or at best invisible. So tell me, Dr. Hasak-Lowy, why did you choose to reinforce this in your story?

In addition to the small black gun, Naren brought to the interview a beautiful wool blanket his mother had knitted for him especially for his trip to the United States. The director had encouraged Naren to bring objects and pictures to the interview, and while both Naren and W privately dismissed this suggestion as too obvious, for Naren the blanket was a prop every bit as important as the gun itself.

As his face grew wet, and Larry let himself become unfamiliar, he felt a sudden need to hide. Even in his own solitary apartment, Larry felt much too visible. He stumbled toward the bedroom, disqualifying the intimacy of his bathroom due to its mirror.

My sense of vertigo intensifies as I realize she's said a lot of this before. Whereas I'm totally improvising, despite all the advice I got beforehand. She's not a mean person, just very focused on the adversarial nature of our relationship.

Naren and W were given no guidelines or limits of any sort. The director, the director himself realized, had no choice but to relinquish all authority to W, who would run the interview and choose the moment of its conclusion. There would be no commercials, no graphics superimposed on the screen, just a brief introduction by W himself. The interview had been promoted heavily during the twenty-four-hour stretch prior to the broadcast, and some estimated 130 million Americans tuned in. In the adjacent control room an unprecedented who's who of TV news production stood dumbstruck, frozen by the humbling profundity of the dialogue next door. More than a few of them later described it as having the otherworldly beauty of time-lapse photography, of an event at once natural and impossible, unquestionably at odds with the typical order of things, in other words, sublime. W, flirting with the edge of antagonism, at first prodded Naren, challenged him, demanding he hold nothing back. Naren directed his responses not to the cameras or to some imaginary viewing audience, but straight at W himself, to his figure and his legacy, until W, nearly overwhelmed, felt absolutely and personally implicated in the history he had returned to report. The tone of the interview oscillated dangerously between vitriolics and reconciliation. W was, for the first time ever, forced to wipe sweat from his brow, not once but twice, while Naren, during the first and second crescendos—seemingly choreographed to occur at the twenty-fourth and forty-third minute, respectively—panted like a wild animal. And then finally, after quietly reproducing the melodic couplet he, his brother, and their boyhood friends would be forced to sing after winning their neighborhood version of kick the can—the couplet a self-pitying apology expressing, in a minor key, the loneliness of the victor—and explicitly explaining to W how this couplet, in all its strange simplicity was the only thing that now made sense to him, Naren thanked W for his empathy, raised the blanket to cover himself, removed the gun and shot himself, expertly, in the head.

The eighty-three-year-old W flew from his chair and crouched over the already dead immigrant. Next door the room filled with gasps and a couple of "oh my God's" but they were surprisingly subdued. W merely touched Naren, lovingly, having wanted to touch him—especially his face—since the first minutes of their first meeting. The retired news anchor was grateful Naren had provided a conclusion, as he himself felt unable to provide one himself. Similarly, he thanked Naren for electing not to shoot himself through the roof of his mouth, and in this way preserving his beautiful face, which W now caressed like a father or a grateful lover.

His crying, he knew, lacked elegance. It was crude and clumsy and truly pathetic. But it was his and he was fully inside it, and the catastrophic character of its form and content, its disastrous architecture, were to be cultivated. Larry, lips convulsing and vision blurred, yanked open the door of his unnecessarily spacious closet and threw himself down upon his mound of dirty clothes. He had recently, in a foolish act informed by his dovetailing autonomy and depression, abandoned key elements in his self-care routine: not showering for days, renouncing deodorant, recycling already worn clothes. As he hugged his neglected laundry, he smelled the worst of himself, his sweat, his crotch, his ass. He moaned hideously, without a hint of self-consciousness, while his red-hot face stretched and seemed to break apart. Pulling the soft pile closer, Larry buried his face in its darkness, almost comforted until jolted right below his closed-tight left eye by the familiar painful plastic prick of his defective, once-despised wallet.

My only hope, I hastily conclude, is to muddle the conversation with fancy terms from critical theory. This wasn't my plan fifteen minutes ago, since (a) it's something I try to avoid even in my academic writing, (b) I fear that it will alienate potential readers, and (c) I don't want it to sound like I really gave this all that much thought beforehand. But she's kicking my ass:

> I was reluctant to reify Indian otherness [I can feel Ted Koppel, fifteen hundred miles away, cringe as I say "reify"], but I could find no way to do otherwise. The truth is, the ultimate focus of this piece, at least that strand of the intertwined narrative concerned with the nuclear exchange between India and Pakistan, is the mediation, indeed emplotment, of this event by the American media, in particular the television media—

She cuts me off:

> So in other words, the instantaneous murder of fifteen million Indian and Pakistani people [I think to interrupt in order to correct her with the actual higher figure, but I am, of all things, quite curious to see where she's going with this] at the hand of your imagination is little more than a pretext for some other idea?

I'm hugely impressed with this response, so much so that I forget that it's my turn to challenge her somehow. Thankfully, Mr. Koppel intervenes, though not exactly on my behalf:

Indeed, Dr. Hasak-Lowy, I find it rather fascinating that, as you put it just moments ago, the story's focus on the so-called nuclear exchange is little more than a pretext for a meditation on the limits of television news. And yet here you are, on television, defending this very move.

I don't blush easily, but I can feel my face growing heavy with blood. I smile the dumbest smile of my adult life. Both are kind enough to give me the last word before the commercial. Here it is: "Yes, Mr. Koppel, the irony is not lost on me."

THE INTERVIEW

K eep in mind that the guy asking most of the questions sweats a great deal, as in constantly, as in he would cause the makeup/sweat artist for Gatorade ads to fear for his or her job. He sweats so much he long ago stopped paying it much notice, so the sweat simply flows, runs, he perspires freely, wetting his collar, undershirts, tie, even his jacket, which he has kept on for this meeting knowing too well what the sight of wet spots under his arm extending well past his elbows would do to this potential employee. He is three inches shorter than the interviewee, but easily has eighty-five pounds on him, making the extensive perspiration slightly easier to comprehend. *In medias res,* obviously:

"So over there at the Kellogg School, over at Northwestern…did you like it? Tell me about it."

"It's a top-notch program. The instructors are all big names in their field, of course. But the key is their summer-placement assistance. I doubt I could have gotten the HP internship last year without their help."

"Sure, sure. Did you enjoy living in Chicago? They have great food there, don't they? I remember fondly the concept of cheese fries." Pause. "So, did you eat a lot of cheese fries there in Chicago?"

Pause. "Sure"—pause—"they're great. A little addictive, but great."

"They're really great, aren't they?"

"Yeah, but you've got to be careful, they aren't the healthiest…" Serious backpedaling. "But there is this one place, the Wiener's Circle, of course the name in itself is classic, but their cheese fries are amazing. The best part, though, is that they are fairly rude; you have to be extremely pushy to get any service if the place is at all busy. And even when you do get served, they act like you're just a big pain. But the strangest thing is, is that I don't believe it was an act, they really *are* rude."

"And you liked that, you liked being treated poorly, being forced to act pushy in response."

Pause.

The interviewee beginning to make up the nearly infinite distance between himself and the man across the desk in terms of perspiration: "Um."

"Never mind. Over there at Kellogg's did they coach all of you about interviewing techniques?"

"Sure."

"What did they tell you?"

"Well"—still sweating, at a slightly slower rate—"they told us all sorts of things, from the obvious to the not so obvious."

"Give me an example of the obvious."

"You know, make sure every answer you give makes you look good, even if you're being asked about something potentially negative."

"Like the 'what are your biggest weaknesses' questions."

"Exactly."

"So answer it for me. What is your stock response for the weaknesses/shortcomings query?"

"I usually say—"

"No, no, no. Pretend I just asked you the question for real."

"Well, when I get involved in a project I often lose myself in it completely—"

"Good, good, the old 'I'm a workaholic' approach, difficult, one would imagine, for a prospective employer to resist. But your phrasing, it could be better. I'm not sure about the 'lose myself' bit, a little too much stress on the out-of-control qualities of the addiction. How about 'when I commit to a project, I commit completely until the project's completed'?"

"Hmm. You're right, it is much more positive, more assertive."

"The term this week is 'proactive,' I believe."

"Yes, I think you're right."

"So enough about the obvious…no, hold on. Answer that question for me, but now be honest. Tell me about a significantly negative quality in your character."

Silence.

"Look, don't worry. I won't consider you unless you do, so think of it as just one more mandatory station in the process. I'll return the favor before we're done."

"Well, hmm, I either like someone or something or I hate them. No middle ground or—"

"You're cheating. That's just a veiled reference to your

intense conviction. That you know what you like and what you don't. That you're your own man, as it were."

"But I hate most everything. That's what I was getting to. It's not just that I like or hate everything, it's that I hate, let's say, four out of five things, people included. It's a default approach to the world at this point."

"I see."

Nothing.

"That couldn't have possibly helped my prospects here. I feel I was just taken advantage of."

"Two responses. Number one, I respect the honesty, I even identify with the worldview. Second, as for the whole taken-advantage-of business, I think that is sort of the point in an interview. It's about me telling you even before you start working for me that the power is located over here with me."

"But that's one of the things they taught us, in the coaching part. They told us to ask a lot of questions in return, during that politely offered moment when you're supposed to ask, 'Do *you* have any questions?' putting that emphasis on the 'you' as if there is something somehow amusing about the possibility of the applicant wanting to know anything him- or herself. They told us to always ask a lot of questions. I was told to always ask one more question than I think is appropriate. They say it communicates to the prospective employer that I'm assertive, and that even though this initially is a turnoff for the employer as he or she tends to find it threatening, that later they find it quite attractive."

"Hmm."

"They did."

"I'm sure you're telling the truth; I suppose that is one of the less obvious things."

"It's on the less obvious side of things."

"Tell me an extremely unobvious strategy."

"Well, bigger companies, companies with a multistage interviewing process, often throw in a lunch—"

"Are you implying that you're not expecting me to feed you, that I'd send you off hungry?"

"Uh, but it's only 9:45."

"And?" Into his intercom: "Sheila, run down to the corner and get a dozen donuts." To the applicant: "What kind do you like?"

"A dozen?"

"For later, what do you like, what kind?"

"Chocolate-glazed, but I'm not very hungry."

"No one is going to accuse me of neglecting my applicants." To the intercom: "Get at least three—no, get at least four chocolate-glazed."

Silence.

"So what about the complimentary, keep-your-receipts lunch? What did they tell you over at Kellogg?"

"Well"—pause, the sound of a comparatively mucus-free throat being cleared—"of course the gesture seems innocently generous and friendly, but it is of course a tool to uncover all the intangibles. Body language, small-talk skills, sense of humor."

"Obviously."

"No, but there are all these secrets. Dos and don'ts encoded into mealtime etiquette."

"Such as."

"Such as never put salt and pepper on your food before you taste it. If you do it means you're not open-minded, that you enter a situation with preconceived expectations."

"What if you get a lunch omelette? You're not going to salt it? Assholes."

"No, but you shouldn't order something like a lunch

omelette, it's too eccentric. You don't want them to think you're strange."

"Fair enough, what else?"

"Avoid messy food."

"Duh."

"Red meat is okay, but not preferred. Pork is a real no-no. Fish is good if it is freshwater. Halibut good, sea bass bad, trout, surprisingly, very good, mahimahi, very bad. Shellfish is best avoided unless it's just a side note to the dish. As in your crab-meat salad. Your best bet is the chicken-breast entrée, especially if it comes with sautéed vegetables."

"Should you order your own dish, or is it okay to duplicate a potential coworker's dish?"

"Duplicates are okay if the employee is at or around the level you'd be hired at. Never duplicate the superior's order, aligning yourself against a coworker of your status. Never. Duplicates are safest when a dish comes recommended as a house special by a coworker."

"What if it's messy?"

"If it is Friday that's okay, because the dress code will be more lenient, leading to an overall eye away from appearance. But this is only if your napkin work is strong."

"Napkin work?"

"Napkin work."

"Okay. What about price?"

"A dollar under the most expensive dish ordered."

"What if they make you order first?"

"Go chicken breast."

"They're out of chicken breast."

"It's only lunchtime—highly unlikely."

"The delivery was supposed to come at 11:00, but it didn't come until 11:45, and prep time is an hour."

"Okay, I'd look for a pasta dish."

"Messy alarm, *eeyoop, eeyoop,* I repeat messy alarm has been activated."

"Cream sauce, not marinara sauce. If they only have marinara sauce, go, excuse me, go fish."

"Nice, nice."

"And to drink—"

"No, let me guess…iced tea."

"Impressive."

"What about bathroom visits?"

"One is best. Actually, one is mandatory. If you don't go at all they'll assume, probably accurately, that you're just holding it in, that you'd make yourself suffer unnecessarily for the company, which at first looks good, but as the inverse of the whole asking questions yourself during the interview, they ultimately don't want someone so selfless as to sit on a ready-to-burst bladder. Two is okay; three is the kiss of death. So your best bet is hold out until deep into the meal for the first visit, leaving the second one in reserve, just in case."

"Okay, enough about the meal. Did they prepare you for brainteasers?"

"Of course."

"So I have nine coins that look the same, but one is gold—"

"Weigh two groups of three. If they weigh the same, take two from the other three. If these two weigh the same, the ninth piece is it. If one is heavier that's it, if, in the initial weighing, one group of three is heavier, see the process for the unweighed group of three just discussed."

"And did they instruct you to blurt it out like a fourth grader?"

"I just thought that…that…"

"Do me a favor, please at least pretend that you're taking me seriously."

"Sorry."

"Don't apologize."

"Sorry."

"That was a joke. I'm going to assume that was a joke, for everyone's sake, I'm going to assume that was a joke. Anyhow. Why are manholes round? There are two reasons."

"Hmmm. Wow. That's a toughie."

"Jesus. You don't have to pretend you don't know it. Just let me finish the question, which I already did."

"Okay. A square can fall through a square hole, but a circle can't fall through a round hole. That's number one. Number two, there are an infinite number of ways a circle can fit in the round hole, as opposed to four ways in the case of the square."

"Is this like a class over at Kellogg? Were you quizzed on this stuff?"

"It's mostly just gossip. You know, the culture of an MBA program."

Donuts arrive. Sheila is not, repeat, not attractive.

"Thanks, Sheila."

Sheila responds with the sound one makes reviewing a long, boring list only to find a mild surprise near the end.

"Bon appétit."

"Really, no thanks."

"You've got to be kidding."

"I told you, I'm truly not hungry."

"They teach about the dangers of sea bass, but nothing about common courtesy? You are my guest, and you reject my hospitality? Unbelievable, really, just unbelievable."

"It's not that, I just thought we were past that."

"'We'? 'We' met about, um, sixteen minutes ago. If you don't eat a donut right now, then this interview is over."

"Fine, fine, okay…good donut."

"As opposed to bad donut?"

"Well, you know, sometimes you forget. It's been a while."

"No, I don't forget. It hasn't been a while."

Nothing.

"How much for the rest of the box?"

"Huh?"

"How much would you need to finish the box, ten more donuts, how much?"

"How much money, you mean?"

"Yeah, how much money, right now, to eat the rest, including the Bavarian cream?"

"Forget it."

"Forget it? What does that mean?"

"No."

"No?"

"No amount, not interested."

"So if I lay down $10,000 in twenties, you walk away, saying, 'No thanks, I'm saving room for the Sizzler lunch buffet'?"

"You're going to give me $10,000 to eat these donuts?"

"It's a hypothetical, Kellogg boy. I'm trying to get a sense of your priorities. How much physical pain would you endure for a sizable cash reward? That kind of thing."

"Oh. They never told us about this line of questioning. What does it tell you?"

"Absolutely nothing. But how much, what is the minimum you'd do it for?"

"Around $10,000."

"So I put down $9,500 and you walk away?"

"Well…"

"Look, it isn't about negotiating. Think, how much would it take?"

Semifocused thought on one side of the table, enjoyment of a cruller on the other.

"Fifteen hundred dollars."

"Really?"

"Yep."

"You don't do it for $1,250?"

"I thought we weren't negotiating."

"Fair enough, I just wanted to double-check. That's pretty steep."

"I don't like being really full. It would mean that the rest of today I would feel horrible, possibly tomorrow as well."

"You wouldn't feel horrible for forty-eight hours for $1,250?"

"I don't know, I'm anticipating a small, but unignorable amount of mental anguish that would take me sometime into the next week. Some strange by-product from gluttony as prostitution. I can't quite explain it, but I sense it would be significant…What about you?"

"Me?"

"Yeah, how much?"

Pause.

"I don't believe you want the truth in this instance."

"What are you talking about?"

"I just think that in this case an accurate response would be a bit much to, excuse me, digest at this early hour."

"I don't follow."

"Nothing."

"Nothing what?"

"That's my answer."

"Huh?"

"Nothing, zero, zilch, nada, zippo, goose egg, for free, I would, I will, I am going to, quite likely, before the day is out, I will consume these donuts. All of them. I may even leave the chocolate cream–filled for last as a small challenge to myself."

"Whoa."

"In fact, assuming Sheila was not feeling generous, it appears I'm paying around four bucks to eat eleven donuts today."

Both men regroup, the word "fat" stubbornly refusing to remove itself from the epicenter of thought-language enlisted to get things back on track.

"So"—slightly more authentic throat clearing—"why do you want this job?"

"Just like that? Just like that we're going to pretend this is a real interview?"

"Call me old-fashioned, but I actually would like to know at some point. Why do you want to work for a soon-to-be three-person company that develops miscellaneous office products? You're not allowed to say it interests you because I wouldn't believe you."

"Well, I am interested in product development and marketing. Those were my Concentrations at Kellogg, and from what I gathered from your ad, I'd do a bit of both here."

"Okay, good enough start, keep going."

"Keep going. I'm also intrigued by the small size of the company. I feel I would thrive in a setting like this, where I'll be required to wear a lot of hats, to juggle tasks. I think I excel in such settings."

"Nice, nice. But more. Why business at all? Why a company that makes support products for home and office computing?

We're talking late nights agonizing over color choices for CD-ROM disk holders. I need at least a little bit of soul baring here. I was hoping you'd be a little more forthcoming, but I need more. Pretend I'm a therapist. Tell me something big. Try to ignore the powdered sugar scattered around my face."

"Something big."

"Something big."

"Something big."

"Yes, something big."

A fair amount of jaw rubbing and tugging. Eyes closed. Interviewee so far from familiar interview territory he scratches his balls, albeit pensively.

"My father, he sold watches. Watches. He was a hell of a watch salesman. Midwest regional salesman for a large watchmaker. Appointments at merchandising headquarters of Sears, JCPenney, Hudson's, Lord & Taylor, Marshall Field's, Saks, Neiman Marcus, you name it, at least annually, huge meetings for the company, plus a million other smaller such meetings at jewelry stores, etc. He sold watches. But with him, with him you had to call it a 'timepiece.' Not that he made you—he'd recognize the term 'watch'—it was just that he had a true, pure admiration for watches, which he called 'timepieces,' and that admiration was so complete, so honest, that you felt you were profaning some higher sensibility with the pedestrian 'watch.' He had this wonderful wrist. Thick, hairy, visibly powerful, flaring out toward his rolled-up white shirtsleeve along a sinewy forearm. His jacket over a chair in some office, he stands grinning, his own model, clad in gray slacks and suspenders. He had this whole 1940s look. This is the late 60s, early 70s, and he's wearing wool, his collars are almost criminally conservative. Even his hair is understated. He sold dignity, he sold integrity. Watergate is on the front page and he's invoking terms like 'pride' and 'honor,' all as a watch salesman. But it was sincere; somehow he meant every last bit of it. Though he knew it was part of the act. I mean, he thought that pride and honor and all that were good things, but he still knew that the link between these abstractions and a $79 timepiece was only imagined, yet somehow he still meant it. It sounds contradictory, I know. It's like he embraced it as necessary, absolutely vital bullshit. To make people believe that their watch could bestow on them a certain wholeness which penetrated down to their very essence. He believed that however nonsensical such an association with watches was, that if people subscribed to it, and it was only ever an issue of the thing as a conviction or not, he believed the world would be a little better if people felt their watches were matters of character. I'm sure you follow."

"Basically."

"He was phenomenal. They made appointments with him. They bought whatever he told them to buy. They hugged him. The rep from Jacobson's asked him to be the godfather of his firstborn. He would enter their offices with his brown leather, oversized briefcase, a briefcase he intentionally weathered in our garage with files and sandpaper, spending no small fortune on polishes and waxes and sealants to achieve the desired appearance, so the briefcase itself, which was a recent purchase, seemed, well, wise. He had it lined with this rich, inviting velvet, the kind of velvet you wanted to touch your cheeks to, and he would open it onto their imitation-oak desks like a faith healer and soon they'd be talking about hometowns and Eisenhower and Mickey Mantle, and he'd get the accounts and sell a half-dozen watches that day, right there, in their offices. Secretaries with half-baked excuses would enter the offices to get a peek at

the new line with their checkbooks 'what-do-you-know'ingly
tucked into their handbags, we were just on the way to the wash-
room to freshen up, let me see those, such lovely timepieces. He
had every sales record, week, month, annual, career, no peers to
speak of, perhaps in sales in general. He was constantly offered
higher managerial and administrative positions, but he refused.
His commissions were quite extraordinary, but more than that
he believed in the traveling salesman, well, of course he did. It
was all part of the mystique, the sentiment, the nostalgia, which
he sold along with the watches. He was something…"

"Which explains your interest in floppy-disk cases. I'm missing something."

"Yeah. Carter. Then came Carter."

"Carter? As in Jimmy?"

"As in Jimmy. Look, don't get me wrong. I'm no huge fan of
the Reagan-Bush era, but Carter, Carter, well, it all happened
when he was president, in office, it happened on, excuse me, it
happened on his watch. The inflation, the gas prices, the unemployment, the hostages, everything. It happened there in the late
seventies. The company was never one of the real heavy hitters.
It wasn't a Seiko or a Timex. Limited advertising. A rare television spot. Mostly ads in papers, and then often as shared advertising, his company's watches featured in an ad announcing a
three-day sale at Hudson's. No mottos. No famous campaigns to
speak of. Who knows, maybe the advertising firm they used were
underachievers. All I know is Carter comes into office and things
get bad. The company is trying to keep its head above water.
Eventually they decide to drastically reorganize their sales division, to try an entirely new approach. More centralized, most
outreach done by mail or phone. Save money on salesmen, re-
duce each year's line by half, a more reliable watch company

putting out a few watches a year in only the most-trusted, long-standing price ranges. Who needs salesmen? It wasn't like they didn't appreciate him. It wasn't like they didn't recognize him as a treasure, as a living-goddamn-legend. But when the decisions are being made that high up, compassion doesn't stand much of a chance. They weren't inhuman, they offered him some other positions in the company, and when he refused, they gave him a respectable compensation package that freed him up to take a couple months off to look for a new job."

"And?"

"And, well, how can I put this? He wasn't the type of man that benefited from time off. As I remember, he took a few days, maybe a week to just take it all in and relax. Him and my mom took a long weekend somewhere. The next week he spoke about fixing up the house a little, taking care of some projects that he said had been nagging him for some time. He started working on some of them. Down in the basement with an old tool set. Then one day I come down there and the dresser he's hauled down to repaint is adorned with about fifty watches. I'm barely ten, but I can already recognize the sound of a man being swallowed whole by an obsession barely worth naming. I try to run back upstairs, like I only came down to look for my mitt or something, when he calls out to me. He tells me to come over. That's it. 'David,' he says, his left hand motioning for me, this tiny smile on his face. I got no choice but to say, 'Yeah, Dad,' like I'm a kid who is thinking nothing other than I guess my dad is about to tell me something, even though I can sense that I've stumbled upon a situation gone wrong. And then he points at one of the watches, an older model he kept, and he starts telling me all about it, when it was made, where, how many different moving parts it has, how often it must be wound, how long it will last, every damn comment preceded by a question that I couldn't possibly answer, a goddamn dialogue with himself, 'Do you know how many moving parts this watch has? One hundred and eleven.' It's not like he's looking at me. He's holding the watch in question like it's going to somehow help him in some way. Eventually I mumble an excuse and escape upstairs. He spends a great deal of time downstairs during the next few weeks. I hear my mother go down a few times, only to come back upstairs with this extremely exhausted, distant look. We're all wondering where he's headed when something happens which has got to make you believe in Freud a bit more. My older brother, Ben, loses his watch at school. We're sitting at dinner. My mother's cooking phenomenal meals night in, night out in hopes of nurturing her husband back to some semblance of his former self. He drags himself upstairs from the timepiece dungeon, unshaven, smelling, shall we say, inappropriate, but we all pretend that it's nothing more than another family dinner. Me and Mom don't notice the missing watch, and Ben is probably too terrified to mention it even to Mom, he's paralyzed in hopeless prayer that Dad will somehow fail to notice. About three minutes into the meal, a meal which kills all efforts at conversation, my father speaks: 'Ben, where's your watch?' His voice is neutral, like he merely wanted to know if it was supposed to rain tomorrow. Not monotone, but the concern, the panic, is remarkably contained. Ben is not as successful at managing the anxiety emerging from his blooming awareness of some ill-timed unpleasantries. He looks, almost jerks his head, to Mom, with a face like he'd like to go take a shit if only he wasn't sure it would cause him to vomit, a face of utter revulsion. My mom is the only possible hope here, but the situation is too naked. She can only say something like, 'Ben, what is it?' but we all know. Of course Dad is the first to say it, to put it into words. 'You lost it? You lost it?' His voice rising slightly. And then just silence. Mom tries to act like she is disappointed, too, as opposed to terrified by the notion of what my father's full reaction may be, but Ben won't answer his query and so the silence returns. After about thirty ferociously long seconds, Dad starts mumbling, 'He lost the damn watch,' over and over, breathing the words through his teeth. And then his hand comes down. His fist. The same one connected to the wrist that used to model his watches. Straight to the tabletop. Fury, absolute fury in one motion. He must have injured his hand. His watchband breaks. His wrist bleeds. The sound makes me sweat slightly as it remains alive in the silence that preceded and followed it, an explosion that ran through the table and through me down to my ankles. Everyone is still, my mother, normally in control, is simply stunned. Surprised, frightened, probably hurt, definitely hurt, like he'd crossed some line she never thought he'd cross without at least informing her first. Like everything was different now. I expected more. Some violence. That he had burst through a barrier into the other side of self-control and rationality. I could hear him breathing, a complex, struggling breathing, like his nose was stuffed up, but he had refused to reroute things through the mouth. I stared, frozen, into my half-eaten chicken leg, intrigued by the point in its evolution the mound of ketchup on my plate had arrived at right then. Ben was hard to observe, with my eyes on my food and Dad's troubled respiration monopolizing my hearing, but I assume he was crying silently. Finally, after a few minutes, I think it was actually minutes, Dad's breathing stopped for a moment, and I, just as a reflex, turned my head to him. He looked back at me, his whole expression softened in some sort of defeat. He closed his eyes, rubbed them with the hand attached to the bloody wrist, his watch collapsing helplessly, lifeless, to the table as he lifted it to his face. Then he said, 'I'm sorry.' He rose, took his plate to the sink, and walked up to his bedroom, where he remained for the better part of six days.

"Then one morning, just when it seems we might have lost him for good, he comes downstairs while Ben and I eat our cereal before heading out to school. The cereal ceremony had taken on a certain pathetic air of luxury and indulgence as my mother, in a desperate effort to buttress our collapsing household, finally caved in and started buying sugared cereal: Froot Loops, Apple Jacks, Cap'n Crunch. It wasn't difficult for Ben and me to hide in the sugary bliss of those almost-electric bright boxes, wolfing down two or three large bowls per morning, staring silently into the nutritional information on the side, until when we left, and this is after brushing, our teeth were almost humming, you could actually feel the cavities forming. So Dad comes downstairs in a nice suit, not his best, but a fine suit. He's shaven, and if you can ignore his eyes and the skin around them, both of which clearly say that he's not out of the woods yet, he looks like he's ready to bounce back. No one asks any questions, and he's not offering much in the way of explanations; he just heads to the garage like any other day.

"Before the end of the week he actually gets flown somewhere for what I imagine was the last interview of the hiring process. He returns home, his eyes both relieved but somehow still suffering. At dinner he makes his announcement. He's been hired to do sales for the Fort Howard Paper Company. What's that, we ask, me and Ben. Mom obviously knows, but she's letting Dad do the talking. They sell paper products, he tells us. We're not quite old enough to know what that means, and we let that be known. They make, you know, things that are made out of paper, you know, napkins, and paper towels, and place mats. And toilet paper? Ben asks, laughing before he measures his words. Toilet paper, too, Dad answers calmly. So what will you sell? I ask. I'll be working on a new, important product. Of course we want to know, but he says it's not important…God, this is pathetic…Sorry."

Nothing.

"Please. Go on."

"You can't see where this is headed?"

"Perhaps, but…but…Hey, have a donut."

"Thanks."

"That's what they're here for. So he's working for Fort Howard, some new, important product."

"Well, well of course, he's selling toilet paper. His reputation is known, and his old company felt bad enough, and they put out their feelers to find him something new, and this is what they came up with. It was an important product. It wasn't just toilet paper, it was the then-new massive-roll toilet paper. I think they were calling it 'Rollmastr' or 'Rollsavr' or something like that, both of which for whatever reason dropped the 'e' near the end. The patent of the company which first put it out had just ended and Fort Howard was hot to expand into all possible markets on this one. They hardly needed my dad; I mean, the thing sold itself. Giant rolls—"

"I'm familiar."

"Giant rolls means less janitorial work because one roll lasted forever. My dad learned all these pi-based equations to explain how many dozens of times more rolls of regular toilet paper were on one of these giant rolls. It was like every inch out at the edge was the equivalent of one or two regular rolls. Also, these rolls prevented theft because they were stored in locked-up plastic cases. This problem obviously needs little explanation, but the universities, in particular, were having a hell of a time with toilet-paper theft. Supposedly at the University of Michigan, toilet-paper consumption during the football season, when the faithful would hurl toilet paper down toward the field after every score, their tails stretching out and flapping in the autumn wind, toilet-paper consumption would nearly double. They knew it was a theft issue. These giant rolls, the Rollmastr put an end to university-sponsored T.P. tossing. Look, it was just a good product. Of course my dad gave it all he got. Within six weeks, every dorm resident in the Big Ten was wiping his or her undergraduate ass with Fort Howard's finest. By the end of the year, all state hospitals and government buildings had fallen in step. It was a coup. Fort Howard pulled the old volume trick that only a corporation of their size could manage and simply wiped out any possible competitors. And, of course, my dad was untouchable, I swear some of the universities were probably feeding their students diarrhetics just to rationalize the warehouse full of Rollsavr they bought after my father rolled through town."

The applicant stares at his shoes, recollecting the early eighties. The interviewer furrows his brow, gazing at the donuts, imagining the exact path to be traveled down the remainder of today's deep-fried time line.

"That's a sad story? What's the big deal? He loses the watch gig and has to settle for butts instead of wrists, big deal. So there isn't much romance to the ass, but his commissions must have been more than enough to fill that void."

"But that's not it. It just didn't work. First off, the wounds of the time off never quite healed. He was unemployed, all told, for over three months, and the money they gave him wasn't intended to last so long. Things got a little tight around the house, and even though he was in an oblivious stupor during the actual cash-flow drought, once he came out it was like he couldn't forget about it or convince himself that it wasn't right around the corner. He got totally obsessed with money. He would drive across town to save three cents on a gallon of gas. I was young, but I already knew that didn't make sense. He knew it, too, but he couldn't see past the money, the actual cash spent on the gas. And this is when the gas crisis is on, so the neurosis, if not psychosis, isn't just his, but on some level is nationwide. The news reports every night, as filtered through that slightly off-kilter mind of his, are telling him his response to gas purchasing is entirely prudent. You've got crazy inflation; gold is going through the roof. He's supposed to be hitting his suburban stride, to be getting the ends to meet effortlessly, and putting a regular amount aside each week. He's supposed to be funding, bankrolling biannual family getaways to places like New York City and the Grand Canyon. The generations of our automobiles which slumber in the garage each evening are supposed to evolve in their majesty at each replacement, from used, to new-but-modest, to new-but-not-so-modest, all the way to deluxe luxury models. This is his role on the planet, one which he had accepted, and was fulfilling quite nicely, thank you, making his family as comfortable and secure as possible in the ominous shadow of the Cold War and the impending doom it supposedly guaranteed. Carter had to come along and fuck everything up. I know it isn't his fault, that he made Begin and Sadat shake hands, that the economy is global and all that, but you put a face to these things because it's the only way to cope. Boy oh boy did he vote for Reagan and Bush. He voted for Dole. It's deep-seated. But back then it all just tore him apart, because he had to keep providing, and even though the financial turbulence was only twelve weeks long, he got stuck in that moment, believing it would, that it had to return. He started saving change with this sense of importance. He would pick up pennies off the ground and nod his head like it was all coming together. He went over every receipt for anything my mother bought, including groceries, asking her, demanding that she figure out what the miscellaneous items, you know, the unnamed stuff on the receipt was for. He had lost all perspective. It had something to do with the switch from watches to toilet paper. With the watches he could pretend that he was the part of something bigger. Some system, some code that stood for something. He really tried with the toilet paper. He spoke about efficiency and reduction of waste. He meant it, he made himself believe it. But it just fell on deaf ears. No one wants to think about toilet paper and the state of the world at the same time. The people who make decisions about toilet paper, the types who order it for ten thousand asses at a time, they don't give a shit about the planet. They're middle-level administrators who somehow got promoted down a dead-end track that ended at ordering janitorial supplies. His enthusiasm, his fervor for sales, that used to be refueled with each sale was just sucked out of him. But of course he refused to become the cynic. He refused to just see it as a job, he had to love it, so he kept on trying to sweep community-college administrators off their feet. He kept smiling and putting on those suspenders each morning, while inside horrible things were brewing.

"And then it happened. We should have seen it. The irrationality over 'the product' along with the financial compulsion. He installed one in every bathroom. A Rollsavr. Institutional toilet paper in my boyhood bathroom from the age of ten until college, where it was, of course, waiting for me. We kept the keys in the cupboard along with the spare towels. Such humiliation. Anytime I brought a new friend to the house, that inevitable moment would come. When they came out, they would just look at me with the facial response for something between a practical joke and a pathetic veteran asking you for a handout. Only a few actually said anything, but the damage was done. It gave the whole house the feel that things weren't quite right, which of course they weren't, that our suburban palace was actually Section 8, that caseworkers came for dinner every Wednesday. It just hung in the air. Dating? Forget it. I didn't bring a girl home, not even for prom. I made up some excuse that we were getting new wallpaper put on."

"Well. Hmm. Okay. I, uh, I thank you for that. There were some real moments of sympathy for you there. But help me out, finish what you started. I asked why this job. I suppose I could offer an answer of my own at this point, but I'd like to see you bring it all together. What's the connection between your father's hardships and this position?"

"Fair enough. Okay. Two things. First, the money. It's not going to make me rich, I know, but your starting salary from the ad looks to be about 20 percent higher than anything else I've heard about. I'm not going to worry about money. I'm here to work and get paid, and your ad promises that this check will be significantly larger than most others. Second, I can't care too much about it. I know that's a dangerous thing to say at this, or any other juncture of the interview. But you're asking. My dad fell in love with the objects he sold. He grew dependent on them. I can appreciate the utility of what I work with. I can own the products myself. I can believe that most people should buy and own them. But I won't let myself love them. They must clearly remain as things in my mind. Product. Don't get me wrong. The gadgets, gizmos, doohickeys, etc., that you market are not meaningless to me. Back at Kellogg, color-coded binders made me believe in my presentations more than I care to admit. But it's passionless stuff, and that's the key. So that's my answer. My dad made one-and-a-half, maybe two mistakes, which I'm not making. That's my answer."

Pause. Mild head nodding accompanied by the bottom lip curling of an impressed, but mostly reserved, spectator. "Bravo. Honest, gutsy, forthright, even a tad insightful. This has been an utterly unboring morning so far. Thank you. The donuts are fresh, which only adds to the ambiance, but you came through there for me. I think that's about it from my side. I'm going to be interviewing some others, so it will be a few days, but otherwise this is your turn to ask me questions, like you said you would earlier. What do you want to know?"

"Reciprocate."

"Pardon me."

"Reciprocate, return the favor, open up. Offer me some nugget of your past, your person. How did you wind up marketing miscellaneous office products? You know, stuff like that."

"Hmm. Bold. Really. I could deny you. I could invoke my authority, just veto the request."

"You could. It wouldn't be right, you already know that. It would cheapen the morning. The donuts would start tasting sour somehow. Also, it would bestow upon me a certain power you can only reclaim by traveling the same route of the midmorning confessional."

"Indeed. Yes. I must. I simply must. But you'll have to excuse me. If I'm going to enter that arena, well I, how can I say this, I've got a date with the Rollmastr."

"Well, now."

"I couldn't resist. It won't be a long wait, I assure you. Make yourself at home. There's still two chocolate-glazed left. Imagine what consumption of either of those would do for your stock here."

Left alone, the interviewee briefly enjoys the inner warmth born of his sense that the interviewer has taken a liking to him along with a larger lightness his confession created as it flooded out of his mouth. Less than a minute into this hazy pleasure, the interviewee is overcome by the impossibility of what has just occurred. He finds himself doubting both the prudence of his decision to spill so many childhood beans, not to mention the coherence of the narrative itself. He has trusted a large man he hardly knows, who still controls all decision-making power worth mentioning. There is no preexisting file in his memory to compare this to, and left alone his impression of what just took place grows frighteningly sinister as his interview anxiety pulls up a seat next to it. He feels his body, a half hour or more in this seat, which judging by its vacant partner chair adjacent, is not as clean as it should be. He wants to stand, most of his mind involved in decisions of this sort send a clear mandate to his leg muscles to rise, but this is wisely vetoed by that part of him which knows that he must be seated when the other man returns. He feels strapped in the chair, a hostage, so he shifts frantically, pulls at his sticky pant legs. His eyes dart about, trying to perform some task of reassurance through nervous movement only realistically accomplished via ambulation. Finally, almost at wit's end, nearly swallowed in panic, he grabs a donut, taking a dangerously large bite as the door opens.

"Well, well, well, how things change."

"You know how it is: You get started, and it takes on a will of its own."

"The story of my life, indeed."

Pause.

"So I was consulting with the Rollmastr just now, and this is what I came up with. I'm ready to go ahead and offer the job to you right now. I'm ready to relinquish my options by revoking the standard 'I've still got a couple of more interviews later in the week,' which may or may not be the truth, I won't tell you for certain until you take the position, for now I'll just say that if there were any such upcoming interviews that I am willing and ready to cancel those interviews. I'm ready to talk terms with you, but I have a number of things to tell you, both in response to your legitimate challenge and in the best interests of what I'm actually looking for here. I'm going to try to tell you a measured amount of what my plans are here, shedding inordinate light upon what we might want to call intraoffice dynamics, something which will play no small role if we decide to work together."

Head nodded in acceptance, lips slightly pursed in confusion.

"I made some money a couple years back in Post-it Notes and those Post-it Flags, you know, those colored-tape labels that—"

"We have an intimate relationship to say the least—"

"Good, so I was involved in the initial creation and production of those products. I wasn't right there among the core group the whole time, but I was close enough for long enough to get a nice payment once all the legal issues were settled. I got somewhere in the neighborhood of the high five figures, after the lawyers took theirs. Post-it Notes are big, big business. So as you can tell, I've got some background in miscellaneous office-support product development and marketing. I've had some successes, and I've worked with some of the heavy hitters.

Needless to say, after the unfortunate turn of events over questions of what my rightful compensation should have been for my contribution to the development of Post-it Notes and Tape Flags some bridges have been burned, and I don't have the option to continue working with the group that made office-product history with those two windfalls. I took my money, invested it wisely over the last year, while I got some more backing from a few outside investors, and I am now perched to start my own company. I've spent a couple months getting this site and setting it up, hiring Sheila, making some initial contacts, asking some questions here and there, doing my research as it were, to get a sense for the plausibility of the half-dozen products I have in mind."

"What kind of stuff?"

"Nothing revolutionary. Obviously I can't get into it until you accept the position. Stuff along the lines of the Post-it Notes. Not actually involving glue and paper; the similarity lies in the minor alteration of an old standby. It's all computers now, you know, all the office technologies. If I had any brains, or luck, I would have gotten involved with the actual computers, hardware or software development, that's where the real money is. But it's too late for that now. I must take solace knowing that there are plenty of parasitic products just waiting to fill the aisles of OfficeMax that people will love to decorate their computers with. I believe the key developments will come in that whole ergonomic area, there are absolutely pant-wetting sums waiting to be earned in wrist-support technologies, but again, I'm way out of my area of expertise when it comes to ergonomics, so I have no choice but to stick with what I know: knickknacks, junk, office crap. But don't read my belittling the wrong way. Offices stink, right, they're dehumanizing, alienating, blah-blah-blah, you know what I mean. And now they're growing frighteningly sterile. Great amounts of organization inside the computers. The laser printers are kept quite busy, but the printouts get filed away or shredded, leaving the offices filled only by that eerie hum and buzz of those silver-dollar-sized fans keeping our motherboards cool. People need to touch things, little trivial objects through which they can manipulate all the information they are paid to be a conduit for. Folders with some character, clips that are friendly, staplers with options. We're talking psychological shelter in this corporate silicon storm. I know what the people need, and I've got a nice little menagerie of concepts just waiting to milk that cash cow of office longing. You'd be my right-hand man. We'd do it all together, you'd just be that extra person for doing all the things I can't do, but we'll be working quite closely together. You're just what I'm looking for."

"Well, I—"

"But there are all sorts of other things you must know. How should I say this? I can't imagine you're going to like me much after, let's say, our third week together. I'm not just saying this based on your earlier comments about hating most things, though that does grant me an extra level of confidence. People tend not to like me. I know right now things look pretty good. The donuts are fresh and numerous. Your story pleased me, and I'd be lying if I denied that a recently moved bowel isn't a source of happiness for me. I'm about as content as I get right now, but don't let the present amiability fool you. Most of the time, I can't get myself to say the things I'm supposed to say to people, things that let people think you deserve some respect. Common courtesy–type things. I went through this phase when I just didn't believe in forced politeness. Then one day I realized it wasn't a phase, but was just who I had become. I knew I ought to snap myself out of it, to smile more, say thank you and things like that. But I couldn't do it. It became clear to me that the price one pays for cruel speech, for blatant insults directed toward restaurant hostesses and airline ticket agents and even neighbors, is not so high after all. That if you're fat like me, and ugly like me, and shiny from sweat like me, that people only like you because they feel pity for you, and the moment you stop responding to that, the moment it is clear to them that you don't give a shit about their compassion, they stop caring entirely, and what remains to be lost by choosing not to hide that your patience has run out and that in general you find these other people unintelligent and oblivious to the truths of the world around them is little if anything. There are those first few incidents, when you realize you have made someone hate you, that as you exit the hotel lobby someone is muttering 'motherfucker' under their breath, fantasizing about subjecting you to odd sorts of violence, the first few times you are affected. You fear that something may follow this incident, some escalation most undesired. But nothing happens. You see, I have had few friends my entire life, so the reality of no one liking me was easier to accept than you might think. I also have a short temper—not much of a surprise, I suppose. I am usually rational, but I make very little effort at this point to head off my anger when I feel it coming on. That I am so aware of my state would seem to suggest the possibility of investing some efforts to change my ways. Perhaps some therapy or even religion. I'm not interested. There are things that bring me joy. I like to eat. I enjoy donuts, of course, as well as mixed nuts. I am fond of baked goods of any sort. I like eating out. I like restaurants such as Bennigan's, TGI Friday's, Houlihan's, Chili's, and Applebee's, because their fare is consistent and their waitstaff is trained to kiss your ass under any and all circumstances. These restaurants also have liquor licenses. It might seem to you that I must be an alcoholic having said that. No. I don't like being drunk at all, but I do enjoy the mild fuzz of a drink or two, when I can concern myself with getting my fork to my mouth without nagging, bigger questions forcing themselves up into my consciousness. I enjoy that. I enjoy renting movies, and I took nearly eight thousand dollars from my Post-it settlement and acquired an impressive home theater with a subwoofer that makes my scrotum vibrate during explosions. I particularly enjoyed *The Matrix*. I will on occasion rent a movie of the adult variety, though I usually don't use the surround sound then; their sound quality is so poor. I was married once for seven months to a foolish woman who convinced herself I had a great deal more money than I did. We had sex on two occasions, her disinterest and repugnance so blatant on both occasions that I failed to ejaculate the second and last time. I have not sought a date since 1983. I do have a cat named William who allows me to pet him for a quarter hour each evening, after which time he hides in a closet out of my reach. I like William, and on cold nights he will sleep with me, which I enjoy. My family is two time zones from here, and this saddens no one involved. I have two nephews who dislike me so much, they stopped cashing the checks I send them on their birthdays.

"As for our working relationship, I will demand of you significant hours at times, often for no reason, just to demonstrate that I am your boss. I will never give you positive feedback unless I forget myself. I will insult you when your performance is a disappointment. Occasionally I will scream. You will be exposed to myriad farts and belches, many of which, including the latter, will make your eyes water. I will call you at home on Sunday to discuss at length trivial matters which could wait until the following Monday. In addition, it will be clearly stated in your contract that you are to work for me at the least for twelve months. There will be no escape clause once you commit. You will be exposed to a half-dozen product concepts which we will develop, so I cannot let you leave once you are exposed. My reserved confidence still allows me to tell you that I expect at least two of these concepts to translate into successful products, and I believe you have a 60 to 70 percent chance to make a small fortune through the royalties and orders, of which you will receive a percentage per your contract. And you must call me 'boss.' That is my confession."

THE TASK OF THIS TRANSLATOR

The underlying cause was Ted's odd but well-funded entre-preneurial ambition. Here was a guy whose not so insignif-icant inheritance, intermittently delivered by bank wire at the command of his healthy as a bull father, who was uninterested in the morbid suspense of wills and impatient sons, might have long ago been squandered had his visions been a bit more grand. Every eight months or so since his eighteenth birthday, Ted would be overtaken by some ultimately small, but at the time monumental, vision, a vision he cultivated and situated in his head alongside his father's own capitalist ascent (having to do with luggage). They never, none of them, not a one, ever amounted to a thing, though a few, bizarrely, developed little lives of their own, this due to lingering ads in the yellow pages and the like. All the same, they kept coming. The fourth of which interests us here. Ted would get an idea, for an invention, a service, a middleman operation of some sort, whatever, and he would first do two things: (1) name it—the invention, service, or middleman operation; and upon the completion of step 1, (2) pay a good friend with graphic-design experience plenty of money to design a logo, letterhead, business cards, ads, and anything else along these lines, seeing how money was not an object, not really.

The fourth such vision, the one of relevance here, came to the destined to be wealthy despite himself aspiring man of means during his third year at a ferociously overpriced, nearly prestigious private college. One of his classes that year, which he took by mistake, he wasn't even in the right building, was named "Transnationalism and Borders" or something like that. Ted read only four pages, right around one-half percent, of the overall assigned readings, but diligently attended the class where he sat silently, attuned to the goings-on with the same steady but vaguely sterile interest with which one follows a sporting event broadcast through a TV halfway across a loud bar. He gleaned nothing tangible from the class, but the word "transnationalism" did grow on him. The instructor, naturally, used the term a bunch, and though this particular student never completely grasped its most limited meaning, let alone larger implications, Ted did develop a real fondness for the prefix "trans." It cropped up in his doodles, and over time its semantic cousins—transportation, translation, transcendence, Transylvania, transplant, transsexual, transmission—whenever they appeared, pricked him somehow. And so a vision was on its way, this one, as mentioned earlier, being the fourth in a longer, still-proliferating series. Ted concluded that all this "trans" stuff had big implications for the future—he did gather from his instructor, who seemed quite passionate about the whole thing, that the future was about transnationalism, or something to that effect—and that a business, one day giant corporation, was waiting to sprout from this trans moment in world history. Ted looked at his trans lists, which would he bring to fruition, transportation was mostly spoken for, transplant too technical, transsexual hardly a money-maker, and so on until he got to translation. His would be a translation institute or company or service that would translate for people when that was needed, and, according to his instructor, this was going to be a lot.

So the first thing to do, obviously, after dishing out over $7,000 for the top-of-the-line graphics stuff, was to hire some translators. The French and German folks were easy enough to track down, but our young CEO was stuck on the idea that the longer the list of languages his company could work with, could translate, the better. Ted wasn't a graphic-design man himself, but he did have an image in his head of the main ad listing all the serviceable languages, descending downward in some authoritative-looking font, properly spaced and all, and that the longer the list, well.

And this is the part that just kills Ben. He, too, attended this center of higher learning, which, again, cost so much that were his parents to have taken and smartly hidden the money required for tuition, room, board, books, phone, recreational medication, trips home—the four-year total coming in just a few bucks over $140,000—in a CD, money market, mutual fund, IRA, 401(k), tax-elusive investment setting, and just kept their child alive and fed, getting him to deliver papers or pizza or processing data or anything until the age of thirty-five just to avoid debt, he could have retired, more or less, thanks to a bull market, which, essentially, would have made him a millionaire. But his parents didn't, so he shared the same floor of a large student-housing complex with Ted the entrepreneur during their first year.

Ben, our hero, took, in order to fulfill the foreign language requirement, an obscure language. This language is a European language, but seriously Eastern European, entirely marginal in pretty much anyone's genealogy of languages, just barely getting invited to the Indo-European family table. Just barely. Balto maybe, Slavic probably. The language that balances out French and Italian on the unofficial spectrum of languages for a romantic evening. This language hardly gets much mention outside of its local habitat, though it is the language spoken by those unfortunates that every fifteen years or so, whether under the auspices of fascist, Communist, or unspecified geopolitical misguidance, rise to international attention as they and their linguistic neighbors do horrible things to each other in the name of nation, religion, ethnicity, etc. Being a language so underappreciated, it rarely surfaces even at gigantic state universities, places where enough people learn and teach, say, Flemish to push a few tables together at some popular bistro right off campus at the end of the semester in order to celebrate this Flemish thing they've built. But thanks to a starry-eyed partially Slavic professor, who wrote perhaps one of the three best grants this decade, enough funds were raised to create a program in this language's instruction. This instructor, who really just didn't get it, was of the mind that once this language program got off the ground and the initial inertia working against it was overcome, the students would sign up regularly, appreciating the sheer beauty of the language, wanting to learn it in order to better understand the unrest that speaks this language, unrest this instructor figured wasn't about to end. Ben, not even remotely Slavic, let alone Balto, in the very early days of that first semester, was helplessly following around a striking romantic interest, who was flattered, but no thanks, who herself was Slavic and who signed up. Ben did, too. It was more of a "I'll just hang out with her in class and see what happens" thing, expecting to likely drop the class and her, or her dropping them both, or just him, but this instructor, boy oh boy, this was no normal language class. It's not that he made Ben passionate about the language, it's just he forced Ben to see how it was his global responsibility to know this language, that to walk away from it, once being exposed on even the most superficial level, was somehow an act of inexcusable sociohistorical negligence. This kept Ben from bailing early on, and later in the semester, just as Ben's transplanted sense of history was wilting, the language was resold to him from a different angle. The instructor couldn't afford to lose students. Future funding depended on enrollment. Not only did he need them to remain enrolled, he needed them to enroll for the second semester and then the second year and on and on. Soon Ben learned that he could do nothing to earn less than an A–; it just wasn't possible. So he stayed on for three semesters, even after the Slavic woman transferred to Indiana. How much did he learn? Not too much. Some basic greetings and conversation, a few hundred words, a handful of strange idioms. A poem by some survivor, victim, witness-type. Enough for Ted to put this language, with Ben as the company's translator, near the very bottom of that impressive list in the ad, nineteen languages long.

"No. No. No fucking way, Ted," Ben at first protested. Ted countered, over a so-called business dinner at a pricey restaurant, that no one will ever ask for translation services in this language. The meal ended with a drunk but still-intransigent Ben. His reluctance was finally overcome in the moment he agreed to listen to Ted make this same point over a bottle and a half of the same dry but full-bodied wine at the same bistro on the same night a week later, again on the company's nickel. Because, really, what's the worst that could happen?

———

The letter arrived four years after the establishment of the translation institute, two and three-quarter years after its last translation services (these in Italian) were provided. It read:

> Dear Misses and Misters that concern:
>   I am making this letter to you for to request your assistances. I am will to travel soon to your country that is yours for meeting with my extensive family in three monthes. Much years ago a difficult event happened and took place due to me that now I do not and did not am communicating with this extensive family. From this I suffer much. My luckiness today permits traveling by me to your country that is yours so to meet and encounter this extensive family that to request a forgiveness. English but however I speak not. Please, then, please I will paying for translation. 19th October this year. I am too wanting meeting with this translating man one week earlier than the extensive family meeting.
>
>   I am thanking you.
>
> Goran Vansalivich

Ted the entrepreneur, who long ago was already on to other not much bigger, let alone better, things, quickly drove his new Japanese sports car to Ben's apartment, letter (already stapled to some nonsensical official memo from Strictly Speaking Translators) in hand, to demand his services. An hour later Ben returned from a pickup basketball game, clad, ironically it now seems, in sweatpants from his alma mater, to find Ted negotiating over his cell phone the purchase of a small cash-machine company, which would finally, not that it matters, make him richer yet.

"Are you out of your mind?" Ben responded rhetorically in his kitchen moments later. Ted, not quite as foolish as we first thought, announced, "Here's your advance, I'll call you in a couple days with more details," casually placed a check upon Ben's filthy counter, and exited. Ben, despite the $140,000-plus forked over by his parents, truly and really needed this money, having maniacally abused his line of credit in everything from the methodical acquisition of each and every rare Hendrix import to his strict observation and celebration of International Sushi Night (which falls on any and all odd-dated Tuesdays). The sweatpants were, in fact, about all he had to show for his eight semesters of liberal-arts education. They're great pants, but still.

This left Ben a bit over two months to (re-?)learn the obscure language in question. He miraculously unearthed some old materials—one textbook and a stack of flash cards—and with his nearly four-digit advance from his friend took to reaching the fluency he never even got a whiff of back on that high-priced tree-lined campus. Two days later, Ben had mastered the material from the second semester and was totally at home with the present tense and words like "dog," "sink," and "prime minister." In the search for more materials, Ben frantically and unsuccessfully searched the Web for his old instructor, who by now was making a killing over at the State Department, then contacted numerous schools, institutions, and bookstores for these same materials, but eventually had to settle on poring through an old copy of this language's dictionary at the downtown library. He did this for three entire days, learning words like "orchestra," "legend," and "diamond." Halfway through day three, trying, as a sort of spontaneous exercise, to describe his burrito to himself in this language ("big," "tasty," "brown," "powerful," "sincere"), he gives up, drives home relieved, practicing resignation speeches (in English) to deliver to Ted, only to find the first half of his exorbitant appearance fee in the mail later that day.

At their preliminary meeting, for which Ben meticulously memorized a host of introductory dialogues concerning instructions to train stations and questions of geographic origins, the man did most of the talking. He was short and slight, with excellent shoes and a striking chin. His eyes were dark green. Ben listened intently and heard:

> My name is Goran Vansalivich and I blah you blah. Blah years ago my brothers (passive marker?) blah by blah. I tried blah to blah (assert myself?) but I could not. Their young children (passive marker?) blah from my country and blah to your country, blah blah blah blah. I tried to explain why I blah not blah blah, but they blah blah blah anyway blah blah blah blah.

Sweating, Ben nodded his head vigorously, sipping his coffee like an aperitif, which Goran would soon pay for, and mumbled, slurring the difference between present and past-tense markers which had suddenly eluded him as he said either "I understand" or "I understood." The man continued:

> Now thirty-five years blah I blah to blah with my family, with my nephews and blah. I try to blah but they blah until I blah and now I can finally blah blah blah, but blah. One week from today at the blah blah next to the blah orchestra, we will blah to blah blah with my family and I will, I hope, blah, blah (kitchen?) blah.

And he gently rested his hand on the table, next to an emptied mug, and looked at Ben, whose toes were flexed against the floor. Ben flawlessly—accent, intonation, and stress aside—delivered the line, "I look forward to assisting you next week," which he had memorized for the occasion, and raised his hand toward Goran, hoping to utter his farewell and be on his way.

But Goran continued, quicker and upset:

But they blah blah do not understand why blah blah blah (threat?) blah blah blah my brother blah blah blah gun from the other man blah blah blah blah blah blah. If I blah choose blah blah I blah blah then maybe blah blah door blah blah blah grave. But if I blah choose blah blah, I blah blah move blah blah (future tense?) not blah together, not blah or blah blah blah, but only, yes, only blah blah blah blah blah blah blah blah. You must blah, you must not blah, yes, I, no, blah blah blah [Goran's hand up around an imaginary throat, his voice inappropriately loud, as the Americans in the place not so subtly turned their heads to see] blah blah, and then boom, my brothers, my brothers blah and I blah, but not, blah, no not blah, they think that I blah, but I did not, no, no, never, no, no, no, blah, oh, blah blah blah blah (idiom meaning "nothing ever ends").

And before Ben and his incomprehension could be exposed, Goran wiped his narrow brow, rose, apologized, and walked out of the café, leaving a brand-new $50 bill on the table for two coffees and the blueberry scone Ben had disfigured beyond recognition.

After the meeting Ben spent the better part of the next two days drunk and/or in bed, the "and" period being a particularly unpleasant gray stretch in between Saturday night and Sunday, when Ben negotiated unsuccessfully with his unfriendly, intransigent sheets. The first activity Ben managed to undertake was a visit to the video store. It meant standing up, moving around his apartment, dressing, leaving home in at least a marginally presentable fashion—teeth brushed, hair attended to, shoes—driving for five minutes, parking, being with other people, milling about, deciding, paying, driving for another five minutes. No small task, but the safest bet in his less than enthusiastic, but unavoidable quest for reinstatement in society.

The store was much too big: forty thousand titles. Some days this is what it took: forty thousand movies. Hours upon hours of transferred-to-video cinematic adventures. Some days he needed the knowledge that he could choose from over forty thousand titles, every last John Candy vehicle, six different Hell's Angels documentaries, in order to be convinced to initiate the rental of exactly one movie. But today he longed for the late 1980s resort-town family-owned convenience-store inventory: fifty to a hundred choices, a few new movies (the term "new release" was as yet unborn), some strange old musicals or a Cary Grant picture, a movie or two with naked ladies, an early Steve Martin piece, and *Star Wars*. Simple enough. But this new store, this "better" store, well, now.

So he milled about for a long while until he felt he was in a very bad museum. He made a mental note twenty entries long of "maybes," though none called out. He milled some more, thinking about his socks. Yawned.

The last station was foreign. It wasn't always; there were days when intellectual aspirations, a dull sense of culture lured him toward this aggressively, self-mannered bourgeois aisle, "foreign." Where French pronouns and high-contrast images of the Indian subcontinent adorn small boxes with promises of a different sort. Where art supposedly resides. Crap. Today seeing a movie did not mean reading a movie. But the milling had become easy and predictable and not so painful.

The first clue was not the language itself, but the chin of the actor in the picture. It wasn't that it was larger than normal, it was somehow sharper and closer to the surface. An angular, nearly threatening chin that looked like his teacher, that woman, Goran, and pictures in Xeroxed newspaper articles. A strangely dominant gene. Subtitled, not dubbed. The original language undisturbed. Better yet, accompanied by English equivalents. Resuscitated and uneasy, Ben seized the tape, gently and cautiously storming the rental counter, longed-for textbook in hand.

Ben raced home, running a lonely red light, not even turning on the radio. Inside his apartment he was aghast at how long it took the signal from the remote control to reach his TV and VCR. His combined mania and fear found him carefully stuffing the cassette into the machine. He pulled over an upholstered milk crate to sit on. Ben watched the movie in its entirety hunched over said milk crate, motionless, keys still in hand.

Over the next five days, Ben viewed the video twenty-six times. The movie was 118 minutes long. Add to this the time Ben spent rewinding, pausing, relistening, transcribing, and imitating, and we're talking ten-plus hours a day of video instruction. The second viewing, separated from the first by a hurried, silver-dollar drip of urine in your underwear piss and the seizure of pen and paper, initiated Ben's transcribing project. The smaller man—clever, but weak and apologetic—spoke softly and quickly, enraging Ben. His cellmate was animated and proud, his words, thankfully, delivered in slow, important portions, everything a speech or sermon:

"I can't help what I've done, but, I, I, I, am, am, am, sorry, sorry, sorry. Heh, heh."

"Apologies and nonsense. Nonsense and apologies. A scoundrel's best friends once he's caught."

Ben hated the little man, and was grateful that he, too, had eventually been captured and imprisoned alongside the leader he betrayed. Like a play unimaginatively adapted for the screen, scene after scene of conversations in the cell. The sadistic guard appearing occasionally.

Ben watched the first third of the movie four times in a row, determined to memorize it in its entirety and move on. On the third day, forced to run out to the convenience store to buy AA batteries for the weary remote control, Ben recited, nearly chanting:

"I made a mistake, an error. I am a man. This is what we do best."

"Wrong! This is what we do most. Our best is fighting for perfection, for justice, for truth. You will not be here forever, Petre...how will you live when you are released? In the prison of their false freedom, or as a warrior for true liberty?"

Halfway through round four of his memorization of third number two, while the tape rewound as instructed by the gallant remote, Ben was struck with the urge to find out how it all ended. His first viewing had somehow evaporated from memory. So he actually sat down, let the pen rest, even granted the remote some time off.

A woman, letters read aloud, a beating and then another. A second guard who is actually an insider. A payoff, or promise of a payoff. Both men swelling into lengthy monologues, sobbing wildly and uncontrollably, no cut for fifteen minutes or more, despair and breakdown, unrefined, unchoreographed, and unedited.

Ben's apartment had been dark or mostly dark for a number of days now. There were unfriendly smells generating from his dwelling and himself. Things, in all its senses, had gotten a bit messy, again, in all its senses.

The ending seemed a bit unresolved, or at least open-ended. The smaller man is persuaded, but by whom? Who is, really, the leader? The leader is revealed, maybe, to have been broken, and is now, with his promised money, a trap? Has the small man been duped into informing once more, this time to his mentor and hero, who is nothing of the sort, really, this time unknowingly? Dammit. The ending, what is it?

Ben didn't like this. He did, sort of, but not really. More captivated than pleased. He had forgotten the whole foreign-language business in the meantime, and watched the film three times beginning to end determined to get to the truth, going so far as to prop a body mirror in a precise position against the wall so that bathroom visits could be made without stopping the tape. He wasn't eating much at this point. Whatever's available. A banana, a can of baked beans at room temperature, a loaf of bread, one slice at a time, the rectangled plastic bag cuddled up against his side like a languid house pet.

Might the whole thing be a documentary? Is that possible? Are they hidden cameras? There are so few edits, so few changes in camera angles, almost no close-ups. Is this real?

Ben searches for the video case, for quoted blurbs from highbrow critics, for a bit of info from the studio or video company or whatever. Some clue to this thing, this devastating thing. The case is not the case, it's the generic, clear-plastic thing. He may as well have rented *Con Air*.

Ben sleeps for a while. He may or may not have decided to sleep. It's either early morning or late evening. The lighting in his apartment is poor to begin with and all the curtains are closed, and somehow got crudely taped to the wall, apparently by Ben. Ben instinctively turns on the TV and VCR from his hygienically unenviable position on the couch. The videotape doesn't respond. Ben panics and curses. The tape, it turns out, has been ejected by the machine. Ben recalls that the machine is designed to rewind the video to its beginning if a tape plays to its end, and then eject the cassette. Ben stares at the edge of the tape protruding from the machine. Its original title and an English translation, *Captives,* that troubles Ben as possibly inaccurate.

Ben lies motionless for a time and takes stock of his situation. Intrigued by the film, but not much else to feel good about. In his exhaustion and hunger, in the dim light of his physiological weakness, he must relax; that is he can only, can't help but relax enough to see the unpleasant trajectory of his entire life in sad, simple focus. At his present position along the path of his days, he is in a mild descent, a yearlong undramatic descent, which followed a shorter undeniably much more dramatic descent of that earlier period, which even here on the nasty couch can only be thought of as "the breakup." The rest, the duly past part of his life, hidden on the far side of the horizon of his misery, is so only a memory as to be doubted. Something to do with potential and promise. Rising overall, unfazed by slight dips. Like the world's population or a retirement account. His present smell can only be described as wrong.

He watches the video again, crawling to the machine, perhaps in a gesture of self-irony. He collapses, again self-irony is a possibility, and watches the film on his back, directly under his television, looking out over his brow, backwards. The only thing certain is that everyone can be bought, it's just unclear who's buying who and why and in exchange for what and who's getting the better end of the deal. In the final account, the middleman is the only obvious winner, and even he seems clueless.

After enduring twenty minutes of angry, chaotic fuzz and hiss from the unsupervised TV, Ben retreats to the bathroom. He sees himself in the mirror and is both disgusted and disappointed; somehow he had expected even worse. He runs a bath, tired and restless. As he disrobes, he is shocked by the sweet, full, rounded scent of his skin. He feels proud of this smell, as if producing such stench was the true project of the last few days, as if this is his greatest asset. He raises a bent right arm, lowers his nose toward and then into a hairy armpit, closes his eyes and breathes intently through his nostrils, savoring the last moments of his repugnance. The odor is so powerful and foreign, he must look at his image once more in the mirror to verify that this is indeed him and not some rank imposter. It is him, though his hair is up to tricks it has never and will never perform again.

The bathwater emits a liquidy version of his smell after little more than a minute. He drains the water but runs the shower at the same time to avoid the cold. The slow, staggered draining of the first tub makes Ben think of calculus, though he's not sure it should. Sitting on his rubbery ass in the now nearly empty tub, Ben soaps himself, paying extra attention to his crotch, which, despite all the water, still garners his suspicion. The second bath allows him to submerge his head and torso, the soles of his feet planted flat on the linoleum wall. He relaxes, feeling his buoyant hair forget its recent behavior. The water is silent in a droning, hummy kind of way. Ben begins a fantasy about a divinely temperature-regulated tub, picturing scantily dressed attendants with steaming water jugs, but he's too tired to develop this any further. He drains the tub, rises with the shower back on, soaps and shampoos himself twice more. He shaves twice, too. Throughout he thinks about the upcoming event, trying not to.

Thanks to his brother's wedding nine months earlier, Ben has nothing but good thoughts about his suit, though there is little else to comfort him here on his drive to the event. He cuts an uncommon path across town, almost due east, from one aging tier of cold-war suburbia to another. Ben has been to London, Rome, Costa Rica, and even Cairo, but he has never ever been on this part of this road, which elsewhere runs right past his boyhood home. The sights say nothing to him; all he can think of, as townships regularly announce themselves every few miles, stating their population and year of incorporation, are high school football teams, stores selling guitar amps, and used-car lots.

The hall is cold and boxy, with a preposterously high ceiling. Goran greets him immediately. Besides the two of them, only the caterers have arrived. Goran's suit and shoes are immaculate, and he holds a glass filled with a clear liquid and a great deal of ice.

"Good evening."

"Good evening."

"Did you find the blah with no difficulty? I am very blah about tonight's blah."

Ben steels himself, trying not to flinch. Fantasies of having miraculously acquired fluency through the video are mostly dashed, though Ben feels a tad more confident. He recites a line from the film. He can't recall, somehow, who said it.

"Please, it is important, please speak slowly, I'm feeling a bit strange this evening."

Goran responds to this with a measured smile, looking

down at Ben's legs and feet as if to check the veracity of Ben's claim.

"Perhaps something to eat or drink." Goran responds, speaking, thank God, slower. "Here," and he reaches up to take Ben gingerly under his armpit toward the caterers. In the poor lighting of the hall, the patch of scarring on Goran's temple, the dermatological ruins of something between bad acne and a burn, shines hideously.

Ben is served a drink by a heavy black woman, who against her black vest and black bow tie is revealed to be merely brown. Getting drunk surfaces as a possibility, but is quickly stifled. Ben is already nauseous.

"Where is the…" He points to where he thinks it ought to be, unable to remember the word, feeling doomed.

"The bathroom?" Ben recognizes the term and repeats it, hoping to prove something to his host. "Over there," Goran points a ringed finger in the opposite direction. Ben hurries, an urgent rumbling in his intestines causing his forehead to perspire. Goran calls something out to him, cheerily, that is absolutely unintelligible to Ben. The intonation suggests the English tongue-in-cheek "don't get lost" or "I'll be here, waiting," but the only word Ben thinks he understands is "tooth."

The unfortunate spectacle of bread-diet constipation mercilessly and suddenly overthrown by a bad case of the willies is best glossed over, so let's just say that even with pants pushed down around ankles, jacket hastily hung on stall-door hook, tie needlessly swung over left shoulder, and ass firmly and squarely planted on toilet seat, Ben is convinced something somehow is bound to get soiled. The seat, even for the slightly tall Ben, is too high, forcing him into an uncomfortable anti-squat position. One bit of graffiti adorns the stall, a symbol or logo of some sort, mostly covered over in a layer of paint close to, but not exactly, the color of the rest of the stall.

Fifteen minutes later Ben exits the bathroom, walks down a short hallway he doesn't remember from the first half of the trip, and enters the main hall. Everyone has arrived. It must have been a convoy or a caravan, for everyone is now here. They stand far away from Ben and from Goran and from the bar and appetizers Goran has bought for them. Ben is stunned once more by the chin. A dominant gene of Machiavellian proportions. Through it the blood relatives are obvious, even from sixty feet. Thanks to this chin and the blond hair of one man married into the family, Ben can construct the entire family tree, which now twists awkwardly in the unforgiving breeze of the reluctant gathering: The men stand suspiciously close together, uncomfortable in suits, hands in pockets, drinkless. Moms wrestle and haggle with their young children, too young to understand the collective boycott of the snacks. Two moms negotiate fruitlessly with small whining pouters. The other women trap their own little squirming bastards between their thighs. Every minute or so, one squirts free and darts toward the goodies. The mother, furious, turns to her husband and buys some assistance with her exasperation. The dad walks quick and angry, his long gait nothing but paternal authority. Upon arrival, the child is instructed to "Come here!" The father reaches his right arm across to grab his child's right forearm. The child is turned, and his ass is slapped, less to hurt him than to propel him back to the group to which he belongs. Each of the four fathers does this or something close to it at least once.

Goran stands away from the group, speaking quickly to an older woman. She and Goran have all the gray hair in the room. The young, boycotting parents have, it appears, no parents of their own. Excitedly Goran speaks to the older woman, clutch-ing her arm like he did Ben's, holding the woman up next to his chest. Her fat face nearly hides the chin, nearly. Her head bobs endlessly. Beginning from the upright position, the bobs pull her head toward her left shoulder. At about sixty degrees, it bounces back upright, in the spirit of a typewriter. Goran appears to love her dearly. She herself is expressionless, though her head cer-tainly moves a lot.

Ben, who is working, returns to Goran in order to help him communicate with this woman. Goran smiles at Ben while clos-ing his eyes. "This is my sister. I have not seen her in thirty-four years. She cannot speak. So sad. She blah a blah last year."

There is twenty minutes of this. Ben stands next to Goran and his shaking, wobbly-headed sister, listening to Goran's monologue, thanking God that he is not being asked to translate. The rest of the family continues to fester. The moms have sur-rendered, and the children gorge themselves on crackers, cubes of white and orange cheese, and carrot sticks. They drink soda dispensed from a special tube, a tube with access to six different sodas. The children force the black woman to prove this by test-ing each one. The mothers sit on folding chairs, too exhausted to maintain the postures and positions their stiff dress requires. The men are a huddle. Ben has no business here and escapes to the bathroom.

Returning to the unreunion through the hallway, Ben en-counters one of the parentless parents. She is a biological mem-ber of the chin clan. The hallway is so narrow, it could not possibly be up to code, that Ben and this woman must synchro-nize their passage, each turning their hips parallel to the wall. She begins twisting before Ben, who pauses and stares, hoping to seize an opportunity. Her bright eyes are blue by blue-gray. Large, the skin around them is taut, crow's-feet radiating down and outward. She cries regularly. Beyond these magnificent, expressive eyes her face is part plain, part ugly. Ben is taller, but she is bigger. Her cheap polyester knee-length skirt reminds Ben of his junior high librarian. She returns his stare, impatient, while Ben registers that he is, if only by default, the best-looking of those assembled here this evening.

"Excuse me." Between polite and annoyed she says it.

Ben starts. "No, uh, mmm, what…" He hasn't spoken English to another person for six days. Confused, her eyes grow. Not to mention she probably needs to use the bathroom. "What, um, what the fu—" He touches his face trying to concentrate, sorting out different abbreviated phrasing for what ought to be a very, very long question. "What the hell is this?" That's his best shot.

She shakes her head. "This?"

"This," he stammers, "this fucking thing," his perplexed arms up to gesture out toward the larger space to his left and her right on the other side of the hallway only to collide with the narrow wall. The embarrassment and pain in his hands return to him his verbal facilities. "What the hell is going on here? Who *are* you people?"

She pauses, looking right over his eyes, like he's been asking her for the time every two minutes for the last hour. "Uncle Goran," she hisses with acidic mockery, "is a murderer." Ben refocuses and does nothing. They stare at one another without understanding. "He killed our parents," she blurts, with all the expression of the lady from 411. "Excuse me," and she lowers her massive right shoulder into Ben's right shoulder and forces him against the wall so she can go and piss.

A few minutes later, Goran approaches Ben, who has been trying to understand what is afoot in his GI tract while attempting to fill in the vast gaps of the woman's sparse narrative, returning to the phrases "prison sentence," "refugee status," and "adoption agency" with most every scenario. "We will start now," Goran says, still smiling.

"Need, can, should, um." Ben fumbles for the right modal verb to construct his sentence with. "Might you say to me what is the thing you are going to say now to all the people here?" Ben inhales, nearly felled by his own syntax.

"I don't know," Goran replies slowly. "I will apologize. You should not blah. I will talk slowly." And he raises his arms toward the two dozen chairs assembled before a podium and microphone. Loudly Goran says to the other family members, "Please sit down."

Ben, quickly rehearsing scenarios of humiliation and failure, realizes the time has come. A couplet of dialogue from the movie keeps running through his mind: "'I'm not who you think I am.' 'Exactly, you are who I thought you were.'" "Sit down, please, everybody," he speaks loudly, almost enjoying the authority of speaking someone else's words.

The family migrates to the chairs, reluctant and lethargic. The men are expressionless. Two of them, both of whom have married into the clan, place themselves at opposite ends of the first row. The mothers round up their little ones. The one from the hallway disciplines her son with the word "dammit."

Goran moves behind the podium, too short for it, but indifferent. A pair of unneeded speakers have been set up, and so Goran's words boom: "I want to thank you for blah here tonight." Goran, still smiling, looks at Ben.

"He, uh, I want to thank you for coming here tonight." Ben returns a forced smile of his own.

"Many years blah, our family blah a very bad blah." Goran pauses.

Ben pauses. "Many years, many years ago, our family had a

very bad thing happen to it. Uh, very bad thing. Real bad." Ben scans the family, waiting to see who will unmask the charlatan first, but they all just stare at Goran.

"The blah blah came into our village and made everyone choose between blah and death." Goran pauses.

Ben pauses. He pauses. He raises his glass, his thoroughly empty glass, to his mouth to stall, feeling his spot in the room sink below the rest of the outlying world, which immediately begins tumbling down on top of him.

Just then the two men seated at opposite ends rise. One is tall, the other is wide. The tall one has a horrible hairdo. Long in back, short on top. He wears cowboy boots with his suit. The other definitely lifts weights. His tie is visibly bottom-of-the-line, and he wears no jacket over his short-sleeved button-down. They walk briskly toward the podium. The room is silent, save for the static breath of the speakers. One girl, happy at the sight of her father, suddenly exclaims, "Daddy!" The bobbing head bobs much faster, like a metronome set for the allegro part of the evening's program.

In the instance before they reach him, Goran turns to Ben and says, each word terrifically enunciated, "I will need your help now."

"Motherfucker," the jacketless one says, also enunciating impressively, in the moment he arrives at the podium. He reaches out for Goran, but bumps the podium. Infuriated, he crashes the podium to the ground. The other one stutters his last step, leans back, and adeptly slugs Goran in the face. Goran goes down and the guy with the bad tie sits on him in order to beat him without having to take his stance into consideration. The translator hurries toward his client, tackles the cowboy, who topples over and onto the other two. The next three or four seconds cannot be fully known without the aid of stop-motion photography.

The main problem is the boot. First slicing up his thigh, it is now, at this very instant cleaving the translator's bottom in two and is firmly wedged into an obvious site of insertion. There are many other things happening at this very instant. The weight lifter is, more or less, lying on top of the translator. Someone's blood, it appears, is on the sleeve of the arm he is grasping. The cries of children and shrieks of women are surprisingly audible, their high frequencies undisturbed by the low, dull thuds and groans of the more proximate melee. But the hard leather cowboy boot, adorned with silver tips, up, yes, up his ass, this is the main problem. Ben's immediate objective is to pull himself up and off of the boot by using the aforementioned bloody arm as a lever. His client's voice, distinctly accented isolated vowels and consonants, can be heard nearby. Ben pulls at the arm to lift himself, but the boot follows, applying equal or greater force. The guy wearing the boots, it seems, is really working over the client, enjoying the stability Ben's ass offers him to hurt the client as quickly and efficiently as he knows how. The body on top of Ben—whose head repeatedly says things like "you motherfucker," "fucking fucker," and "cocksucker motherfucker cunt" in a distinct, but difficult-to-place East Coast accent—shifts a bit. The client pulls the man's hair—Maine?—using his fingers to truly hurt the other man's face.

It occurs to Ben that Goran isn't just making sounds of suffering and pain. There is also something akin to laughter. The big man has rolled off Ben; the boot is nearly disengaged. Two women—he knows by their shoes—are angling into the pile, scolding the combatants, using their handbags for some unclear purpose. It occurs to Ben that Goran just may be the kind of man who views the relationship between a $3,000 suit and a brawl as anything but mutually exclusive. Much to Ben's dismay, there is a counter-roll, though the boot has been successfully dislodged.

At that moment, the pile is dismantled by the two stockiest female family members and one of the caterers, who drag the attackers away by their feet. The one who had been on Ben thrashes and flops, fishlike.

Goran rises, decidedly dignified for a man bleeding from both nostrils. The wives of the two men scream at their surly, seething husbands in unintelligible unison. The children have been hurried to the exit by the other mothers. The two men who did not participate in the brawl stand silent and stone-faced next to the woman with the bobbing head. It shows no sign of slowing, though the return point is now closer to seventy-five degrees.

Goran sits in a chair, tilts his head back, and begins a series of facial contortions. Throughout, he systematically checks the flow of blood from each nostril, dabbing the area around his philtrum with a different digit at each new expression. He settles on none of them, instead grabbing a thick pile of small, square napkins.

From among those invited, only the two other men and Ben remain. The wives, the bloody husbands, and the head have all disappeared. The caterers stand far away, safe behind a table, drinking soda and picking at the remaining cheese. The two men sit down. Both dark featured with shiny black hair. Their faces clearly come from the same source, though one of them seems to have taken his a bit further. His nose, ears, lips, and even chin are bigger, wider, thicker, and sharper than his brother's. Ben, his ass throbbing, looks at Goran, who no longer smiles as he tries to repair his face with cocktail napkins.

Goran holds a bright, newly reddened one at a distance from his face, considering it like a hand mirror. He speaks in slow monotone: "They will not tell their children I killed their parents. I did not."

"You won't tell your children he killed your parents. He did not." Ben looks at Goran as he says this, his chest swelling as the words come and go effortlessly.

"He did!" one of the brothers protests. "Bastard!"

"I did not," Goran says calmly. He pauses. After a few of his more discreet efforts fail, he gives up, twists the tip of a napkin and casually inserts it in his right nostril. Half-nasal, he continues: "I did not blah them, but I could not blah them. I wanted to blah them, believe me, but I could not." This "blah" is the same word repeated.

"What does"—and he says the sound of the unknown word to Goran—"mean?" Ben asks.

Goran removes the napkin tip, studying its saturation. "To do something so they don't die."

"He wanted to prevent it from happening, he wanted to save them," Ben's voice pleads with the brothers, "but he couldn't. But he wanted to."

"They made me watch," Goran says to the napkin. Reinsertion.

"Nonsense," one of them says.

"He's lying," says the other.

Ben turns to Goran. "They think that you are…that this… that this is nonsense and lies…what you said."

Goran takes his eyes off the napkin, studying Ben with similar interest. "I loved my brothers and sisters. I wanted to die instead. Now I want my nephews and blah to be my family." Ben continues looking at Goran and vice versa after the latter finishes speaking. Ben looks over at the taciturn brothers, back at Goran,

and then at his own shoes. His bottom smarts, but less. He starts
to translate, but one of the brothers beats him to it:

"We shouldn't have even showed up today. We only did because Aunt Sonja asked us to."

As Ben begins to search for their words in Goran's language,
the other brother continues: "She can't talk, and she can barely
write. It took her ten hours to write a one-line note. She wrote,
'Listen to him. Nothing more. Listen. Please. To him.' Well, we're
listening, but that's it."

"Yeah. Fuck him," the other adds by way of conclusion.
Their anger reveals itself through the bottom of their chairs,
now squeaking around the floor as they use their legs to spit out
their contempt.

Ben thinks he might have a very crude paraphrase for that
last part, and could do the rest no problem, but Goran interjects,
"The blah is the blahest. The one who does not die is the one
that wishes most to die."

Ben raises his hand to both parties, asking them in two languages to hold on and wait and shut up, please, now.

Suddenly warmed up, Mr. Big Face continues, addressing
mostly his brother, who nearly smiles, apparently enjoying the
intimacy of their antagonism. "I mean, how does a guy like him
even get into this country or out of his own? He's a known crim-
inal. It isn't just his own that he kills. He's notorious."

Ben feels a jolt of promise as he recalls the image of the very
page upon which "notorious" and its equivalent were printed in
the library dictionary. Though it may have actually been "nocturnal."

"I wait my whole life since that blah day to blah to everyone,
to my family that I am blah, that I hurt no one." Goran looks
down, moving the bloody napkins around the tabletop in a vari-
ation on solitaire.

"Please, stop, please, hold on," Ben continues, nearly laughing in his powerlessness.

"If I could, if I were that kind of man, if I knew I wouldn't get caught, I would kill him right now," the littler-faced one declares proudly. "I was cheering for Earl and Tommy. Quietly, because, after all, the kids. But he deserved it."

Outside of the brothers, who take turns, everyone is speaking at once. Ben is nearly speaking sign language, having vigorously added all known gestures to his bilingual gibberish in order to silence the room, but no one pays any attention. Goran regularly slams a fist upon the table each time he proclaims his innocence. The brothers counter by pointing their fingers, at Goran, at Ben, at each other.

Gritting his teeth, stomping his foot, and half spinning around in his exasperation, Ben invokes the translator's authority with a spirited "Shut the fuck up!" He repeats it in English, justly confident that Goran will understand. The startling, heartfelt integration of urgent tone and intense mini-dance was the kind of thing that might have earned him an ice-cream cone or another pony ride from his mom a decade and change ago.

The hall is silent. Ben sits down, unable to decide where and how to start, uncertain as to the source and nature of his interest here in the first place. Goran has built a large asterisk, the bloody napkin ends gathered into a single point, their still-white tails radiating outward. The brothers help each other put on the suit jackets they had removed moments earlier. Ben bites his lips and shuffles around a half-dozen mixed-up phrases in his head.

Finally Goran removes a checkbook and pen from inside his suit jacket. He writes a check, tears it out, and hands it to Ben. It is written in the amount of $25,000. A local bank has issued this check, printing on it Goran's full name and a local address. "For each family," Goran says.

"He wants to give this to every family," Ben says handing the check to the one with the exaggerated face.

"For what?"

Ben translates.

"They will believe me."

Ben translates.

The brothers whisper to each other, alternately shaking and nodding their related heads.

"Not enough," one rejoins.

Ben translates.

Goran writes another check, tears it out, and hands it to Ben. "Thirty," Ben announces.

A brother snatches the check from Ben and studies it. He reaches into his own inner-breast pocket, removes a pen, and writes on the check. He stands up to hand it directly to Goran, but Ben intercepts the check and reviews the alteration. "They want fifty each," he informs the client.

Goran motions for the check from Ben, then writes on it. As he finishes a brother walks toward Goran to take the check. Ben raises his arm to chest level, stopping the brother, and instead takes the check himself. "Forty-two-five."

"Fuck him," one says fed up, turning the first word into a diphthong.

For a few moments no one speaks. The caterers are carrying trays and boxes of liquor out through a back door.

Then Ben speaks his best idea in years, the kind of thing that comes to him thanks only to the chaotic distribution of dumb luck. "What if," he rubs his unique chin, "what if he pays you thirty now and another twenty in five years, but only after he checks with your children that you're telling them the truth?"

"What was that?" Goran asks, as if he has missed a potentially crucial line in a movie.

"What truth?" one of the brothers challenges.

Ben holds his index finger up to Goran and speaks to the brothers. "That he didn't kill anyone."

The brothers consult each other by looking at each other. One says, "And if we don't?"

Ben clumsily explains the deal to Goran, who seems intrigued. The translator turns back to the brothers.

"That's the deal. Yes or no."

Goran slowly walks Ben to his car through the crisp air of the parking lot. "When I return in five years, I want you to be my blah again."

"Your what?"

"My translator."

"Oh. Of course."

Goran reaches into his breast pocket and hands Ben a check. "Thank you." The short wealthy man walks away toward an idling car.

In the poor light of the parking lot Ben needs a few moments to make out the many digits on the check. His entire torso surges as a number of internal organs—lungs, heart, colon—respond instantly to the good news. Meanwhile, the cold night makes Ben's jaw and mouth jump involuntarily, causing his teeth to click and crack together spasmodically, resulting in an irregular shoulder bounce, all of which are summarized in a dull hum Ben does not notice. Failing to wrestle control of the top quarter of his body, Ben simply nods his convulsing head and mutely smiles his open and closed mouth, unable to remember how one responds to "thank you" in Goran's language.

RAIDER NATION

Tony, who is a difficult man, came over on a Sunday. Lucy was brought along. The purpose of their visit was to watch the Oakland Raiders play a football game of great consequence to their fans. My father, who only wants me to be happy, gave me a high-quality television as a gift to mark the beginning of my graduate studies. This television measures forty-three inches from corner to diagonally opposed corner. In addition, the television has a feature through which it is possible to view a second channel in a small rectangle superimposed upon the larger screen. It is even possible to move rapidly—that is, "surf"—through channels on this small screen. Then, if one happens upon a channel whose present content is more compelling than the incumbent content upon the larger screen, one can press a button that causes the small screen to trade places instantly with the large. In general, I do not watch a great deal of television, but this feature, I find, encouraged me to think twice about such infrequency.

Tony learned of my television and its high quality after bringing me home from work. Though, as I stated above, I am a graduate student, I wanted to supplement my stipend. I elected to find work as a bank teller near the university campus. Because I am a loyal student of Marxist literary theory, I believed, at the time I began working at the bank, that spending numerous hours in a space of such highly concentrated capitalist activity would be illuminating. I was incorrect. I no longer work at this or any other bank. The job also forced me to wear a tie, an additional thing that brought me no pleasure.

I met Tony during the time I worked at the bank. While for me this job was, I feel, well below my capabilities and certainly not the type of labor I expect to one day devote myself to, it was for Tony—or as my dad might call him, this Tony character—a golden opportunity to make something of himself. Again, I ask for your apologies in light of my patronizing assessment of Tony's potential. But in this I know I am not incorrect. Many details of Tony's past are unknown to me, but I was able to gather enough facts in order to extrapolate that Tony's relationship to our nation's laws was not, in the eyes of our nation's law enforcement, agreeable. Indeed, whereas I terminated my tenure at the bank on my own volition, Tony was the object of a termination, and could have been the object of incarceration if his cousin and bank manager, a Mr. Alex Nunez, had chosen to pursue in some official fashion Tony's failed effort to steal loose change and other miscellaneous monies from the bank.

Prior to my resignation and prior to Tony's termination, we worked together at the bank for three weeks. Tony initiated a small series of conversations with me about such things as: my identity, my feelings about working at the bank, my interest in marijuana and psychedelic mushrooms, and my thoughts about

Jennifer Stenerson, in particular her breasts, Jennifer being another teller at the bank. I was, I believe, cordial, though many of
Tony's inquiries left me mildly perplexed. At some point during
a majority of our brief exchanges, Tony—my father would perhaps also think or refer to him as that joker Tony, joker in this
case suggesting not a penchant for clever witticisms, but rather a
deceptive and perhaps mendacious constitution—would find
a reason to strike or clutch one of my hands briefly, as part of a
larger expression of his agreement or excitement. During these
incidents he would often exclaim "hell yeah" or "that's what I'm
talking about," such as the time I blushed and concurred, reluctantly, that Jennifer Stenerson's breasts were, yes, very pleasant to
gaze upon. My apologies to Jennifer and any other people who
believe this admission to be offensive.

I never initiated conversation with Tony, but this had little if
any effect on his recurrent efforts to socialize with me. At the
end of one day, as I was leaving the bank, Tony offered to drive
me to my apartment. I informed him that I lived no more than,
I estimated, seven blocks from the bank and that my short walk
home was, in fact, a source of pleasure. Tony then asked me, I
suppose rhetorically, what the fuck I was talking about. Next
Tony compelled me to walk with him to his automobile. I do not
recall if he put his hand on my back and pushed me, or if he
merely acted as if I had already agreed to accept his offer. I am
easily influenced in situations such as these. This trait of mine
made me wary of any and all contact with a person like Tony.

As I approached his car from the back, I recognized it to be
a 1994 or 1995 white Toyota Corolla. Though the make and
model were unremarkable, the car's owner—that is, Tony—had
enhanced the car in numerous ways. Its muffler was unusually
large and very shiny. A similarly large spoiler fin was affixed to

the trunk. I also immediately noticed that this vehicle boasted large tires that actually protruded four to six inches out from under the body. These tires had silver rims that were as shiny as the muffler. Finally, the back windshield was decorated with the logo of the Oakland Raiders football team. This logo features the face of a powerful man who wears an old leather football helmet that provides his face no protection. As such it is little surprise that this man wears an eye patch, like a pirate or the deceased Israeli military leader Moshe Dayan. Behind the man's head are two crisscrossing cutlasses. The frame surrounding the man's head is in the shape of a shield. Though we were in Berkeley, California, I was not surprised to see Tony's car declare its support for the Oakland Raiders, since Oakland and Berkeley border one another, and as such it is not uncommon to see similar endorsements of the Oakland Raiders on the cars and clothing of Berkeley's inhabitants.

Due to his manner of driving, Tony's car gets poor gas mileage. Throughout the short trip to my apartment, Tony only accelerated and decelerated, boldly, except when forced to a full stop, during which time he devoted himself to the manipulation of his elaborate car-stereo system. This system was quite able to create loud sounds at very, very low frequencies, making me suddenly cognizant of my lungs and rectum. Tony grinned at me often and nodded his head, I believe in order to communicate to me his pleasure at sharing the might of his car-stereo system with me. As a driver, he was disrespectful of stop signs.

In front of my apartment building I thanked Tony for transporting me, but before I was able to exit the vehicle, he swung his right arm over my headrest, turned his head, and reversed quickly into a vacant parking space on my street. "Bri," he said, "hey man, I need to make a call and my cell's at the crib. Can I, you know?" My name is Brian. I don't believe he waited for my response, though it would have been yes.

Tony described my apartment as being "tight," and I thanked him. He held his phone conversation in my bathroom, with the water running, so I cannot reproduce his conversation here. His voice crescendoed a number of times. Upon exiting the bathroom, I noticed that Tony had rolled up his shirtsleeves. All male bank tellers must wear a shirt with buttons and a tie. Short-sleeve button shirts are acceptable, but Tony never wore such a shirt. Now I knew why. Along the inside of his left forearm, in large black Old English lettering, a tattoo read 𝕿-𝕯𝕺𝕲 and the symbol between the "T" and the "D" was in fact not a hyphen but a crucifix, dripping blood. In my opinion this tattoo was not flattering.

"What is 'T-Dog'?"

"Shit," he grinned, "that's me, Tony DeAnza. T to the motherfucking D-O-G." He danced briefly. Then he removed a book from a shelf. "*Postmodernism: The Cultural Logic of Late Capital*—what the fuck is this?"

I could not formulate an appropriate response to this question, despite, or perhaps because of, my overall fondness for the work of Fredric Jameson. But no matter, as T-Dog, as I will now call him—at least for a while—noticed my television.

"Damn, B, nice set."

I thanked him.

"You got cable?"

"Yes, this is a basement unit. It is the only way I can get a signal." In fact, my father, who said it was no problem at all, arranged for me something called DIRECTV, which uses satellite technology to deliver to my television a vast number of stations. I find the choices overwhelming.

"Shit, we should check out the Raiders on this mug. They're gonna take it this year." T-Dog then pretended as if he were clutching and throwing a football.

I was somewhat convinced. "Um—"

"Bri, man, can I ask you a small favor?" he asked, touching his ear and inspecting his shoes. "You know how we work at a bank and banks give out loans and shit?"

I nodded.

"You think you could be like a bank for me, for like a week or so?"

I felt my cheeks redden, and I was sad to realize that T-Dog was very much in my apartment with me. I knew my cooperation was inevitable, and this saddened me yet more.

T-Dog demonstrated his appreciation for the $150 check I wrote to him via an especially powerful hand slap. I was promised that my money would be returned by the end of the following week, and that I couldn't possibly know what a favor this was. As he said this, his small brown round eyes widened, and this was the first moment during any of my interactions with him so far that I did not fear him, and there would only be one more like it. I am easily made to feel threatened, and this is why I am most happy reading difficult books in quiet libraries by myself, even though Marxist literary theory is no longer valued by most contemporary scholars. T-Dog was aggressive, brash, confrontational, and unpredictable. As such he scared me. But during the above moment he did not, because he forgot and let me see, for a moment, that he was actually just desperate. Once this moment passed, his eyes changed back to their usual shape; then it was no longer possible to believe that he was still desperate, even though I remembered he was. This is a hard thing to express. But, of course, I knew I was giving, and not loaning, T-Dog my money, a fact that was unpleasant and distracting, since, as my job at the bank indicated, I was not independently wealthy, despite being irrevocably bourgeois, I believe, by circumstances beyond my control.

One week later, T-Dog was relieved of his duties at the bank. While I did not view him as a particularly valuable member of the bank staff, a certain part of me, in combat with the rest of me, continued to hope that T-Dog might indeed fulfill his role in our lender-borrower dynamic.

Four days later, as I left the bank, T-Dog summoned me to his idling car. This invitation did not bring me joy, but that part of me which persuaded the other parts of me that I was soon to be richer said "see" and made me walk to his car. In fact, as that part was saying "see," I could hear my father saying, with a hint of skeptical optimism, well, would you look at that. "Get in, bitch," and he opened the back door. I cannot be absolutely certain that T-Dog addressed me as "bitch," but this remains my best guess. Assuming this is an accurate reproduction, I am more confused than insulted. T-Dog invited me into the backseat because the passenger seat was occupied by a woman. I had initially intended to pretend that this was just a woman and slowly make it clear that this woman is or was indeed Lucy, but I can't see any point in such misdirection. But of course at the time I did not know she was Lucy, though I was about to know.

T-Dog's powerful car-stereo system was again producing a great deal of sound that I felt through the car seat. The music featured a woman whose voice compelled me to picture my own erection. T-Dog introduced me to the other passenger, "B, man, this is my lady, Lucy."

Lucy turned to me and smiled. Her teeth were very straight

and white. "Hey," she greeted me. I made an effort to smile in a fashion that might be interpreted as casual. I'm not certain if I succeeded.

Soon they were inside my apartment. This was not my plan, but T-Dog appeared uninterested in my interests and desires. I served them cold, nonalcoholic beverages. They sat on my couch while I faced them from a kitchen chair. Today T-Dog was wearing a small white undershirt. In addition to his eponymous tattoo, there were miscellaneous symbols and letters on his shoulders and across his chest. The tattoos were of a low quality, and thus hard to decipher. Again, I did not find them attractive.

Lucy, or Lu-Lu, as T-Dog referred to her, wore black jeans which cut into her waist and a yellow cotton blouse with frills on the sleeves. This blouse was largely unbuttoned, and in order to conceal her breasts, she wore a tight undershirt, not entirely distinct, in regard to cut or material, from T-Dog's shirt. Only in opposition to T-Dog's thin, shallow chest—which was unable to fill up even his meager tank top—Lucy and her breasts made a great impression on her undershirt. This impression was indeed not limited to the shirt itself, since due to the scope of her breasts and the neckline of her undershirt, a portion of each breast was hidden neither by brassiere, undershirt, nor cotton blouse. It is challenging to estimate the amount of boob evident, in light of their three-dimensionality. I am tempted to describe merely the vertical length of her exposure (two and one-quarter inches, approximately), but this would be insufficient. The insufficiency of this description stems from the fact that each exposed partial breast clearly had a horizontal quality, that is depth. Though this depth decreased as my eyes rose toward her neckline, ending in an area where it was impossible to know if this was breast or not, at its thickest point this dimension was the opposite of trivial. My knowledge of geometric formulas, though once adequate to earn a 770 on the math section of the SAT exam, is now frustratingly limited; otherwise I could estimate both the surface area and volume of visible breast. In truth, the volume was not visible, as Lucy's olive skin was not even translucent. But this volume mattered greatly, because of the contours it created in the surface area itself. Most important—and here I have no choice but to invoke a postmodern cliché—was the presence of the absence, both of light and breast, in a valley created between the breasts. This was her cleavage. To cleave means both to split or divide and to adhere or cling to. I spent much of the time Lucy and T-Dog were in my apartment that day trying to understand this dark line between her breasts. This forced me to spend much of my time looking as if I was doing anything but trying to understand this dark line. It was during these latter interludes when I thought about geometry and the word "cleave" and whether or not I would be disappointed by the likely evaporation of Lucy's cleavage were she to appear naked before me.

"So, man, wassup?" T-Dog inquired.

"I am busy with my studies, and with my shifts at the bank," I replied.

T-Dog addressed Lu-Lu, "B, man, he's a fucking genius, dog. Check out all these fucking books." He read a series of titles: "*The Ideology of the Aesthetic, History and Class Consciousness, The Politics of Modernism: Against the New Conformists,* shit, what is this shit?" In truth, T-Dog had some difficulty reading aloud these titles, but it is hard to fault him for this.

"I study Marxist literary theory," I replied, not feeling that this was an intelligent strategy.

T-Dog next removed a small Ziploc bag from his pants. It

contained something white. He asked Lu-Lu, "Hey, get the stuff out of your purse." So actually, he did not ask.

The white thing was cocaine. Next, the following conversation did not occur:

Me: T-Dog, why do you choose a drug that is known for its high cost, when I believe it is the case that you have limited funds? For after all, was it not I who loaned you money recently? Cocaine has never, I believe, been the official drug of any austerity plan. According to an article I once read on stimulants, speed offers similar effects at a radically reduced cost.

T-Dog: B-Dog [I was grateful to be called B-Dog], it's just a motherfucking eight ball. Lighten the fuck up.

Lu-Lu: Yeah, B [also acceptable], we're just trying to have a good time.

Me: I even must wonder whether or not your decision to indulge in my residence is not a provocative gesture by which you demonstrate to me in the presence of your girlfriend that rather than fulfill your obligation to me as a borrower, you instead choose to squander your surplus wealth on a most expensive narcotic. And I am taken aback by your decision, despite my awareness of the bold tendencies in your character, to undertake this thoroughly illegal activity without asking me, your host, for any permission whatsoever.

Instead, I watched T-Dog prepare two long lines of powder on the hand mirror he received from Lu-Lu. His concentration almost caused me to believe that he was capable of greater things. Lu-Lu focused on T-Dog, and lifted her head once to me in order to smile. She did not appear to feel that their behavior was inappropriate. In addition to thinking some of the thoughts which I have reproduced above, I made repeated efforts to swallow the suddenly vast amounts of saliva in my mouth. I wondered how a militant Marxist might feel about the drug trade, but my concentration was poor, and so my conclusions are not worthy of space here.

Though I was not close enough to witness the phenomenon as I now wished I had, I will pretend I did. T-Dog and Lu-Lu, in quick succession, placed a tightly rolled-up $20 bill under a nostril, brought this bill toward the mirror's surface, and through the force of a focused inhalation, summoned a line of white cocaine to travel—against the never-waning force of gravity—up and through the $20 bill and into the attached nostril. I recognize this phenomenon to be well known, but to see it, in particular the fact that the bill was brought only *toward* the mirror and not onto the mirror itself, thus forcing the cocaine to rise off the surface and through the air before reaching the $20 tube, this was a lesson in human ingenuity. I wished I were small enough to stand on the mirror in order to watch this scene enlarged, each tiny grain of cocaine like a giant snowflake falling quickly upward. Would I also have wanted to be small in order to amble through Lu-Lu's exposed breasts? Would an inch-tall B-Dog have been able to leap from the mirror onto the hem of her shirt, brought near as she lowered herself to the mirror, her wondrous chest expanding as she inhaled?

Though our triangulated dynamic was always far from equilateral, as the cocaine took effect their (Lu-Lu and T-Dog's) corners radically collapsed toward one another (their angles thus approaching ninety degrees), thereby sending me away toward infinity (my angle almost at zero). Lu-Lu and T-Dog began professing their desire for the other. Then she rose, and perhaps with the music from the car ride reproduced in her head, danced in a sexually inviting manner. Of course, T-Dog was receiving this invitation and not myself, but there I was. Her invitation was expertly designed to spawn an affirmative RSVP. In particular, Lu-Lu moved her hips and buttocks in an irregular circular fashion, occasionally shifting tempo or direction in such a way as to give a thorough demonstration of the impressive skeletal-muscular potential of this sexually relevant region of her anatomy. I wished to be as fortunate as T-Dog.

Then, without asking for my permission, T-Dog rose and took Lu-Lu's hand. He said to me, smiling, "Shit, B, I gotta do this." They retreated to my bedroom, from where I heard each of them say "yes" and "yeah" numerous times. Tony's climax was audible, Lu-Lu's was not, regrettably. I assume they had sex in my bed. I should say, in my bed, they had sex, I assume. Because I know that whatever took place happened in my bed. Afterward it smelled of sex, and may have been damp. It is naturally impossible to know what type of physical acts were undertaken, but my hunch is that they indeed had sex. That night, many hours after their unceremonious departure, I refused to fulfill my command to change the sheets. The smell kept me awake for hours, until I retreated to my couch, where I touched myself and attempted to visualize Lu-Lu's chest. He still owed me money.

And then some time passed. Autumn became winter, but it was difficult to believe this to be meaningful, as the temperate climate of the Bay Area precludes the possibility of the extreme weather many associate with winter. Perhaps our earthquakes are a response to this. The semester concluded. I spent long nights researching and composing seminar papers on the rise of the novel and the emergence of the private sphere. The quality of these papers was of great concern to me, but my professors had yet to return them in the self-addressed stamped nine-by-twelve-inch manila envelopes I provided. The campus and its adjacent residential areas were noticeably vacated by students. My father called approximately every forty-eight hours to invite me to join

him for the holiday season in his spacious home in a new development in Orange County. Through the phone I considered the
sincerity of his regular invitations; they were most sincere. I was
forced to manufacture a suspicious series of poor excuses to
fend off his advertised hospitality, a hospitality summed up in
the words, hey, fella, what do you say? I lied that I was still writing papers, that many close graduate student friends were remaining in the area for the break and had invited me to spend
free time with them, that the bank could not operate without my
labor. My father made efforts to persuade me, but never ques-
tioned the truth-value of my excuses. I loved him for this, and I
found myself hoping, as I wandered the empty, lonely campus
during the evening, that he instantly detected my lies, but chose
to decide that I must be misleading him for reasons only I could
understand, and that in time I would gladly accept his invitations
so we might enjoy each other's company like we had when I was
much younger.

The University of California, Berkeley presents its student
and faculty with an extremely long winter break. As Christmas
came and went, as the media dissected the nature and meaning
of the holiday buying season, as the sky remained cloudy and
damp, I recognized with some anxiety the fact that nearly three
weeks remained before the resumption of classes. My peers, the
larger faculty, the larger yet undergraduate populace had, starting
around Thanksgiving, declared their eagerness for the arrival of
winter break. I, too, in the moments I found myself the addressee of such a declaration, described my affection for the
concept of institutionalized vacation. And, I must admit, the initial minutes following the placement of my twenty-one-page
paper on a neo-Marxist reading of Ian Watt's famous study were
moments of relief and levity. But the rest were not so. My apartment, asked to host leisure activities, seemed confused. I read

books, I attended movies, I even went bowling with my only close friend in the department, a woman name Ilse, who has been writing a dissertation on Joyce and Lacan since 1991. She is a superb bowler, but cannot and should not be relied upon to relieve one's sense of loneliness for more than an evening. Her sadness is remarkable.

And so I took to shopping in Berkeley. There are many stores around campus selling merchandise directed at the 18–24 market group. I view these shops with cynicism, as they prey on the disposable income, which rarely comes from their own work, of the largely privileged undergraduates. Moreover, I doubt even a small percentage of this consumer populace has any awareness of the extent to which they have been conditioned to fashion their identities through an intricate series of purchases: for clothing, music, hair products, etc. I apologize for this preaching, but it is important you understand how my decision to undertake shopping as a regular activity represented a drastic departure from not only my typical behavior, but from the strongly held political beliefs and ideological convictions informing this behavior. But I was despondent. My father had not called in nearly a week. I hated and feared January. The company of other customers and store clerks was oddly pleasing. Initially, I spent long hours browsing the shelves of Berkeley's stellar bookstores. I made a series of acquisitions, retreated to coffee shops, and read, inspired by stimulants. But I was restless, and this satisfaction was short lived. Next came the record shops, then the clothing stores, and finally, with but a few days until classes were to resume, a handful of stores targeted at the trendiest consumers, for whom commodity fetishism is a never-fading beacon. These stores sell T-shirts that appropriate the logos of well-known corporations in order to present a message related to sexual activity, narcotics, or corporate malfeasance (the latter I found entertaining). Others sell more outlandish clothing, skateboard equipment, or drug paraphernalia.

And it was in such a store, where I pretended, with great apprehension, to be in the market for an eighteen-inch translucent green water pipe, that my path recrossed with T-Dog's. Peering over the display case, I felt a violent slap on the back. I assumed it to be law enforcement, and froze in terror. "Well look who can't resist the chronic now!" he said by way of greeting. After my heart rate subsided, I discovered myself to be pleased to see him.

"Hello, I'm…"

"Shit, that's cool, B, what the fuck do you think I'm here for? To buy chewing tobacco?" T-Dog's jocularity was a welcome counterpoint to my own emotional state, and I hoped to prolong our conversation or even make plans to meet at a later date.

"How is Lucy?" I inquired.

"That slut, shit," he responded. I was surprised and excited, that is, both surprised and surprised to be excited.

"What happened?"

"Man, B, Lu will fuck anything. I mean anything."

"Was she unfaithful?"

"She will fuck anything."

"I'm sorry to hear that."

"The bitch."

Tony then consulted his beeper, and I feared he would disappear. "Tony," I said, "do you recall that once you said that you would enjoy watching the Oakland Raiders play a football game on my television set? Are they going to be televised in the near future, because if they are I would like to invite you to watch a game on my television. Which you said was an excellent television."

"Do they have a game soon? You gotta be fucking with me. B, this is the motherfucking playoffs. It's on, tomorrow. New England. Winner plays in the conference championship and the winner of that goes to the goddamn Super Bowl. The Super Bowl. Do they have a game soon. Man, where the fuck have you been hiding?"

"Well, would you like to…"

"I might, maybe. I can bring somebody, right?"

I purchased twelve premium beers and a large bag of potato chips so that I might construct an appropriate setting for the viewing of a football game of such consequence. Some of the thoughts in my head between my chance encounter with T-Dog and his arrival for the game itself concerned the wisdom of my invitation. That Tony DeAnza is what my father would call a "bad seed." That he would seek to take advantage of me a third time. But perhaps my funds would be returned. Perhaps he would bring Lu-Lu and a friend, or if not Lu-Lu, then a friend of Lu-Lu's and Lu-Lu's friend's friend. Or perhaps, simply, he and I would watch a suspenseful, competitive football game and celebrate as our team vanquished its worthy opponent. Or perhaps, despite my knowledge of contemporary theory, the Russian language, and Dostoyevsky's entire oeuvre, perhaps I am a very foolish man.

"Let me tell you something about the Raiders. They don't fuck around. Bottom line, B, they *do not fuck a-round,* period. Back in the day, before they moved down to LA, the Raiders were *hardcore.* After games, they'd go to the bars, hang with the Hell's Angels, and if you stepped to them with some weak shit, shnapp! They'd take you the fuck out. You think they dished out the punishment on Sunday afternoon? Try Sunday night when the bars start closing. Them mugs was crazy. And now, man, Al Davis and Chucky Gruden, they don't give a fuck either. Davis sue his fucking moms, if he think he can win. Chucky Gruden look like he's insane in the fucking membrane, I mean look at that motherfucker. Silver and Black my man, Silver and Black. 'Cause the fans is all about that. Man, these motherfuckers be dressing up like Darthmotherfucking Vader, summoning up the Dark Force into the Black Hole. Pirates and Road Warriors, wearing shoulder pads with metal, *real metal spikes* coming out. Monsters. Plain and simple monsters. 'Cause there's rules, and then there's Raider Nation. You come into Raider Nation and forget about it, ain't no motherfucking rules in Raider Nation. Shit, me and my boys went to the Dolphins game. Third quarter in the bathroom, some pussy-ass Dolphins fan thinks he can roll solo taking a piss wearing his Marino jersey. Shit. Me and the boys, we beat his ass, I mean *beat his ass*. You wear a visitors' jersey in Oaktown and you declare war. This is motherfucking Raider Nation. I ain't no Raider *fan,* I am a proud, bleed Silver and motherfucking Black, citizen of Raider Nation!"

T-Dog had, midway through his speech, mounted my coffee table. His can, his third can of beer, was held out at arm's length, like the Statue of Liberty's torch. Many of his references were lost on me. Lu-Lu applauded and offered, "Raiders! Wooo!"

"T," I addressed him, "are the Raiders considered a dirty team?"

"Shit!" he responded. "They're the fucking Raiders. Are they dirty?"

T-Dog and Lu-Lu had been here for less than fifteen minutes. I was astounded to see Lucy. As she descended the five stairs into my apartment I realized that she was beautiful. Her

head and face were recently attended to, her lips painted, a clip
pulling her straight black hair up and back. The poor lighting of
my entranceway reflected off this hair in a perfect band of
sheen. T-Dog was already assaulting me with a violent greeting,
a mutated handshake and hug composed of fists and squeezing.
Lu-Lu, recently, had meticulously and deliberately tried to make
herself attractive. In order to come to my home. Perhaps it was
for T-Dog. Perhaps she did not even know of this evening's
destination. But she had and here she was, and perhaps it was
intentional and perhaps it was for me, not T-Dog.

"So what do you say, B. Who's gonna take this motherfucker?"

"I hope the Oakland Raiders win, because I'm certain such
an outcome will bring you great joy."

"Joy. Shit. Such an outcome would bring me joy and
500 bucks. And you your 150 that I owe you. You know I didn't
just forget about that shit. That ain't me, man."

"Brian," Lucy said. "Tony told me how important it was for
him to pay you back." He nodded.

"I bet straight up, forget the spread, with this asshole I know
from my building. Grew up in Boston. Thinks Larry Bird's better than Jordan. Guy's a fucking idiot. We bet 500 bucks. And
he's good for it."

"But if your team fails?"

"Shit."

"Shit?"

"They won't lose, Brian, Tony's Raiders will not lose." And
she rose from her spot on the couch, raised her hand, and slapped
it with Tony's. Then she approached me, hand raised, and I, too,
raised my hand, and she slapped it. She and I were not experts in
the area of hand slapping, and the meeting of her thin, painted

fingers and my limp palm—a palm that has not clutched a football since the days of Brezhnev—made no sound at all, and surely would not have held up well to scrutiny by the powerful men who first invented this celebratory gesture. But we took pleasure in it, grinning at one another. "They won't lose, they will not lose."

I could not watch the game. For a host of reasons:

(1) I do not understand the rules of football. I gather that one team makes efforts to advance the football in the direction of and then beyond the opposing team. Carrying and throwing the ball through the air are standard means for advancement. It appears that there are a nearly infinite number of schemes and strategies whereby the team in control of the ball attempts to frustrate the opposing team's equally infinite number of schemes and strategies aimed at preventing the team in control of the ball from moving the ball forward in the first place. I think. All of which is regulated by a mobile tribunal located on the field. These men regularly interrupt or punctuate play by informing the television cameras of a particular transgression, none of which was discernible, but all of which were accompanied by clever arm movements. When leveled against the Raiders, T-Dog invited the tribunal to open their mouth so that he might "stuff" his penis down their throat. Their authority was fascinating, but ultimately impenetrable.

(2) T-Dog, who appeared to have a thorough knowledge of these strategies and the code of the tribunal, which challenged my worldview. And this made me feel shame, for I knew that he was actually not dumb, but just unmotivated. But then I was revealed as inferior to him in the presence of Lucy, who knew less than T-Dog, but much more than myself. But also in contrast to my ontologically dubious direct initial response to the game was T-Dog's. Even for him this was excessive. He had quickly availed

himself of the alcohol I provided free of charge, and this an-
nulled any and all of the very, very few inhibitions typically guid-
ing his behavior. And he was so very excited, for not only was
this a game of great consequence for his team, a team he had so
cathected, but moreover his immediate financial future rested on
its outcome, such that were this to have been a telecasted debate
between a panel of New Critics and one of Deconstructionists,
and were Tony to have wagered on that with an asshole who attended Harvard, Tony would still not have been my first choice
with whom to view what could otherwise be an interesting and
instructive television event. Monitoring Tony, I feared for our
immediate setting in its entirety. For my modest furnishings, for
Lu-Lu, for myself, for Tony, for anything resembling decorum.

(3) I wanted the Raiders to prevail. This urge surfaced suddenly. I wanted Tony appeased. I wanted my loan repaid. I
wanted happiness and joy to fill my apartment. I wanted their
season to continue, so that perhaps Lu-Lu would return with
Tony and a friend. I did not want this to be the end. But I was
not only helpless to determine the outcome, I was unable, except
in the most general sense, to detect whether any given exchange
on the field brought the Raiders closer to victory. I am at home
with this feeling of helplessness, as I believe it to be the deter-
mining sign of the subject in the age of Late Capitalism. But
one's—or, more precisely, my—ability to mitigate this naked
exposure to the cruel whims of the early twenty-first century
through a thorough, balanced study of its very unruliness, this is
all I have, I feel. Perhaps this is an epistemological irony, or even
an ironic epistemology. Perhaps it is. But this is why I study diligently, this is why I must know things. Instead, here I was both
impotent and dumb. On two occasions—in response to complex, and to my mind fateful melees—I asked T-Dog, "Was that

a good development for the Oakland Raiders?" Each time he responded with rhetorical evasion: "Does that look like a good development, motherfucker?" Until I realized that my efforts to educate myself or at least follow these events were quite possibly making Tony yet more volatile (see #2).

"Tony and Lucy, I am hungry and would like a grilled cheese sandwich. Are either of you interested in a grilled cheese sandwich? I make a superior grilled cheese sandwich. You can choose from—"

"What the fuck are you talking about?"

"Just that I am going to make myself a grilled cheese sandwich, and I was wondering if you or Lucy would care for one as well. I have mild cheddar and Havarti and pumper—"

"Naw, man, I can't eat cheese, it gives me diarrhea and shit."

"You're lactose intolerant?"

"Yeah, whatever, what the fuck's it to you?"

"I'll have one."

"Great. What type of cheese and bread would you prefer, Lucy? As I mentioned, I have a mild cheddar and Havarti. I myself might have some of both, and as for bread—"

"Why don't you show me how you make it."

"I have pumpernickel and wheat. What? Oh, that would be great—"

"Hey, you girls want to take it to the goddamn kitchen already? Fucking Raiders here."

"Okay, Tony. I'm sorry to hear about your condition. Would you like peanut butter and jelly or some pretzels, perhaps?"

"B."

"Yes."

"I'm good, but you're starting to get on my fucking nerves. There's chips here, I'm cool."

I closed the door separating the living room from my kitchen, but T-Dog and the game remained quite audible. Lu-Lu was in my kitchen and so was I, and no one else was.

"Here is the cheddar and Havarti. The wheat is standard Oroweat, whereas the pumpernickel is from Semifreddi's. This is a bread of extremely high quality, but, of course, not everyone likes pumpernickel. Also, I put a brown mustard on mine, but again, that's optional—"

"What are you going to have?"

"Oh, I will definitely have pumpernickel, and as I mentioned earlier, I may take a bit of both cheeses. There is some tomato if—"

"Fucking Raiders! Hell, yeah! Touchfuckingdown!"

"Whatever you're having will work for me."

I was shuttling back and forth between my open refrigerator and my counter, a distance of perhaps three feet. Lucy stood on the other side of the counter and aimlessly fingered the few items scattered there: a can with three ballpoint pens, sixty-four cents (two quarters, a dime, four pennies), and a scrap of paper with a bibliographic reference I had needed to verify. Lu-Lu's presence radically altered the standard atmosphere of this, my kitchen. It was in many ways the first time I considered my kitchen to be a place. Even from a wholly subjective perspective, I am not certain that she was beautiful, but she struck me as femininely competent. She was a woman who was good at being a woman, whereas I was a man who was less successful (at being a man). T-Dog was perhaps a bit too good in some areas, but overall quite bad in most. Thus, I was grateful to be interacting with her one-on-one in my domestic space.

"Brian, why'd you invite Ton here?"

"Shit. Shit. Shit, shit, shit."

"I am not sure. Why do you ask?"

"Well, he owes you money. He is not very nice to you. I mean…"

I wanted to ask Lucy why she agreed to serve as T-Dog's companion. Why she allowed him to have a relationship with her vagina. But even thinking these questions threatened to ruin my pleasure.

"My invitation was spontaneous, and perhaps not intelligent."

"C'mon, Gannon, you fat pussy!"

"You see, the key to grilled cheese is to grill at a low temperature with the lid in place. Many people grill the bread quickly, leaving the cheese unmelted, which is unfortunate."

I looked at Lucy, who was looking at me with an unremarkable expression. Her eyes were brown and outlined heavily in black. I wondered how much she spent annually on beauty products. She was holding the edge of her mouth in her teeth. The entirety of her breasts was concealed this evening, which, though disappointing, was probably for the best. I looked back down at the glass lid. Steam had covered it, and I found this satisfying.

"Lucy, when did you first encounter Tony?"

"We met at Laney College."

"In a class?"

"Yes, in a class. What, you don't think we're smart enough?" I reddened, but Lucy was smiling, less insulted, I suppose, than aware that this was an option I made available to her.

"I am sorry. T-Dog just doesn't…"

"We were—"

"Ah, fuck a cock!"

"We were in a marketing class. Actually, Ton didn't finish."

"You did?"

"You know it. Getting my degree in the spring."

"In?"

"Finance."

"Congratulations."

I turned the sandwich. The dark bread appeared to be properly grilled and the cheese was already melting. I felt proud.

"Do you like him a lot?" I said it. Staring at the spatula.

"Sometimes. He did a good thing for me once. It makes me not mind him like I probably should."

"'A good thing'?"

"Yeah, we fucked up once, but he stuck around and helped out. I was surprised, but there it was."

"Here's yours. Now on to my sandwich. First I have to let the pan cool. If you forget this step, there is a good chance you will scorch the butter."

"Brady, you bitch-ass whore. Hey, what the fuck you two doing up in there?"

She stuck her head out. "Eating, stupid, what do you think. Who's up?"

"Raiders, Lu, but they're killing me. And it's snowing like crazy, check it out."

She left. Then: "Bri, come look at the snow!"

The field was white. I felt sympathy for the players, who were required to pay attention and concentrate. As a child, in Chicago, before my father and I relocated to Los Angeles, I always discovered that snow, though intriguing, had a scattering effect. I retreated to the kitchen, and Lucy soon followed.

"This is *gooooood,* Brian."

"Thank you."

"Mmmm."

"And so you are happy to remain with Tony?" I asked, courageously.

"For now. Until something better comes along."

"You require a surrogate?"

"Huh?"

"Tony will need to be dislodged? There will need to be a replacement? You would not just terminate relations unilaterally, without a backup mate?"

"No, I guess not. That's just me. I'm always with someone. It's a bad weakness to have." And she chewed, pensively.

My sandwich was properly fashioned, but I discovered myself to be uninterested in eating. In truth, I was not exceptionally hungry to begin with, and only offered to make grilled cheeses in order to escape T-Dog and the game. But looking at my designated sandwich, which I knew to be exemplary, I became aware of my anxiety. The game was nearing its conclusion, and Tony was most certainly going to respond to its denouement.

Lucy had returned to Tony, while I remained encamped in my kitchen, cleaning meticulously. First the area and items dirtied by grilled cheese construction. Then the counter and sink. Then my refrigerator was scanned, and questionable items were removed for disposal. I swept the floor. I rewiped the countertop.

"Hey, B, what the fuck? I came to watch the game with you, man, what the fuck?"

"Oh, I apologize, I was just tidying up in the kitchen." I returned to the other room. "Have I missed anything?"

"You've missed all kinds of shit."

"The Raiders are up 13–10, fourth quarter, only a few minutes left," Lucy informed me.

"Well, that is good news. They seem positioned to win."

"Yeah, man, but they were up big before."

And so I sat down, reluctantly. The snow on the field was considerable, and appeared already to have been dirtied. The players continued battering each other, at times audibly. This was the fourth reason I did not enjoy watching, and I feared it was the first reason Tony did. He was standing opposite the television. I began to attend to my socks.

"Shit, B, stand up. Lu, stand up. Shit's coming down to the wire. We got to pay attention."

We obeyed and the three of us stood shoulder to shoulder, watching the television and listening to Tony. I decided to try to focus on the game. The Raiders were attempting to prevent their opponents from acquiring any more points. Set against the images on the screen was the commentary of the announcers, who increased the tension, unforgivably.

Each play seemed to spell doom for someone, but the teams somehow continued, neither conceding defeat. And then suddenly, the quarterback of the New England Patriots was struck violently by a member of the Raiders. This quarterback, a Mr. Tom Brady, did not see the Raider, a Mr. Charles Woodson, approaching, as he (Mr. Brady) was standing with his back to the path of the then oncoming Mr. Woodson. And though Mr. Brady was likely glad to have his head protected in the face of such unrelenting hostility, his helmet severely restricted his peripheral vision. Mr. Woodson, a trained and talented professional, struck the upper back of Mr. Brady with such force that he (Mr. Brady) failed to maintain his purchase on the football, for which the sport is named. As a different Raider defender, a Mr. Greg Biekert, fell upon the recently liberated ball, Tony and Lucy celebrated in the following manner:

—screamed and hollered, quite loudly

—hand-slapped and hugged, me as well

—playfully mounted (Tony did) my sofa and imitated the act of sex

—cursed the recently battered Mr. Brady, many of his relatives and associates

"Ton, man, c'mon," Lucy instructed. And then: "Ah, shit, they're reviewing it."

"Reviewing what? It's a motherfucking fumble. Woodson cold-blitzed his ass." The carousing ended with Tony standing again in front of the television, still holding the last can of beer, which he had nearly opened to mark his celebration. Lucy returned to the couch in order to bite her nails. I attempted to make sense of the scene, but my attentiveness and sharp mind were limited in the face of football's obscure policies and regulations. The urge to ask surfaced, but I doubted Tony was interested in providing a tutorial at this particular moment.

My apartment remained silent for a number of minutes, save for the voices of the commentators, who reviewed the sequence a dozen times in order to speculate on the outcome of the judge's deliberations. Mr. Woodson's sneak attack proved more impressive and debilitating with each reading. As an uninformed novice, I decided the Raiders should be rewarded for their cleverness, however ruthlessly aggressive.

When the judge finally delivered his verdict, the details of which struck me as unusually opaque, I expected Tony to do something very bad. But he did not. He did not respond. He did not move at all. He remained in front of the television, unopened beer in hand. Lucy, recognizing the potential urgency of the situation, tried to soothe her beloved, offering encouragement and optimistic predictions, but Tony would not respond.

The game continued, each of us alone, waiting. We were

forced to watch the opponent obtain three points. The sixty minutes of game-time expired. But in the spirit of American capitalism a tie was deemed unacceptable, and the players were thus required to take part in what Tony called "fucking bitch-ass overtime."

As a physically unimposing man, I must say, at least in the abstract, that my favorite element of the unwieldy universe that is football is the fact that a little man with no particular aptitude in running, jumping, or hitting is allowed to occupy the critical role of kicker. And as a Mr. Adam Vinatieri of the New England Patriots obtained three points for his team, when even a single point would have sufficed, and as his teammates quickly surrounded him to celebrate and communicate their approval, I tried to take pleasure in this irony of the weak over the strong in a game designed to celebrate power and violence.

But then there was Tony. He had not moved in the last twenty minutes. Lucy had ceased her efforts at interacting with him, while her eyes began doing horrible, nervous things. Now the game was over. Midway through his paralysis, I had imagined him exhaling in a vaguely existential manner when the Raiders proved victorious despite being forced to surmount such a strange and considerable obstacle. However, I did not, perhaps I could not, visualize the consequences of the present outcome. Lucy and I looked at one another. I spelled "trepidation," visualizing the letters in thirty-point font and searching, in vain, for its etymology.

While Tony had been sweating mildly throughout the game and during his petrification, I now believed, though it was hard to be certain, that he was crying, or at least tearing up. His breathing, to be certain, had grown erratic, and the first sounds were only now emerging. "Fucking rules, man...Fucking bullshit...Shit...We won...Fuckers." And variations of this sort for a minute of two.

And then, without notice, Tony brought back the hand clutching the beer can and threw it, furiously, toward my television. The screen surrendered, its glass penetrated. For an instant there was an unusual light, the nature of which still fascinates me. The can remained lodged in the punctured machine, and so the beer, the liquid beer, ran down the dead box and onto the floor.

Lucy was the first to respond. "What the fuck, Ton? Why you gotta be doing shit like that?"

Ton quickly looked to her and then to me. His face was an interesting blend of outrage and supplication, and I realized, for the first time, that despite the potential for violence in this man, that I suddenly had the upper hand. His act was a transgression, and as its apparent victim, its currency was for me to spend.

"The television should be unplugged, I believe." Tony obeyed and unplugged the television.

And with that I exhausted my interest in controlling the situation. I was grateful to my father for his generosity, but I harbored hostility toward the device, and whenever I saw that bumper sticker, most ubiquitous along the progressive streets of Berkeley, "Kill Your Television," I had always recognized a pang of concurrence. I had no interest in demanding anything from Tony, I was simply glad that he would now cease to be a threat to me, his debt now repaid.

Lucy approached the dead television and inspected it. After some nudging the can remained stuck. She turned to Tony, "Ton, man, you fucking idiot, man, get the fuck out of here! You know how much a TV like this costs? You already owe Bri 150 bucks you can't pay him, and now this? Go. Just go. Get a fucking job. You loser."

Tony turned to me, still silent. My tendency for reconciliation surfaced, and I nearly informed Tony that I was not angered and that his destruction of my television, despite its unjustifiable character, did not greatly disturb me. But instead I remained silent, maintaining my power.

When the door closed, Lucy again tried to remove the can from the television. The moisture on the can made this difficult. "You will cut yourself. Don't bother, though I like to recycle cans, there is no other reason to separate the can from the television."

Lucy turned and came to me. "I'm really sorry about Tony, Bri. I shouldn't be surprised, but I am. I thought he was done being like that." She had clutched my hand.

I went to the kitchen and began to eat my cold grilled cheese, facing the sink. Lucy came in a minute later. She grasped the muscles connecting my shoulders to my neck and massaged them. This felt alarmingly good. I ate my sandwich, grinding my molars with pleasure.

The phone rang and Lucy answered instantly, as if this made sense.

"It's for you."

"This is Brian."

"Brian, fella, how are you?"

"Hello, Dad."

"You won't believe what I just saw on television. Wow. Talk about wild."

"What was that, Dad?"

"You don't care too much for football, do you? Because this was, let me tell you, an absolute lulu of a game."

"Well—"

"It's a playoff game between the, between *your* Oakland Raiders and the New England Patriots. In New England. By the end of the game it's snowing like mad and the whole field is white. Absolutely incredible. Like a bunch of kids out there. And it's all coming down to the wire when Charles Woodson, one of the stars of the Raiders, just blindsides the Patriots' quarterback. On a blitz. You know what a blitz is?"

"More or less."

"It's nearly like cheating, but really it's just a big gamble. Anyhow, boy oh boy does this gamble pay off. Woodson absolutely clobbers the QB, who never saw him coming. The ball flies out of his hand, the Raiders get it, and that's it, right?"

"One would think."

"Game over, right? But they review it. They've got this screwy review rule now, and they review, and they decide—jeez, I can't even remember the explanation. Somehow the refs say it was actually an incomplete pass or some such nonsense. Can you believe that? We're talking about the season here, and if you ask me the championship, because the winner of this game, I believe, has the inside track to at least get to the Super Bowl. I mean...oh, forget it, I'm just boring you to death, you couldn't care less about football."

"No, Dad, it's alright, thanks for the report, because I'm certain local members of the community will want to speak with me about it, and now I'll have something to contribute: 'Woodson was robbed, the rules are unfair, whatever happened to justice?'"

"You can say that again. Anyhow. Man, I feel sorry for the Raiders fans, that's got to be tough. Hey, who was that that answered the phone? Since when are there women in your apartment, kiddo?"

"Oh, that was Lucy, just a friend."

"Just a friend, huh. Well, listen, it finally dawned on me, I keep inviting you down here, but what do you care about down here? Your friends aren't here and you say you like it so much up there, so I was thinking, I could come up next weekend. I got some business I could take care of, I'd get a hotel near you so as not to bother you too much, but we could see the sights, and I could take you and your friend Lucy out to a nice dinner. What do you say?"

"I—"

"You know, because I miss you, kid."

"Sure, Dad, that would be fine."

"Great, great, that's just great. Listen, do you need anything? Clothes, money, anything. Sometimes I forget to ask. You got everything you need? Everything you want? Hey, and how's that TV of yours?"

"Everything's fine, Dad, really, everything's fine."

"Turn it on for the news, you'll see, they won't even talk about anything else. It'll take them years to get over this one. Years."

HOW KEITH'S DAD DIED

Keith's father died of a heart attack at 2:58 A.M. on a Tuesday night, so it was officially Wednesday, though in Keith's father's mind it was still Tuesday because he hadn't yet gone to sleep, or hadn't yet been able to fall asleep, though he had briefly tried a couple hours before he died.

Keith's father started suffering from intermittent insomnia a little less than two years before his death, and, in fact, about six months before he started having trouble getting and staying asleep, he started having trouble in his sleep. He began, in his sleep, murmuring unintelligible sentences with considerable emotion, and on the rare occasion that his wife heard actual words, they didn't fit together in any logical way as far as she could tell, until one night his soft murmuring turned into loud mumbling and then actual screaming, so she rolled over to hold him, which didn't slow him down, and though she thought that

it might be a big mistake (though she realized later she was con-
fusing nightmares with sleepwalking) she decided to wake him
up. When she did he calmed down immediately and was fully coherent soon after, at which point he thanked her for waking him
in order to stop what she thought must have been his suffering,
though he could not remember anything other than something
having to do with a car and a boy.

Keith's father placed his head on his wife's bare chest, one of
the three most common positions they rotated through in bed
each night, which was Keith's mother's favorite position and
thus quickly helped her to relax, and in less than fifteen minutes,
during which time Keith's father said "Yeah, something about a
boy and a car" four times, Keith's mother had fallen asleep, while
Keith's father, whose head was still on her chest, felt more awake
and alert than he had in years. For the next hour he was convinced he would not fall asleep again that night, and began fearing that something was going wrong, but more than that he was
frustrated knowing that the following day would be a struggle on
only the few hours of sleep he was expecting to have. In a last-
ditch effort he decided to listen closely to the sound of his wife's
breathing and heartbeat, which, much to his surprise, helped him
to fall asleep.

During the next few months Keith's father's murmuring,
mumbling, and screaming slowly increased along with the time
he spent awake with his head on his wife's chest trying simultaneously to diagnose the problem and relax in order to fall back
asleep. Finally a night came when he could not fall back asleep
despite rousing his wife awake enough to make quick love to her
with the hope that ejaculation would help him relax, which it did,
but not enough to fall asleep. So he went downstairs and had
some toast and watched TV, flipping through the different cable

stations, but focusing mostly on an airing of Steve Martin's *The Jerk,* which he had remembered liking the first time he saw it almost twenty-five years earlier, but which did not amuse him at all at 5:00 A.M. on a Friday morning, which still sort of felt like Thursday evening to Keith's father, who was forced to cancel his morning appointments, which finally convinced him to take his wife's suggestion to go see someone, because at this stage in his life, which was from one perspective the last stage of his life, his work had become his greatest source of satisfaction, and his wife was greatly invested in the idea that this was just a stage (though certainly not the last stage of his life), because though she was pleased that he so loved his work (this prioritization of his work over everything else had never been officially stated by either of the two, though she still recognized it as true), she was not gladdened by the fact that he had begun to gradually extend his hours of work while slowly increasing the number of anecdotes he brought home from the office, which were usually just updates about patients she knew only as names. Keith's father sensed that he could only be boring his wife with tidbits about the marriage of some patient's brother, but he needed to share with her the sensation of deep satisfaction he gleaned from every passing moment of work, a sensation that coated the trivial in a thick layer of splendor, that had as its source the realization that he had definitely made it as an optometrist, that he had used his talent as an eye doctor as a foundation upon which he built a stable practice that brought in good money, and though Keith's father could have easily come to this conclusion years earlier, he was something of a pessimist when it came to money and was expecting something to go wrong, until when it didn't for so long he eventually accepted the idea that he had carved out a nice little niche for himself, and so every day at work became a constant reminder of this success, which didn't surprise him once it finally happened, though he had years earlier convinced himself it would be unwise to expect such a scenario to actually materialize, and so every day at work after this realization was made, Keith's father conducted his examinations with a relaxed confidence he just couldn't believe was his own, and he especially liked that he had long since memorized all the letters and numbers on the many charts he would show to a patient during a typical exam, this allowing him to turn his back to the patient and the chart in order to prepare something for later, while still being able to listen to the patient tentatively read a series of letters to which Keith's father would say in an authoritative but compassionate voice, "Okay, next line," and Keith's father could sense that while he was always an above-average optometrist he was getting much better, so much better that he concluded he must be among the finest optometrists in the world, which turned every day into an unannounced challenge with himself to perform without error in the different aspects of his job, and so when he had to cancel appointments after not falling back asleep at all, and after already suspecting that his performance was slipping, if only by degrees, Keith's father decided to take the necessary steps to address his new condition.

When he announced to his wife his intentions to "see somebody," she produced instantly the name and number of a good doctor she had gotten from a friend, which surprised Keith's father a little bit, but not much as he interpreted it as just one more example of his wife's devotion to him and general know-how, though in truth a large percentage of their friends were seeing or had seen doctors who specialized in sleeping disorders, hypertension, and other conditions (which they treat with an updated menu of medication) that like divorce seemed to be everywhere, though Keith's father had no idea that so many of their friends were among those dealing with such conditions, including his wife's closest friend from whom she had gotten the number. Keith's father went to see the doctor, who shook his hand warmly and then asked him a battery of questions about his work and marriage and general health, and then asked Keith's father to tell him the details of his condition from its beginning, which Keith's father did with relative accuracy, and the doctor then asked while pursing his lips if there were strange or reoccurring dreams that Keith's father could recall, and Keith's father said that there was something very vague about a boy and a car, and the doctor nodded and said nothing more about the dreams, while Keith's father took a little deeper breath than normal because he had just lied to his new doctor, because, in fact, the dream about the boy and the car was about a dead boy and a car crash. Keith's father had concluded to himself that perhaps this was a repressed trauma that was fighting its way back into his consciousness, something he may have witnessed at a young age, which, he concluded, would make some sense due to the new inner strength he felt since he had crowned himself king of the optometrists, a transformation which may have signaled to that part of his brain controlling the release of such forgotten memories that Keith's father was now ready to deal with the trauma again after nearly half a century, and Keith's father suspected that there were doctors who perhaps through hypnosis or some other semilegitimate method could extract the memory whole thereby allowing Keith's father's life to return to normal, but Keith's father wasn't interested in therapy of any kind that would demand a second trauma in order to exorcise an earlier one, and that even if this first trauma was dealt with, Keith's father concluded, there would likely be some other repressed baggage holding the next number and waiting anxiously for its turn to invade Keith's father's dreams, so Keith's father opted to lie to his doctor, hoping that the medication the doctor would soon prescribe for him would remedy the situation.

Keith's father's new doctor did indeed prescribe some medication to help him sleep more regularly, and though the doctor told Keith's father that it might take a little while to find his proper dosage, after only a few days Keith's father decided he had enough, because while he was now sleeping without difficulty, he was not feeling like himself when awake, but instead like his intellect had been severely dulled, as if his IQ had dropped between fifteen and twenty-five points overnight. His wife tried to convince him that he was still fatigued from the previous period of poor sleep and that his body was just getting adjusted to the medication and that in less than ten days he could see his new doctor again who would undoubtedly lower his prescription, and Keith's father nodded his head to all this and agreed with her intellectually, though at this point he didn't trust his intellect at all, whatever was left of it, and called his doctor less than thirty-six hours later, trying to sound coherent, which he still was, because he had in fact greatly exaggerated the negative effects of the medication after working himself up during lunch alone at his office when he convinced himself that he was just starting out on a long, painful journey filled with nights of poor sleep and days of sleepy confusion, and that he was doomed to become just one more average eye doctor who could certainly manage his clinic, but not with the stunning competency with which he had earlier, and that sadder than this, at some point he would no longer be able to remember what it was like to operate at such rarefied heights of professional expertise, and would instead only be able to vaguely remember that he once indeed was exceptional, and because of this he called his doctor asking if they could move up his date to review his dosage, and the doctor asked him some more questions about his sleep, and Keith's father rushed through the answers trying to explain that the sleep wasn't the problem, and the doctor suggested he lower his prescription by a certain amount, which Keith's father quickly did, and as a matter of fact already had done the day before having decided that it was unlikely the doctor wouldn't suggest it anyway.

In the days following, Keith's father felt more lucid, but certainly not like his old self, and one night he woke up and had trouble falling asleep again, and he decided that very night that this medication just wasn't going to work, so he stopped taking it the next day, which angered his doctor a little as he realized what he had already suspected during their phone call of a few days earlier, that Keith's father would be a difficult patient, too neurotic or anxious, but the doctor tried a second medication anyway, though he was hoping the first would work, largely because the pharmaceutical company that made it, in particular the Midwest distribution and marketing division of this company, offered him undisclosed financial compensation if he prescribed it to a minimum number of patients each year for a set time span, which it appeared Keith's father would not reach, and while the doctor had recognized immediately that there was something plainly unethical about such a relationship between doctor, patient, and multinational conglomerate, Keith's father's doctor thought the medicine was as good as any of the others, all of which he thought were objectively only okay. At this point in his career, the doctor had begun to doubt seriously the effectiveness of virtually each new drug, as he believed they were being given to people whose chemicals had finally fallen in line behind the other malfunctioning aspects of their lives, and he began to liken himself to someone who paints over cars on the verge of rusting out completely, only degrees better than plastic surgeons, and he felt a depression he assumed was similar to that of many of his patients, with the only difference being that he knew many more technical terms with which to name all its different faces, and he took a monthlong vacation the year before during which time he experimented on himself, and though he felt better, he could sense that something deeper was still festering untreated, so he stopped taking medication, knowing that he was functioning fine to begin with in terms of job performance and impulse control and ability to make small talk with all the people in his circle of friends whom he had begun to resent for treating him with respect in large part because he was a doctor who made them all feel better, or at least referred them to doctors like him that made them all feel better, and he had begun reading books about Chinese and other Eastern medical traditions and concluded not only that holistic treatment was clearly more effective, but that this truth would eventually be accepted by Western medicine, and when it did he would be looked back on like a latter-day phrenologist.

Keith's father tried to be optimistic with the second medication, and after a week he thought that he felt a little better than he had with the first medication, but he concluded that there was no reason to expect that he would find a medication that allowed him to sleep better without some side effects carrying over into the daytime, and his wife accepted this reasoning, though she tried to convince him to give this medication a little more time hoping that eventually his body would recalibrate itself and he wouldn't just feel like his old self, but would indeed actually be his old self. He wanted to believe this was possible, so he stuck it out for two weeks more, and though he felt the negative effects lessen, they didn't go away entirely, and at his next appointment with his doctor he told him that he was no longer interested in trying to treat his condition with medication, which his doctor accepted with virtually no resistance, which surprised Keith's father until he realized that he had initiated the treatment on his own and was certainly at no obligation to continue with it if he chose not to, though in truth his doctor chose not to resist because he was in the process himself of leaving his profession, feeling more and more each day that he was the part of something dreadfully wrong, and within the next two years he would move to China to study its medical techniques, which, though it relieved his conscience would so alienate his circle of friends and ex-patients that it would only lead them to a stronger belief in the type of treatments he once advocated, as they all assumed that he had gone crazy, and two of Keith's father's wife's friends, both of whom were medicated, eventually found themselves discussing this doctor at Keith's father's shivah, blaming the doctor for failing Keith's father, who could still be alive today, one said, had he stuck with such a treatment.

In the first few weeks following the termination of Keith's father's brief experiment with medication, Keith's father enjoyed nights of sound sleep while he stormed through long workdays in eager coherence until he convinced himself that perhaps the whole episode was just a phase and that the dream or nightmare had simply caused a temporary ripple in his sleep patterns and that his body or mind or consciousness or whatever it was that dealt with things like this had gotten used to it or managed it somehow by storing it somewhere or treating it as the liver treats alcohol or some other ingested impurity, and Keith's father's wife listened to this theory and said well I hope you're right, I suppose anything is possible, but doubted that such a thing was actually possible, though she realized she had absolutely no expertise in this area and suspected that the pessimism she had internalized as she came to terms with the notion of living with a highly medicated, and likely uncured, insomniac had more to do with her fears than anything objective or rational, but despite this just couldn't get herself to believe that it was really all over. About three days later, in nearly the same inexplicable manner, Keith's father began to have his doubts, too, concluding that such an end to the episode was too good to be true, that the rest he was now enjoying was likely caused by the relief he felt at being unmedicated, and, indeed, eleven nights after renouncing his second medicine, Keith's father woke up around 2:30 A.M. after murmuring from about 1:45 on, and only managed to fall asleep two hours later after watching a dubbed film on one of the movie channels that took place at a generic Mediterranean resort where men with large mustaches and women with bad teeth plotted, murdered, and made love to each other in strange places during long scenes in which the mustaches and teeth were overshadowed by European breasts and staged moans by anonymous voices, and while Keith's father found the movie mostly ridiculous he mustered up enough intent resolve to masturbate to the lovemaking between the head of the drug ring, who was also the owner of the resort, and a new waitress with a large chest, who turned out to be an undercover police officer who eventually caught and arrested the drug lord, though Keith's father never found this out as he quickly went upstairs even before their first sex scene was completed, having achieved orgasm well before the two on the TV.

Keith's father's insomnia returned and with it came a new, higher level of anxiety than anything Keith's father had experienced previously, as simultaneously and frantically he tried coping with its return, while denying its potential severity, while convincing himself he would outlast or overcome it, while fearing it would eventually spell disaster for his entire life as he then visualized it, and here he would picture fragments of nightmarish scenes that all involved the packing of boxes, his office closing as he cleaned out his desk, his wife stacking family pictures in a box (which once held the family's first microwave), and he became erratic and irritable, snapping at his wife often, something he rarely if ever did previously, and she would accept these blows trying not to blame him for his condition, while going through a similar series of impossible steps for coping with the new situation, until everything came to a head one evening, when Keith's father first screamed at his wife for misplacing a remote control, to which she apologized and then retreated upstairs where she broke down in the bathroom (the same bathroom Keith would break down in during his father's shivah) using the same fan technique to blanket the sounds of her crying, and it was only after ten minutes that Keith's father realized something was wrong, and concluded rightly that she was upset, and so he rehearsed approaches for discussing the new situation along with the latest episode, settling on a pledge to try medication again, and he went up to the bathroom and knocked on the door and said, "Honey, are you okay?" and she said, "Go back downstairs. I'll be down soon," in a voice that betrayed her efforts to sound normal, and when she came downstairs with her red cheeks he announced his decision to her, and she sat silently for a moment and then began speaking softly about how much she loves him, and then about how hard this has been, and how she isn't sure how much longer she can endure something like this, her voice steadily increasing its volume, and she began

crying again, and was soon out of control, and Keith's father became removed and found himself wishing she would stop, but
she would not, and Keith's mother kept expecting her husband
to come over to her to comfort her, and moments before he finally realized that he should do just that, her melancholy tears
had made way for bitter anger, and she accused her husband of
not caring about her in "this whole thing" until she finally shifted
into a guilt-including mode asking with injured contempt and
stuttered breathing, "How, how can you not care?"

Keith's father sat in silence for over two minutes while his
wife's slippery red face stared at him from ten feet away on the
adjacent couch, which didn't directly face him, as all the couches
in the living room faced only the TV directly, and Keith's father
mostly stared at the carpeting alternating between thoughts
about a possible retort while wondering how many years old the
new carpet was, deciding along the way that it was at least seven
years old, and that it was therefore odd to still consider it the
"new" carpet, and when he looked up at his wife's swollen eyes
and crossed arms, he decided to just start speaking despite having no response in mind, still feeling a faint buzz in his stomach
from her accusation, which he suspected meant that she wasn't
entirely inaccurate, though he knew he did care, and he tried to
start explaining this to her, and how sorry he was, but that was all
he could find to say, so he repeated it over and over, I'm sorry,
I'm sorry, I'm sorry, and her face hardened as he repeated it,
though each time he said it he meant it a little more, until the
image of his wife packing the pictures appeared to him for an instant but from an entirely different perspective. Shame overwhelmed him, and during his fifth "I'm so sorry" his voice
broke, and he stammered halfway through the last word, while
his vision began to cloud, and a flood of tears followed, and he

staggered clumsily toward his wife and they held each other shaking hysterically and feeling desperately helpless, and their moaning and sniffling echoed back and forth, both of them unable to retreat from their respective peaks of frightful misery long enough to actively comfort the other, until Keith's father's near-hyperventilation caused him to belch awkwardly, which amused him slightly, allowing him to subdue his crying in order to stroke his wife's hair and back until her crying slowed as well.

They stayed awake a few more hours, first in the living room, then in the kitchen, then in their bedroom, discussing both the events of that evening along with those of the past two months, and though few concrete plans were made, and Keith's mother cried on and off while downstairs, the shared crisis of that evening, along with a renewed sense of common purpose, saw the evening end in a mood of mellow, tender affection, as each in his or her own way reasserted a commitment to "fighting through this thing" (while embracing and in between soft kisses of surrender rarely exchanged at other times), until Keith's parents fell asleep exhausted, Keith's father's head rising and falling gently on his wife's chest.

The next morning, which Keith's father arrived at on the back of an uninterrupted sleep, offered him little of the reassuring optimism so abundant the night before, and indeed outside of the fact that the hysterics of the previous evening had sapped him to such an extent that he slept soundly, Keith's father was unable to salvage any palpable detail in which he could reinvest his impoverished sense of hope, and though he knew that he and his wife had reaffirmed that they were on the same team as it were, and that such support from his wife was certainly valuable, it did nothing to solve the problem itself, and here Keith's father differentiated with no uncertainty between solving the problem and coping with the problem, and decided that no amount of the latter done well could make up for failure in the former, and that for all the previous night's accomplishments, which he realized were urgently needed, it still left him an insomniac without recourse, which his wife hadn't thought about as she hummed to herself in the kitchen that weekend morning feeling renewed and actually in love with her husband, who, she could not avoid realizing, she loved a little more because of his crying, which reassured her of something in him that only crying demonstrated, and she knew this to be somehow wrong, but decided that since it was already over with that there was no point in denying herself the satisfaction it brought her, however much she was clear with herself that she would never wish upon him again such a trying experience.

As she hummed to herself in the kitchen while preparing coffee for the two of them she decided that the day should be devoted to them, and she imagined them sharing the newspaper, and discussing its content, and then making love, and showering together, which they hadn't done in years, slowly getting dressed, and walking to a nearby restaurant for lunch, where they would talk about trivial things like the new shop in the same strip mall, and they would hold hands across the table, and she would even bring up his eye clinic to see how proud it made him, while she would answer his attentive questions about her real estate classes and clients, and their waiter would be charming, never forgetting to keep their water glasses full, and the sun would shine strongly into the restaurant forcing her to put on her sunglasses from time to time making her feel like a movie star, and when the meal was over they would walk home slowly, never feeling rushed, momentarily reviewing the meal, saying that it was pretty good, especially her soup, and when they got home there would be a message from Keith, or his sister, Lisa, and they would sound happy, but more than that they would sound unaware that their parents were still so much in love, and then they would drive to an outdoor art fair, and they would go their separate ways for a little while, only to converge almost accidentally later on, each eager to show the other the things they were considering buying (and it would be important to buy things that day, things that would be on display in their home, to always remind her, or them, of that special day), and they would buy a fragile glass bowl or a colorful photograph, and then return home after running into some friends they hadn't seen in a while, friends they both actually like but never seem to see, and they would make enthusiastic and sincere small talk and show each other the things they bought, and both couples would truly approve of the other couple's purchase, and they would separate from the other couple and say to one another almost simultaneously that it's a shame they don't see them more, and would resolve to call them in the near future (and, of course, the other couple would say the same thing), and once back home they would take a nap, still a little worn out from the day before, and then shower again, this time separately, and go to that Italian restaurant and then to a movie, or even rent a movie, and watch it together undressed under the down blanket that they can only use sporadically due to his allergies, and they wouldn't make love again, they would just fall asleep downstairs, and she would wake up at three or four in the morning, but she wouldn't wake him for obvious reasons, and eventually they'd wake up together, and it would be the next day, and they would look at each other still half asleep, a bit confused and disoriented, until they remembered where they were and all that had happened, and then they'd exchange a mischievous smile, feeling like two kids at a slumber party, and she imagined all this as she walked up the stairs to the bedroom with two cups of coffee and the newspaper tucked smartly under her arm, and as she turned into the room she smiled at him, while he returned an empty, defeated gaze that chased away her fantasy with such velocity she had to close her eyes to keep from losing her balance.

The monthlong depression Keith's father entered that morning made both his and his wife's lives nearly unbearable, so much so that he tried medication again, this time an antidepressant, which led to a manic episode at the eye clinic, where Keith's father found himself nearly paralyzed one morning as the intensity of holding his face so close to that of his patient's for ninety seconds or so while he checked the patient's eyes' ability to converge, for patient after patient, enveloped him completely. He had become slightly irrational, giddy, excitable, and the license to hold his face so close to someone else's, someone whom he knew but not very well, to smell their breath and listen to its rhythm, to actually feel this breath on occasion, threatened Keith's father's self-control, and though there was never a danger of Keith's father using this opportunity to close the few-inch gap separating him and his patients, he did find himself extending this period of the exam, redoing aspects of the test, improvising others that revealed no information whatsoever, until Keith's father had stopped recording much of the important results, and after the last exam of the morning, Keith's father found himself masturbating in the office bathroom, something he had never done before, and ejaculated to the voice of his secretary, which was suddenly suggestive. The guilt Keith's father felt staring into his semen on a few pieces of Kleenex with his pants lying next to him on the floor (he had removed them entirely in his mad haste), while his secretary continued talking un-

knowingly on the phone, offered him a window of coherence
wide enough to call his wife and tell her it was important that he
stop taking his medicine immediately, and he threw out the rest
of the medication he had at the office, canceled the remainder of
the day's appointments, and drove home slowly and in fear,
where he told his wife a carefully measured fraction of the
morning's events, which did include his masturbating but not the
thoughts he had about his secretary while he masturbated, and
his wife slowly said "oh" and made a sad face and leaned over to
kiss his forehead, and then she led him upstairs where she helped
him undress and get into bed, after which she closed the blinds
and disconnected the phone in the room, and he collapsed a few
minutes later though he did not expect that this would happen,
and when he woke up he felt nearly like his old self and realized
with great relief that he would likely not need to be institutionalized, something he had convinced himself was surely unavoidable as he put his pants back on in the bathroom at his office
after masturbating about having sex with his secretary while giving her an eye exam.

    After renouncing medication once and for all, Keith's father
felt himself submitting to his new reality as an inescapably per-
manent state, while he tried harder than anything else to please
his wife, as he became more and more convinced that she would
eventually leave him for one reason or another related to his situation. He even agreed to go to most large gatherings they were
invited to, something they usually avoided at his request, and it
was at a party for a good friend of his wife's best friend that
Keith's father found himself speaking with a man named Bill
Michaelson, who made a suggestion that would solve, if only
briefly, Keith's father's insomnia.

    Keith's father crossed the threshold of the host's house

while inhaling deeply in order to combat the familiar sense of doom that had enveloped him each time during the last month he confronted a situation that was not entirely predictable (they had taken to renting movies and ordering in at least one night each weekend). He held his wife's hand and actually squeezed it tighter as she wrestled her hand from his grip in an effort to greet the host, leaving him vulnerable, like the little boy he considered himself to be as she drove the few miles from their house to this one while his head rested clumsily on the passenger-side window, because he was too exhausted (partially from lack of sleep, partially from wearing himself out by worrying day after day that he was damned and helpless) to make certain that they were heading the right way and that no errant driver was careering toward them, something he normally did when in the role of passenger (which was itself rare), though it was patently unnecessary and aggravated his wife, and so he left it to her to get them from point A to point B, which she was more than capable of doing, but as he let her do it all on her own, he couldn't help but feel the way he used to feel when staring out a car window forty years earlier as his mother drove him about, too young to be aware that he may be in danger or nearly lost, and now as he relinquished (or was forced to relinquish) his ever-present sense of awareness and responsibility while the edge of his forehead knocked gently into the window as the car hummed along, he concluded that his relationship with his wife was now based on his needs, not abstract needs which were actually veiled desires, but basic needs since he no longer readily found the energy, constitution, or self-confidence to drive across town, pick out his clothing, or pay the bills, tasks she took on more and more, and as she pulled her hand from his to hug the hostess while he stood silently trying to smile he longed for her to return to him, just as he used to miss his mom while waiting anxiously in the family car as she ran inside some store to run a quick errand.

Keith's father's wife was whisked away immediately by her best friend, who rushed to meet Keith's parents at the entrance, having waited impatiently for them since her arrival twenty minutes earlier, under the auspices of showing Keith's father's wife a new painting the host couple recently purchased, while in actuality dying to tell her best friend that she was indebted to her for coming at all, since she just realized how little she can stand this whole circle of friends, and Keith's father's wife stood nodding, slightly relieved to be in the presence of such familiar pettiness, while Keith's father barely recovered from his wife's exit in time to extend his moist palm to greet the hand of his host, whose name he mumbled with slight enthusiasm, and the two men in unison inquired of each other's condition, one saying "how are you," the other choosing the more informal "how are ya," to which one responded "fine," while the other said "okay," and just like that the host had turned away from Keith's father who instantly noted that it was up to him to move from his spot near the doorway and enter the buzzing party, so he scanned the large living room until he spotted the buffet, which he began walking toward hoping, almost praying, to find a pasta salad among its contents.

Halfway across the room, Keith's father tried to slow his steps fearing that he was jogging toward his destination, while he smiled awkwardly to each guest he thought he made eye contact with, though due to his paranoia he actually smiled to a number of guests who hadn't noticed him at all, until he finally reached the buffet, which boasted a Chinese chicken salad, a fruit salad, an elaborate, multitiered cheese-and-cracker structure, and its twin, an equally impressive vegetable and dip tray, and at the far end of the table, a pasta salad. Keith's father grabbed two carrot sticks as he moved toward the pile of red plastic plates layered alternately with matching napkins, snatched one up, eagerly guessing that the trip down the buffet and subsequent eating would likely last at least fifteen minutes, after which time he could hunt down his wife without appearing desperate, who would hopefully point him toward an acquaintance or two with whom he'd struggle to make small talk until he escaped to plead with his wife to leave as soon as possible, who would likely be ready to leave as well, but would still resent having to leave because of him, and they would drive home in silence, his head resting again on the window, while feeling even more childish than during the drive over, as in his haste to leave the party he would have forgotten to urinate, despite knowing full well the effects three glasses of 7UP (they would have no ginger ale) would have on his bladder.

Keith's father moved slowly down the generous buffet, pleased that because they had arrived a little late (which would ensure a shorter visit in general) the buffet had been visited by most guests, and outside of a couple picking aimlessly at the vegetable tray, he had the buffet to himself, which still boasted large quantities of each item, including the pasta salad, which appeared to be pesto based, and after loading his plate with representatives from each dish he made his way to the adjacent drink station, which he was even more delighted to have to himself, as he was able to put his plate down while pouring himself a beverage (they did in fact have ginger ale), and with plate in one hand (upon which he had wisely placed fork, knife, and napkin) and beverage in the other, Keith's father scouted out a tiny alcove that offered only one chair, which was presently vacant, and while he knew that such self-imposed isolation was clearly in

conflict with the protocol of such gatherings, Keith's father decided he could claim extenuating circumstances, namely, that if
he was able to enjoy his meal without having to expend energy
simultaneously in fruitless small talk, it would likely rejuvenate
him long enough to function at a near-normal level for perhaps
a half hour, and therefore eating alone was in fact still in the best
interest of the collective, so Keith's father hurried toward the alcove, again forcing himself to slow down halfway there, until he
heard his name called out, which he ignored, but couldn't resist
the call when repeated, and turning his head reluctantly saw a
grinning Mel Kaplan approach him, and while greeting Mel and
bracing himself for the customary Mel Kaplan pat/slap on the
back, Keith's father tried to accept the fact that the alcove chair
would remain vacant.

Mel Kaplan said, "Al Weintraub, how the hell are ya?" and allowed himself a hearty chuckle, while Keith's father, who called
himself Alan, was compelled once again to notice the striking
physical similarity between Mel and his onetime business partner, Michael, Keith's father's brother. Mel told Keith's father to
come over and eat with him and took Keith's father by the arm
and began directing him in the opposite direction toward the
crowded living room until they arrived at the edge of the largest
sofa, where Mel reclaimed his place, forcing Keith's father to
drag over a plastic chair, which Mel noticed only as Keith's father
sat down, causing Mel to erupt in an "Oh, jeez, Al, I'm such a
putz. Here, take my seat," to which Keith's father raised his hand
trying to communicate to Mel that he was fine in the plastic
chair, but Mel was already standing up next to the plastic chair,
so Keith's father, whose self-pity was now fully activated, moved
himself to the sofa, which, despite its smooth black leather, was
not terribly comfortable.

Before Keith's father had an opportunity to begin eating, Mel introduced him to Bill Michaelson, saying, "Al, this is Bill Michaelson, he did some consulting work for your brother and me a few years back," and turning to Bill, Mel said in a lower voice, "This is Michael's brother," and Bill grinned and extended his hand to Keith's father, who steadied his plate with one hand and shook Bill's hand with the other, and Bill said, "It's a pleasure," and somehow seemed to mean it, so Keith's father invoked his customary "glad to meet you," though this time with sincerity. Mel was already talking to both of them, almost lecturing to them, apparently picking up where he left off when he went to grab Keith's father, who was slightly annoyed by the high volume of Mel's voice, but recognized Mel's story as an opportunity for him to eat his meal uninterrupted, and that if he could steady his eyes on Mel and nod periodically, he could actually let his mind wander elsewhere, and thus almost be eating alone, and this realization satisfied Keith's father immensely, causing him to smile as he nodded to Mel, which Mel noticed and seemed to be pleased by, which only caused Keith's father more pleasure, as he realized that he was deceiving Mel, who was looking more and more like an ass to him, all the while enjoying an above-average pasta salad along with occasional forkfuls of an equally solid Chinese chicken salad, and Keith's father was now grinning noticeably, so tickled was he by his good fortune, and he briefly allowed himself to look down at his plate in order to stab a particularly inviting pasta shell filled with pesto and pine nuts, which Keith's father had recognized earlier as the finest morsel on his plate, and Keith's father brought his fork down on the noddle with exaggerated fury, which instantaneously made him nervous, but looking up quickly at Mel and Bill he was relieved to see that neither had noticed, so Keith's father slowly brought up the shell to his mouth and actually closed his eyes intending to savor his prize, and he placed the fork in his mouth, bit down slowly, slid the fork back out, feeling the pasta shell collapse onto his tongue, and for a moment he let it rest there, his eyes still shut, until he heard Mel's gravelly voice, "Oh, jeez, I've bored another one to sleep," and Keith's father quickly opened his eyes trying to recover, feeling foolish with two sets of eyes on him and an enormous shell in his mouth waiting to be chewed, and he thought for a second about trying to swallow the shell whole, but realized the danger of such a stunt, and so he smiled for a moment, then mumbled something about trying to concentrate in order to figure out if the pesto in this salad was more garlicky than the pesto his wife made, which no one responded to, leading to an awkward silence until Mel declared, "Enough about me and my stupid stories. Al, what's new with you, how's the eye business?"

Keith's father paused for a moment, unable to decide what to say or to remember if this sort of question was actually seeking more than the briefest response, and he knew he did not feel like speaking any more than was absolutely necessary, so he elected to treat Mel's question like a polite gesture more than a curious inquiry, and said that he was fine and that business was going very well, and paused again under the guise of taking a sip from his ginger ale, thereby giving Mel an opportunity to seize the conch from Keith's father, who was holding it loosely and reluctantly to begin with, and indeed Mel burst out quickly saying, "Michael tells me you've been having trouble sleeping," which stunned Keith's father, even though he had long ago concluded, along with essentially everyone else he knew who also knew Mel, that Mel was terrifically annoying and without tact, which even Michael thought, but recognizing that, and being quickly reassured this evening that Mel had not changed, Keith's father still had trouble believing that Mel would actually mention something both highly personal and equally dull as a topic of conversation, and Keith's father knew it was up to him to respond, but couldn't think of anything to say, and actually wanted to strike Mel or at least tell him that his sleeping habits (and he certainly wouldn't say sleeping "problems") were none of his fucking business, but didn't have the resolve, energy, or courage to do either, and was resigning himself to discussing his insomnia with Mel when Bill, who was speaking for the first time since greeting Keith's father, asked Keith's father in a voice many degrees quieter than Mel's if he exercises.

Keith's father, along with Mel, was surprised by this comment, though Bill was not at all, though he momentarily regretted forcing the topic so blatantly, as he had planned on discussing exercise at some point that evening (preferably more than once), since it was the only thing he was presently interested in at this point in his life that he expected the people at this gathering to be able to relate to at all, doubting that it was appropriate or even possible to make conversation with anyone present about ham radio, bow hunting, or amateur pornography, his other current passions, and indeed he had only gotten interested in exercise at all when he finally got fed up noticing the fat on his sides, which shook unflatteringly in the videos he and his wife made of themselves having sex, though he was now an advocate of regular exercise on its own merits, and quickly reassured Mel and Keith's father that there was some relevance to his comment, as he informed Keith's father that when he started exercising he noticed he fell asleep quicker and slept more soundly. Keith's father only replied to this with a slight nod of his head and murmured something, as he was still stuck on Mel's earlier comment, but Bill didn't hesitate to ask Keith's father again if he does indeed exercise, and Keith's father said not much, which was his way of saying not at all, and Mel volunteered that he plays tennis once in a while, which was his way of saying he played tennis in the last three years, and soon Mel was offering tidbits of his tennis-playing experience, which Keith's father noticed through the fog of his disbelief was being entirely ignored by Bill, and Keith's father began to feel a sense of camaraderie with Bill, who was leaning toward Keith's father slightly in order to offer that Keith's father ought to give exercise a try, and Keith's father said that he would, and by this point had recovered enough to know that even though his plate was still half full of pasta salad he would be wise to search for his wife, and so he began to rise while telling Bill that he would look into exercising.

Soon he was on the other side of the room, where he took a deep breath and tried to come up with a new strategy, but before he could figure out a way to get back to the buffet without Mel getting curious, his wife placed her hand on his shoulder and asked him how he was doing. He told her he was alright, and she took him and introduced him to a couple named Evelyn and Dennis, who had a son who was considering going into optometry and who, it seemed to Keith's father, had taken it upon themselves to find out the pros and cons of such a career, which didn't bother Keith's father one bit, as it gave him a chance to talk at length about the many hurdles he had cleared in his quarter century in optometry, and Evelyn appeared to be extremely interested in everything he had to say, so much so that Keith's father felt enough confidence to lean over to his wife to ask her to please go get him some more pasta salad, who returned his request with a puzzled look and then a silent trip to the buffet, and Keith's father continued speaking and answering their questions for nearly twenty minutes until his wife, who was annoyed by his long-windedness and the way his monologue reminded her of many of their dinners alone after he returned from a long day at the office, and who wasn't even enjoying herself much to begin with, told Keith's father she wasn't feeling well as soon as Dennis excused himself to go to the bathroom, and within five minutes they were back in their car on the way home, a rejuvenated husband behind the wheel.

The trajectory of Keith's father's near-euphoria had nearly come to an end by the time he and his wife got into bed, and he was becoming distant and silent when his wife asked him what he did at the party before she found him, but he wasn't interested in discussing his time with Mel and Bill, so he said only that he had sat with them briefly and that nothing much occurred, and his wife asked him if Mel hadn't "pulled a Mel," which indeed he had, though Keith's father didn't feel like talking about that either so he said no, and she asked who the other man was and he told her what he knew and then as an aside mentioned the exercise comment, which he hadn't taken seriously at the time, and his wife said, "Really?" but nothing more, though the idea brewed in her for a while, until two days later at dinner, with Keith's father deep into his depression again, she suggested he give it a try, but he didn't even respond, busy as he was meditating on his exhaustion.

Before he knew it, they were walking briskly around the neighborhood, which roused him enough to say that walking wasn't exercise, and she laughed at him and told him she would be glad to buy both of them running shoes tomorrow, which she did, and the following evening, this time before dinner, she convinced him to put on his new shoes to go jogging, and he resisted briefly until she taunted him into accepting the challenge that he was unable to run around even half the subdivision, and they were soon outside, but neither of them made it more than two hundred yards, and so Keith's father was reduced to walking, forced to watch his wife's demonstration of how to use one's arms to get a "workout" from walking, and Keith's father laughed at her again, refusing to think of walking as exercise, but did it anyways half-mockingly, half-seriously, until by the time they did a full loop around the subdivision, he was sweating noticeably. Back at the house they both showered, Keith's father's wife asking him over and over, "Now didn't that feel good?" though he only felt more tired, and between his contempt for the concept of walking as exercise and his fear that he would only be that much more tired than usual the next day, Keith's father responded with a "we'll see." That night he slept without waking once, which he still did a couple nights a week, though his wife was quick the next morning to attribute it to the exercise, and she succeeded in dragging him out with her four nights that week, while he went out each time still claiming skepticism, stating that his only interest in the whole thing was to build up enough endurance to not have to walk, which he declared was an insult to the concept of fitness, but as the week progressed he found himself sleeping more regularly, until one evening during a slight drizzle he grabbed his shoes and went out on his own while his wife was attending a real estate lecture at the nearby community college.

By the time two weeks had passed, Keith's father was becoming convinced that the walking, which was still just that, was having some positive effect, but he realized that he would be unable to actually run for a while, having not exercised prior to this week in over five years. In addition to this, it was raining often, so he suggested buying a stationary bike, which his wife agreed to

immediately, and she bought for him the most expensive bike at
the local sporting-goods store, complete with an elaborate panel
of red lights that could communicate to the rider a wealth of
information concerning calories burned and miles ridden, and
Keith's father was genuinely impressed by the device, which they
put in the living room, and he rode it for a little while, during
which time he announced repeatedly, "Now this is exercise," and
later that night when he woke up and couldn't fall back to sleep
easily, he went downstairs in his restless frustration and rode the
bike again, returned upstairs, showered, and fell asleep with little
effort.

The next morning, Keith's father, with a broad smile on his
face, relayed to his wife his successful experiment of the previous night, and Keith's mother responded that she knew he had
been riding because she heard the machine clearly from their
bedroom, and Keith's father felt a pang of guilt, as he had convinced himself the night before while riding the bike that the
machine wasn't very noisy, though he knew it really was, and he
asked his wife if it kept her awake, and she said she was able to
get back asleep, and he asked, "Right away?" to which she answered, "No, not immediately, but I did. It was no big deal." The
two of them sat in silence for a few minutes, each one sipping on
their morning coffee, Keith's mother reading an editorial she
would explain later in the day to a friend as "completely asinine,"
which was written by a man, about the high frequency of mothers with careers who are unfulfilled by their work and miss the
joys and rewards of a more traditional maternal role, and Keith's
mother found herself so incensed by the writer's argument that
she decided by the article's end that while the author's ignorance
and blatant sexism were certainly deplorable, it was the newspaper's decision to give space to such views that irritated her, as she

assumed that while views like this certainly still existed, publications like her newspaper had long ago recognized them as lacking any validity, and had therefore stopped printing such nonsense.

Though Keith's mother didn't regret the seventeen years she spent raising Keith and Lisa, and though immediately after Keith's bar mitzvah she finally decided to get a real estate license, and in the decade-plus since had learned a great deal about a complex field while making some significant sales along the way, Keith's mother did envy those men and women who had been in the same career since their early twenties. In fact, Keith's mother believed that due to her aptitude in real estate sales, if she had started seventeen years earlier, she would undoubtedly be a salesperson/agent of significant stature, likely earning six figures or more annually, and Keith's mother was reviewing these beliefs in her head, beliefs she reviewed from time to time, and was arriving at the idea of writing the newspaper a letter, something she had never actually done, but considered doing a few times a year, when Keith's father broke her train of thought along with the morning silence by suggesting that they move the bike into the basement. Keith's mother, still more interested in possible openings for her scathing letter ("As a woman who has been on this planet for nearly a half century I have seen enough to know that prejudice is not about to go away, nevertheless I had thought that mainstream publications like your own had progressed enough to realize that sexist sentiments like those expressed in your April 20th editorial, 'Homesick Working Mothers,' deserve no place in the debate concerning women, working, and the family.") than in discussing Keith's father's bike, nodded her head and said okay, hoping to continue thoughts about her letter, but Keith's father said, "Yeah, that's a good idea," and stood up tugging her arm saying, "C'mon, let's move it right now," and Keith's mother, bothered both by the distraction and unenthused by the idea of moving the heavy bike so early in the morning, asked Keith's father impatiently if he was crazy, and Keith's father repeated his "c'mon," this time with a giggle, having realized the ridiculously juvenile eagerness of his plea, but still wanting to move the bike and not convinced that his wife was entirely unwilling to participate, until Keith's mother offered that they move the bike after Keith's father returned from work, which they did. That evening Keith's father slept straight through the night, but the following night he woke up a little after 2:00 A.M. and went to the basement and rode the bike, and while the noise of the bike was fainter than before, it still woke up Keith's mother, and the following morning she brought this up to Keith's father, a bit of news that struck him as devastatingly ominous, until later in the day when he thought up the idea of soundproofing the basement.

Keith's father immediately called a local building company he had seen advertised on local television where it claimed that no job was too small, whose phone number Keith's father remembered because it spelled B-U-I-L-D-E-R, and two days later Keith's father left work early to return home, and met a man there from the company, who did not appear in the commercial Keith's father noted with slight disappointment, who measured the basement and quoted Keith's father a few prices, and counter to habit, Keith's father selected the most expensive material the builder offered, and before the end of the next week the job was completed. Keith's father convinced his wife, standing with purse, keys, and the day's groceries in the living room, to test the soundproofing, and so he went down to the basement, rode the bike for thirty seconds, ran winded back upstairs, and asked his wife "Well?" and she said she thought she heard something but wasn't certain, and Keith's father ran back downstairs, loudly recited the slogan of the building company which had installed the tiling, ran upstairs, and raised his eyebrows at his wife, who responded that again she thought she heard a mild hum, so Keith's father ran back downstairs, shouted, "I'm going to break your neck, you motherfucker!" while pointing at an imaginary adversary, and ran back upstairs, and his wife, this time with no prompting, said she could hear that he was yelling, but couldn't hear what he said, and that it was not loud at all, and then she asked him what he yelled, and Keith's father, overjoyed by both his satisfaction in solving the noise problem and his more general pride in the wonders of technology, hugged his wife and told her he had screamed, "I love you, Barbara!" and she giggled a bit and said that she didn't believe him, but hugged him back anyways.

That night Keith's father woke up at half past 3:00 A.M., and his hazy, waking frustration stemming from a dim awareness of his insomnia was soon overtaken by a lucid enthusiasm to take advantage of his effectively silent exercise bike, so Keith's father hurried down the two flights of stairs to the basement, thought to grab an old radio from Lisa's vacant room, and slowly exclaimed, "Oh, yeah," as he closed the door behind him. In the weeks following, Keith's father found himself engaged in nocturnal rides every two or three nights, and though the rides required him to wake up an hour or so later the following morning, Keith's father was feeling better about his situation than he ever had, as the post-ride shower in combination with the physical exhaustion from the workout almost always sent him straight to sleep. In addition, Keith's father began to notice the effects of the exercise on his body, a body that had never drawn much

attention, either positive or negative, a body that was average in
nearly every sense, shoulders of unremarkable width, legs neither long nor short, neither skinny nor flabby, a body that developed a pouting belly during the Reagan, Bush, and Clinton
administrations, but now Keith's father was noticing that his
pants were a bit looser, that his legs were a little firmer, and were
able to bound up the house's stairs effortlessly, and while Keith's
father had never fancied himself an athlete of much merit,
Keith's father was beginning to understand that such regular intensive workouts were helping him attain a level of physical fitness he had never enjoyed at any point in his life. This degree of
fitness immediately reminded him of his brother Michael, who
was an all-around phenomenal athlete, and who once upon a
time had been a baseball player of significant merit, whose larger
frame in tandem with years of practice made him one of the top
first basemen in the city during high school, when they still lived
"in the city" during a time when baseball was *the* sport. Michael
received a scholarship to the state university to play baseball and
started his freshman year, he even had a tryout with the Indians,
and was offered a spot on a minor-league team, which he considered taking, but the money was horrible, and he still enjoyed exposure on the college team, where he hit .318 his sophomore
year, and he assumed the offers would be around after he got his
marketing degree, but in his junior year he missed the first half
of the season when he dislocated his elbow, and when he finally
came back his timing was off, while a promising freshman had
replaced him at first base, and so the coach had him pinch-hit almost every game, telling Michael that he didn't want him putting
unnecessary strain on his arm by playing the field, but this gave
Michael too much time to think about his batting troubles, and
soon he was in a genuine slump for the first time in his life, and
Michael, who could once recognize a pitch by the way the ball

came out of the pitcher's hand was now second-guessing himself, and he batted only .248 that year, with one lousy home run, and during the winter Michael tried to strengthen his arm, but his confidence was shot, and he barely played his senior year. After graduating he didn't bother to seek out any tryouts, but instead took a job with a janitorial-supplies company, where he found a new arena in which to compete, and Michael's early success at the company helped him relocate his self-confidence, and soon the executives at the company were noticing Michael's skill as a salesman and were boasting to the rest of the employees about Michael's talent and competitive spirit, which they attributed to Michael's baseball past, which was slowly reworked into a more-storied career in which the elbow injury occurred at the semipro level, when a spot on the actual Indians had all but been assured, and Michael didn't bother to correct anyone, and even batted cleanup for the company softball team, where he was the league MVP from 1971 to 1977. He played in every league he could make time for, and though a small belly was developing he maintained an athlete's appearance and disposition, and it was only in the late 1980s, during a championship game, that Michael destroyed his knee trying to break up a double play, he couldn't even run for eight months, and his frame started to expand, which everyone, including Keith's father, was reluctant to point out to Michael fearing that he would not be receptive to anyone's advice about how to take care of his body since Michael's reputation had always made him the family expert on diet and exercise, and after Michael's knee healed enough for him to play softball again, he returned to his leagues claiming that it was only a matter of time until he got back into shape, but his knee collapsed soon after despite the enormous brace he wore, and this time the doctor said that the damage to the knee along with Michael's weight made it unlikely he would be able to play again, and Michael pretended to be stoic, announcing that he was glad his career had ended at its peak, and that he wouldn't become one of those old guys who could barely run to first base, but his weight continued to increase, lowered from time to time by different diets, and at some point, only months before Keith's father's insomnia first surfaced, Michael finally decided that there was no hope in ever losing enough weight for it to matter, not as long as he could lose weight only through a particular diet without the aid of exercise, and Michael was frequently reminded by his wife Joanne that he could swim if he wanted, but Michael hated swimming and considered with horror the notion of himself in a bathing suit, and so Michael's weight steadily increased, while Keith's father's weight, which had all along been normal among his peers, suddenly started going down, and the chiasmatic trajectories of Keith's father's and Michael's weights came clearly into focus coincidentally at precisely the same time their misunderstanding over Keith's father's request for a business loan began (to expand the clinic), and this role reversal in bodily pride was never ever vocalized by one or the other when the two brothers were together, but neither one could ignore it was happening, and while Keith's father felt sorry for his brother's situation, and regretted that his new level of fitness undoubtedly compounded Michael's despair over his ever-expanding girth, Keith's father was elated for the first time to think of himself as in possession of a body worth noticing, and this brand-new pride only swelled as Keith's father's belly disappeared, a development which his wife noticed with joy as well, and soon the dedication Keith's father brought to his work, which he was once again able to uphold thanks to the bicycle, was being applied to his exercise regimen as well.

Keith's father was initially pleased with himself for thinking to bring Lisa's clock radio down to the newly dubbed "exercise room," especially as the radio allowed him to create even more noise that only he would hear, and at first Keith's father enjoyed trying out the different stations, waiting for little surprises to be broadcast to him, songs from his childhood, ads from strange companies that could only afford radio time in the middle of the night, bizarre loners calling talk shows to explain away some government conspiracy, but over time the novelty of the variety wore off, the general strangeness grew predictable, and Keith's father found himself impatiently pedaling while waiting for something interesting to come over the airwaves, and though he had smartly pulled up an old table next to the bike and placed the radio on it so he could adjust the stations without interrupting his biking, the incessant turning of the dial and the annoyance he felt as he arrived at either end of the frequency range knowing that he'd have to backtrack a third of the way before he was likely to hear anything new, let alone anything good, finally made him realize that radio just wouldn't do. So one night, while listening to a Spanish talk show for no particular reason Keith's father got off the bike, went upstairs, and hauled back downstairs a large but officially "portable" radio/tape deck/multi-CD player that Keith's mother bought on a whim two years earlier, but which sat mostly unused in the living room at the edge of the kitchen unless Keith's mother remembered to turn it on when preparing something in the kitchen. Though Keith's mother had initially bought the item in order to own a CD player, and the machine could actually hold five CDs, there was only one CD in the house, a collection of Barbra Streisand singing show tunes, and while Keith's mother liked Streisand's voice she found the accompaniment unbearably syrupy, and hadn't bothered to buy another CD, so the CD player was unused over the last eighteen months.

Keith's father had actually considered bringing the larger

machine downstairs a few nights earlier, but recognizing the dearth of tapes and CDs in the house, he saw little reason to move it, sensing as well that the move could conceivably aggravate his wife, who might claim that she likes having it there and does indeed use it regularly, but as Keith's father was trying to imagine what it might be like to be bilingual he somehow recalled a certain tape that he suspected might be in his wife's car. After bringing the radio downstairs, Keith's father searched quietly in the kitchen for his wife's car keys, found them, and then went out to the garage feeling comforted by the sight of their two cars waiting loyally until they were called upon again. Keith's father opened his wife's passenger side door fearing that her alarm would go off even though he knew how to deactivate it before this would happen, but the thought of his failure to do so and the subsequent blaring of the horn was only too easy to visualize, and so Keith's father looked down at his wife's key chain from which it was possible to control the alarm, double-checked that his finger was on the proper button, and deactivated the alarm.

Once inside the car, Keith's father turned his attention to the armrest between the driver and passenger seats, which also functioned as a tape holder, and began fumbling through its contents, past the many real estate tapes his wife liked to listen to, until at the bottom he found the tape he was looking for, *Louis Jordan's Greatest Hits,* a tape Keith's father bought for his wife a year or so earlier when Keith had come in for what turned out to be a lukewarm visit, during which time Keith dragged them into a music store wanting to show his mother some of the new music he was listening to, and Keith's father knew at the time that he ought to go with them, but didn't trust himself to refrain from sarcasm as he thought both that so-called "college music" was horrible,

which he based on almost ninety seconds of listening experience, and that Keith was acting arrogant and detached from his
parents, in particular his father, who had stories he wanted to tell
his son, so Keith's father drifted around aimlessly in the store
until he was pulled to a bin that held tapes priced $3.99 or less,
and though Keith's father had no intention of buying anything,
bargain priced or otherwise, he couldn't resist the gravity of the
cheapest merchandise in the store. Keith's father browsed casually up and down the large bin, which mostly contained titles he
had never heard of, until he saw the Louis Jordan tape, which he
immediately reached for in order to check if "Five Guys Named
Moe" was included, which it was, and Keith's father smiled,
walked to the counter, and bought the tape, which he presented
to his surprised wife when they met up outside. She exclaimed,
"How adorable" and actually hugged her husband, while Keith
asked what the big deal was, and his mother asked/told Keith,
"You don't know who Louis Jordan is?" and Keith shrugged
"no," and his mother proceeded to tell him that if it wasn't for
Louis Jordan he may not be alive, because the first time your father and I spoke to one another it was about one of his songs,
and Keith, who was annoyed to have not found any decent CDs
in the store, but because he wanted to take advantage of his
mother's offer to buy him something wound up buying a CD he
didn't think he'd actually like, did not bother to ask her what
song she was talking about, and Keith's father noticed this blatant disregard, but Keith's mother was still excited by the surprise and continued with the story in which the first thing Keith's
father ever said to her, other than the time he was introduced to
her right before of course, was that he doubted anyone actually
knows five guys named Moe, and that she found that so funny,
and they just started talking after that, and the rest is history, and

Keith nodded a bit and said, "Huh," and Keith's father, back in his wife's car staring at the tape, was still amazed that his wife had found such a moronic comment funny at all, since it was the improvised product of his impatient desire to say anything in order to get her attention as he stood next to her in a diner while mutual friends they were each with who had just run into each other were making small talk, and Keith's father recalled his wife's face from that moment, her slightly awkward smile and accompanying overbite, which he found so attractive, looked at the picture of Louis Jordan on the front of the tape case, thanked him out loud, left the car, and returned to the basement.

Keith's father found Louis Jordan's music appropriate for his late-night stationary bike rides, and as he listened to the tape over and over he found himself singing along with the words he had by now memorized—not just saying the words, but truly singing, and Keith's father discovered that with no one around to hear him, he unabashedly belted out the lyrics with even more vigor than the vivacious Louis Jordan himself, and Keith's father was initially surprised by this development, as he rarely whistled or even hummed a tune, let alone sang, though Keith's father did recollect a brief stint he had in his synagogue's choir, which lasted only a few months when he was twelve, during which time many of his friends who weren't in the choir suggested brusquely that Keith's father was sexually attracted to men, and Keith's father remembered liking most of the songs the choir sang, but that their rehearsals conflicted with baseball practice, and there was no question in his house if Michael was going to play or not, and so Keith's father, who enjoyed baseball somewhat, decided to give up the choir to play baseball as well, and since that time singing and music in general had played a minimal role in his life. But now he was definitely singing and definitely enjoying singing, and before the end of the week Keith's father was able to come up with a short list of vocalists he thought he might enjoy singing along with, and that weekend he went to a music store (a different one) and bought Louis Jordan on disk, along with disks by Frank Sinatra, João Gilberto (with Stan Getz), Ella Fitzgerald, and Louis Armstrong, and Keith's father was satisfied with each disk, though he quickly realized that certain styles fit better with different parts of the bike's "hill" program, which started out smooth and then slowly progressed to higher degrees of difficulty, during which time a special mechanism in the bike offered extra resistance to the rider. Keith's father took it upon himself to figure out how to use the CD player's "program" function, which took longer than expected, but after nearly a half hour of failed experiments, Keith's father mastered the program command, and over the next two weeks he arrived at the following menu of songs, which lasted almost exactly as long as his eighteen-minute "hill" program and followed the ride's crescendos and decrescendos of difficulty almost perfectly:

Frank Sinatra, "Bewitched"—opening two-plus minutes, no hills.

Ella Fitzgerald, "You'd Be So Nice to Come Home To"—almost three minutes, minihill into brief flat stretch.

João Gilberto, "So Danco Amor"—three and a half minutes, end of flat stretch, beginning of major hill.

Louis Jordan, "Ain't Nobody Here But Us Chickens" and "Five Guys Named Moe"—nearly seven minutes of hill climbing.

Louis Armstrong, "I Gotta Right to Sing the Blues"—
just under three minutes of cool-down riding.

Keith's father quickly learned all these songs by heart, and in
no time was able to mimic each singer's technique, and as his endurance improved and leg strength increased he was able, when
the urge struck, to free his arms and hands to acknowledge his
imaginary audience or play along with the horn solos in the final
four songs, solos he had memorized as well. Keith's father's new-
found love for music and singing, which he cultivated proudly
during the biweekly implementation of his effective method for
combating the very insomnia that had so threatened his well-
being only weeks before, propelled him to the far reaches of joy,
even beyond where he found himself after his official ascen-
dance to the position of the world's top optometrist, because
this pleasure was borne on the back of his own private emanci-
pation, and outside of the problems he felt he was having with
both his brother and son, which Keith's father was certain would
be cleared up soon, he decided that this was as happy as he had
been since the early years of his marriage, and this positive association with his marriage inspired Keith's father to invest new
energy into his relationship with his wife, which included long
leisurely walks, weekend trips to small-town bed-and-breakfast
inns, and an increase in lovemaking so sharp that the two of
them joked about calling Guinness just to check.

Keith's father was reviewing these developments as he rode
through the most difficult section of the "hill" program, singing
along with Louis Jordan when a pain shot out from his chest, the
pain of his heart failing, of his pump giving out, and the pain ran
through him so swiftly that he was engulfed in fear before he understood what was happening, and he never would understand

that this is how he would die. His right hand reached for his chest and the heart inside it, but the urgency of his body trying to save itself sent his hand past its target, and unlike the thousand or so times he had casually, even absentmindedly, placed this hand on his chest in preparation for the Pledge of Allegiance, when he never once considered that his palm was marking his heart, this time, when that was all his body wanted his hand to do, he missed, and the last self-initiated movement of his body, a desperate last gesture to grasp this unfair pain, would end as his bent, contorted hand struck his shoulder, and the force of this self-inflicted, unintended blow combined with the quick collapse of his frame sent his figure capsizing off the left side of the bike, his right foot ripping itself free of the pedal's toe grip in the instant before the just-struck shoulder and the head normally above it met the floor. Louis Jordan continued singing and playing his saxophone, and when he finished, the machine exchanged CDs as it was programmed to do by Keith's father, whereupon Louis Armstrong followed the other Louis just as he had the other nights and sang lyrics, some of which Keith's father was never quite able to decipher, this due to the manner in which Armstrong's singing mimicked, impossibly, his horn playing, though Keith's father sensed the lyrics celebrated, in an indirect way, the singer's affirming conviction in the power of song, and for that matter art, to transform cruel suffering into transcendent, if unruly, beauty, and Keith's father, in contrast to his experiences with Sinatra, Fitzgerald, and Jordan, could never manage to accurately accompany the trumpeter's vocals, since for the imaginative Armstrong lyrics seemed to be little more than a pretext to express himself with an unpredictable daring that ultimately went well beyond the words themselves, that thus rendered language a medium and little more.

A few measures after he finished singing, Louis Armstrong played the same thoughtful solo for Keith's father as the sweat on his skin began to evaporate, and when the song was over, and when the bike had long since turned off as it does automatically when the rider stops pedaling, its red lights extinguished, the CD player made the final sound of the night, as its laser glided back to its resting spot, buzzing softly the whole way.

ACKNOWLEDGMENTS

Thanks:

To Joey Garfield, Tracey Kaufman Grossbach, Josh Lewis, Beth Rubin, Amy Scheffler, David Wish, and especially John Schott and Naomi Seidman for taking me seriously early on. To the sadly short-lived Berkeley Jewish Studies Creative Evenings and to Comp Lit's Writers Reading series for warm, intelligent audiences. To Rosemary Graham, Ayelet Waldman, Michael Chabon, and Etgar Keret for believing in me and offering professional guidance. To my University of Florida colleagues and comrades for continued intellectual stimulation and for valuing this project, too. To Jonathan Cohen and Matthew Rohrer for remarkably reliable encouragement and endless support over many years. To my agent, Simon Lipskar, for your honesty, insight, patience, persistence, and for always getting it. To my editor, Tina Pohlman, for your intelligence and enthusiasm, and for bringing me on board, not once, but twice.

To my family: the Lowys, the Levins, the Hasaks, and, in their roundabout way, the wonderful Ariel and Noam.

And to Taal, for listening thoughtfully to every word multiple times, for never doubting, for helping me do this when I should have been doing other things, for, quite simply, making this happen in a million other ways every single day.